SANDSTC

Rachel McNeely

ROMANCE

BookStrand
www.BookStrand.com

A SIREN-BOOKSTRAND TITLE
IMPRINT: Romance

SANDSTONE LEGACY
Copyright © 2009 by Rachel McNeely

ISBN-10: 1-60601-249-5
ISBN-13: 978-1-60601-249-9

First Printing: June 2009

Cover design by Jinger Heaston
All cover art and logo copyright © 2009 by Siren-BookStrand, Inc.

PUBLISHER
www.BookStrand.com

DEDICATION

This book is dedicated to my husband, who has always believed in me and encouraged me to follow my dreams. You are my hero.

And to my critique partners: Lara Santiago, who has been encouraging and helping me since we met almost five years ago; to Kristen Painter, thanks for the wonderful web site and helping me with my grammar; and last but not least to Carrie H., who always has the right suggestions on how to make my story better. You all are the best.

SANDSTONE LEGACY

RACHEL MCNEELY
Copyright © 2009

Prologue

Sandstone Ranch 1862

Judith Collier paced across her small living room. Heat lightning flashed outside the window, and the sun sank into the west leaving an empty haze in the distance. Daniel should be home.

She wrapped her arms tight around her waist trying to stave off the fear seeping through her body. Hearing a noise, she hurried to the front door and strained to see in the gathering dusk.

Daniel appeared from between the trees. He rode slumped over his horse.

Dismounting, he walked slowly toward the house. When he raised his head, Judith gasped at his ashen face and the dark void in his eyes.

"Daniel, what is it?" Judith's hand went to her throat.

He handed her a crumbled letter. Smoothing out the paper, she read the short note. Jess, Daniel's brother, died September 17 at Sharpsburg, during the battle of Antietam.

Tears flooded Judith's eyes, and the words blurred. Daniel's boots striking the stairs brought her head up.

"No, Daniel," she wailed and ran after him.

He stood in their bedroom throwing pieces of clothing into a blanket to be rolled and fastened behind his saddle. Judith grabbed his arms to stop him. He flung her off. She reached out for him again.

"No." He held her away, his hands tight on her upper arms. "I'm finished listening to you. I should have joined the battle long ago. It's not too late."

Blue eyes frozen like icicles pierced into her, and she flinched. She jerked out of his grip.

Daniel turned back to his task and then took his hat and the rolled blanket. Maneuvering around her, he rushed down the steps.

Judith ran after him. "You can't leave me. You said you loved me." Her words stopped him.

His voice harsh, he snapped at her. "Love has nothing to do with it. I must go, or I won't be able to hold up my head. My brother is dead."

Anguish was written across his face in the deep grooves of his cheeks and the tight lines around his mouth. But all she felt was her own pain. "I can't stand for you to go." She placed her hand over her heart, "If you leave, you'll never come back, and I don't want to live without you."

She moved close, her fingertips brushing across his lips and along his jaw. Deliberately, she moistened her lips, tempting him to forget his obligations.

He didn't respond. She dropped her hand and stepped back. She didn't know this cold stranger.

* * * *

Daniel took a last glance around the room and at her. Fading sunlight shined in ribbons across the polished wood floor, and it glittered in her reddish gold curls. Tears clouded her hazel eyes.

He'd loved her since the first moment they'd met. Daniel clenched his teeth. The course of his life had changed. He fought the urge to pull her into his arms and kiss those full sensuous lips. He had to go. He couldn't allow her to change his mind, not this time. He'd been wrong giving into her before.

"You don't love me, or you would understand." He flung the words at her. "I have no choice." Knocking his hand against the frame of the door, he ran down the steps and away from her.

* * * *

She watched him disappear into the shadows of the nearby trees. "And you have chosen death," Judith whispered. And for what, honor? She wanted to spit the word out. He had left her here alone.

Her hands hugged her stomach. She was barren. They'd barely been married a year. The love they'd sworn on their wedding day mocked her. Love was nothing but a figment of a woman's imagination. Men had honor, women had love, or thought they did.

Her chest burned from the sting of his words. His anger ripped out her heart. Bile, hate, and pain warred with the love she'd felt. It clawed at her insides.

A gray mist floated before her eyes. She moved toward the staircase, like an old woman with shuffling feet. Tentacles of despair wrapped around her like a lover's embrace. The ripping pain inside her body made her gasp for breath.

She'd embrace the anger and hate, as much as she'd filled herself with love for him. She climbed the steps one by one, leaning against the banister.

If only she could scream out her agony. It spewed around inside her and overflowed into her throat, scalding her. Finally, she stood in their room. The place she and Daniel had filled with love and joy.

Her knees buckled, and she fell to the floor. She grabbed her throat. Something horrid tore at her. It gushed up her airway, stopping her breath as it clawed from deep inside. It hurt like the pain of a million knives, burning and cutting, until it erupted out of her mouth. An unearthly noise echoed off the walls. Judith's body shook and writhed. A shrill laugh pounded in her ears. Did it come from her?

Chapter 1

February, 2008

Déjà vu flooded Katie Weber and sped her heart rate the moment her gaze fell on the Red Barn Dance Hall.

Vivid memories of hopeful adolescent fervor, over the boy she'd had a crush on, flashed in painful recollection. Her first heartbreak had occurred in this place, when one boy in particular had not asked her for a dance.

If only her existing problems were as insignificant. Her fiancé and subsequently the home they bought together was now gone. The only intrigue in her life involved a cryptic inheritance letter regarding a local haunted house called Sandstone. She shivered at the thought.

"And here we are." Sara Leach, her best friend, pulled into the crowded parking lot and shut off the car's engine.

Katie sighed inwardly wishing she had curled up with a good book instead of coming here tonight. "Wow. It hasn't changed a bit since high school." She glanced at Sara's exuberant expression. Katie forced herself to smile and prepared to endure the evening.

Sara turned to her. "I'm glad you decided to move back to Treehaven after your split with Eric. Your folks don't mind you rooming with me instead of them?"

Katie picked up her purse and shawl and walked with Sara toward the entrance. "No, they'd like to have me home, but they understand. It's difficult to move back in with your parents. Especially when you've had your own home and thought your life was going in another direction. I hope you realize you may have my company for a while."

"No problem. Tom and I aren't planning to tie the knot until fall, so you have plenty of time."

They entered the building and stood inside the door to let their eyes adjust to the dark room. Candlelight gave a soft glow to the area. Tables sat around the large dance floor, and the band, stationed at the north end, tuned their instruments.

"There he is." Sara pointed to a man waving from the other side of the room. "Tom said he'd get here early enough to save a good table." She grabbed Katie's hand, and they threaded their way around the crowded dance floor.

Tom Cole stood to greet them. He still looked the same, stocky, muscular arms from playing football in high school and college and leathery skin from too much Florida sunshine. His wide smile greeted Katie, and he pulled Sara to his side and kissed her.

"Welcome back, Katie. Sara said you're home to stay."

"That's my plan."

"Good." Tom motioned to the waitress, and they ordered their drinks. After she left Tom leaned back in his chair. "Hope you ladies won't mind, but I invited a friend of mine to join us. He's in town for the weekend."

Katie eyed him warily. "This isn't a set-up for poor Katie, is it?"

"No." Tom shook his head vehemently. "It never entered my mind, honestly. You might remember him though. Jake Andrews and I were in the same high school class."

Jake Andrews?

The mere mention of his name made Katie's heart flutter and her knees weak. Her old crush in high school. Her first instinct was to run, but manners kept her seated. Would he remember her? Cheeks burning, Katie recalled her too obvious behavior during that time. Sara's voice broke into her thoughts.

"Didn't he have a reputation as a trouble maker?" Sara asked.

"Totally unwarranted. He's a good guy." Tom glanced around when the music started. "Dance with me."

Sara put out her hand. "Smooth change of subject," she said and joined him on the dance floor.

Katie watched as Tom held Sara close. Two steps into the dance, he leaned down to whisper in her ear. The gesture made Katie envious, but happy for her friend. Katie's past year had been difficult. She should have moved home sooner, but she'd lingered on in New York, unsure of what she wanted to do. Now on her first outing, she was going to see Jake for the first time in years.

"Here are your drinks, honey." The waitress sat the glasses on the table and left.

She'd just picked up her glass when she saw a tall, dark haired man standing under a light directly across the room. She'd have known Jake Andrews anywhere. He was etched into her memory. Tom and Sara stepped off the dance floor to greet him and Tom motioned toward their table and then danced away with Sara. Jake headed in her direction.

Oh, yes, he was good looking at fifteen, when she'd had many a fantasy about the bad boy senior. Even after all these years, he still sent shivers of excitement down her spine, especially when he directed those sexy blue eyes at her.

Everything about him seemed bigger. Not heavy, but taller, with broader shoulders and a more confident air about him. He stepped to the table and a smile spread across his sensual lips. She felt warmth flush her cheeks.

"Sorry, I don't mean to stare. You look familiar," she said, to cover the truth that he was all *too* familiar.

"Jake, have you met Sara's friend, Katie Weber?" Tom asked, as he and Sara came off the dance floor. "Have a seat."

"Hello, Katie." Jake reached across, and his large hand covered hers. She started to pull away, but he held her fingers securely in his grasp. Now not only her face felt warm, but her whole body zinged with awareness. When he released her hand and sat, she almost sighed with relief, except his chair was right beside hers.

Katie listened to the conversation flowing around her. She didn't really listen to the words, but enjoyed the husky tone of Jake's voice. A panicky feeling came over her when Tom and Sara went back to the dance floor.

In a room full of people, their table seemed isolated from the rest. They were alone and he stared intently in her direction.

"Do I have a wart on my nose?" she quipped.

"No." He reached out and pretended to brush something off of the tip of her nose. He jerked his hand back to his side, and she moved further back in her chair and took a large swallow of her drink.

"I do remember you from high school."

His words flowed over her like warm honey. "Please don't remind me," she said. "High school is such an embarrassing time. I was so awkward."

"Not really. If you mean the time you almost fell because of a dropped pencil, it was hardly your fault."

No, but my drooling over you was pathetic.

"Let's dance." He put out his hand.

She slowly rose. He pulled her into his arms and swung her into the crowd of dancers. His grip was firm and warm, and he embraced her tightly against his hard chest.

His spicy male fragrance floated around her, and she resisted the urge to cuddle even closer. This was not like her at all, especially the past year. She'd avoided men like the plague. But then this was her old dream come true.

"You're very quiet." His voice interrupted her thoughts. "Is it me or you just don't talk much?"

She had to chuckle. "My friends and family would laugh at that remark. They'd say that they can't shut me up."

"Then it *is* me."

"You're a man."

"I am." He tipped his head, curiosity in his expression. "So?"

"Not my favorite gender right now."

"I see. Bad break up?"

She nodded and waited for him to say more, but he swung her around a couple of other dancers and held her tighter.

Jake danced well, and Katie was sorry when the music stopped. They joined Sara and Tom at the table.

Sara leaned over and whispered in her ear. "Want to go to the ladies room?"

Katie nodded, and they excused themselves. She followed Sara to the alcove where the ladies restrooms were located.

"What do you think?" Sara asked, as soon as they got inside. "He's still as good looking as he was in high school, and if I remember correctly you had a big crush on him then."

"That was a long time ago."

"True, but I can feel the vibes dinging off you," Sara said with emphasis.

Katie frowned. "Am I really so obvious?"

Sara held up her hands in protest. "Only to me because I know you so well. Anyway you and Eric broke up almost a year ago, even if you did just come back home. It's time to get out and meet new people. Give Jake a chance."

"Yes, Mother."

"OK, I'll get off your case," Sara said with a laugh.

The men stood on their return.

Tom had ordered chips, salsa and another round of drinks. He, Sara and Jake reminisced about high school. The band started to play again, and Tom and Sara returned to the dance floor.

"You didn't eat much." Jake motioned to the chips. He stared at her for a second before adding. "I'm hungry, and I understand the old root beer drive-in still has the best shakes and burgers. How about going for a ride?"

"A ride?" she asked.

"To get a burger and afterwards we'll go for a drive to get some fresh air."

"I hardly know you." She fibbed, as her heart pounded in her chest.

"Not true. We went to the same high school and have some of the same friends," he said.

"I have to let Sara know where I'm going."

"I'll wait here."

She glanced around and saw where they danced. "I'll be right back."

* * * *

Jake watched her talk to Sara, who looked in his direction. Sara said something to Katie, and she also glanced his way.

He'd caught his breath when he'd first walked up to the table. Katie had raised her head, and those hazel eyes, flecked with gold, met his. Her soft voice had sent a warm ache through his body.

What was the matter with him? She wasn't his type. He'd known that in high school and even though he'd been attracted to her, he'd steered clear. Her family would have never approved of him dating her. His reputation always preceded him. His recent taste in women favored tall, willow thin models. A woman who knew the ways of the world and didn't want more then he was willing to give was less complicated. Katie Weber exemplified the type of woman he deliberately avoided. Home, house and hearth were written all over her. And yet he still invited her to leave with him.

A sense of relief washed over him when she headed back in his direction. Her smile warmed every cold corner of his heart. Wow, better watch it, he warned himself.

"Ready?" He asked. When she nodded and picked up her shawl and purse, he put his hand on her back and led her outside.

"I forgot to mention I didn't bring my car tonight." He stopped beside his pride and joy, a black Harley Road King Classic. "Have you ever ridden a motorcycle?" He studied her expression, first one of surprise and then a cautious smile.

"Once, with my brother. It's a little scary." She glanced around at the dark night.

"At night, it can give you a great sense of freedom. I'll take the back roads. There won't be much traffic or we can go back inside." He sensed her struggle.

"No, this is fine," she whispered.

He unfastened an extra helmet from the back seat and pulled out a leather jacket from the saddlebag. "I'll put your purse and shawl in here." He took them and refastened the pouch.

"You're very prepared. You must take lots of women for rides."

"I do." He laughed at her expression. "But they're usually ten or twelve years old and one of Tom's nieces."

She was so open in her expressions. He caught the quick flash of relief before she turned to put on the jacket. He adjusted her helmet strap and then his.

"Put your arms around me. Ready?"

Her arms tightened around his middle, and he heard her soft yes. Vowing not to scare the pants off of her, he left the parking area and drove into the dark night.

A sliver of moon cast silver light across the dark trees. He traveled the back roads and watched for the street just inside the city limits where the root beer place was located.

After parking the bike at an outside table, he took Katie's hand and went to order. "Burgers, shakes, and fries?" he asked her.

"No fries, I'm not that hungry."

He put in the order and carried it back to their table.

Katie bit into the cheeseburger. "Hmm, it's as good as I remembered." She smiled at him. A few cars drove by, and the faint sound of music floated through the air from the inside eating area.

"Hope you don't mind staying out here. The food seems to taste better outdoors."

"I agree. I used to stop here at least once a week with my brothers and sisters."

They ate in companionable silence. Jake enjoyed watching her face. There was no pretense about her. He hadn't enjoyed a date this much in a long time. Well, if he could call this a date. After they finished, he cleared the table and helped Katie back onto the bike.

"Where are we going?"

He knew exactly where he was headed. "Wait and see."

A ribbon of water sparkled through the darkness, and Jake turned the bike onto a narrow, hard packed, dirt road. He stopped at the edge of the St. John's River and parked the motorcycle.

He helped Katie unfasten her helmet. "Did you enjoy the ride?"

"It was wonderful, once I got over my initial fear." She walked closer to the water. "This is a beautiful spot. Private and yet you can see a bridge in the distance and cars crossing."

"It's one of my favorite places for thinking." Why the hell did he say that? In fact, he'd never brought a woman here before. Katie loosened his mouth and his brain.

She smiled and touched his arm. For as much as he wanted to pick her up and take her home, she was not for him. Her hand shifted toward his collar. He stepped away with a pang of regret.

Katie was the youngest of the Weber clan, a large, well known family that had lived in Treehaven for many generations and held a place of respect in the community. They'd never let her associate with a man who was expected to end up like his father, a criminal, who died in prison. No matter what he did, he'd never live down his family's past. The residents of Treehaven had always eyed him with suspicion.

"Now you're the one being quiet." Katie moved closer to him. The soft look in her eyes meant trouble.

"We'd better head back."

"So soon?" She shivered.

"You're cold."

"Not really." Her eyes stared into his. "Please let's stay. I don't want to go yet."

Her sultry voice wrapped around him and sent heat along his nerve endings. She crowded him and he liked it. He pulled her against his hardened body, tipped her head back and kissed her rosy lips. Her soft gasp parted her mouth, and his tongue delved inside to taste her sweet as honey flavor.

She pulled her head back and stared into his eyes. "You may change my opinion of your gender."

Jake reluctantly stepped away. He raked his fingers through his hair. "Look, we need to slow down. I'm not going to be around much longer. This is my first trip to Treehaven in almost a year."

"Good, I don't want a serious relationship."

"Just that word sends fear spiking through my head. You're not a one night stand kind of girl."

* * * *

The cool night air blew across Katie's heated body. Jake's kiss had ignited an aching desire. She yearned for him to take her back in his arms.

But she'd never considered a one night stand. "You're right, I'm not." Her face flushed with embarrassment. She'd thrown herself at him and although he'd seemed interested, he had his emotions well under control.

Jake released a deep sigh. "Sometimes I hate being right."

She sent him a winsome smile. "Take me home? I'm rooming with Sara."

"Sure." He went to the bike, handed her the jacket and adjusted her helmet. His warm fingers brushed against her chin, and she shivered. He'd noticed, but didn't comment and they were soon on the road and then parking outside Sara's townhouse.

Katie handed him the jacket and helmet. "Thanks for the ride."

"Don't forget your shawl and purse." He held them out to her.

When she reached out to take them, he pulled her close. "And don't leave without a proper goodbye." His warm lips brushed against hers.

Katie put her arms around his neck and leaned against his hard body.

She opened her mouth, and the kiss deepened. Then she slowly stepped out of his arms.

"And don't you forget that," she whispered, and she walked to the townhouse. She forced herself to not look back. As soon as she closed the door, she heard the motorcycle roar as he sped away.

She recognized an undeniable attraction between them. She'd never completely forgotten him.

Katie went in the living room and sat in the dark remembering her first close encounter with Jake. She'd been going down the stairs to her next class when she stepped on a dropped pencil. She immediately started to skid when strong arms pulled her close against a hard chest. She'd raised her eyes to find Jake smiling at her.

"Are you hurt?"

She almost didn't hear him for staring at his mouth.

"What? Oh, no. I'm fine. Thank you."

Other students brushed by them in their hurry to get to class. But for a second, time stopped for Katie. She'd had a crush on Jake all year and this was a dream come true, to be standing in the circle of his arms.

Gradually, he let her go. He ducked his head. "Got to go. See ya." And he strode off.

Katie stood in the same spot for several seconds before someone nudged her along.

Strange that memory was so clear it seemed to have happened only yesterday.

Katie went into her bedroom and turned on the light. It was just as well Jake didn't come to Treehaven very often. She had enough complications in her life. Jake had been wise to step away from her when he did. On Monday, she had an important business meeting and who knew where that might lead.

Chapter 2

Katie glanced at her map and searched the edge of the roadway for the sign. There, Sandstone Ranch. She slowed and turned onto the dirt road.

Her car bumped along the narrow, rutted lane. Katie watched for any sign of life. No houses in sight and tall pines edged along the sides. She saw a curve and slowed.

The old house sat in the middle of a large yard. Someone had recently cut the front and side grass, but in the back pink, white and blue wildflowers bloomed.

A huge old oak reigned majestically across the front lawn. Moss hung off the tree limbs like lace trimming, and the full canopy of branches created a circle of shade in the stark sunshine.

The two story white frame house with faded green trim had a wide porch that ran across the front and wrapped around the north side. The house leaned as though the weight of the porch pulled tiredly at the old frame. Palm trees waved against the pale blue sky and the lone whistle of a train added to the melancholy mood.

Katie stopped her car. A slight breeze ruffled the leaves of the oak. No one was here yet, and with all the town gossip about this place being haunted, she hesitated to get out of her car.

She picked up the envelope lying on the seat beside her. When she'd first received the letter, she thought it was a scam. Her Dad assured her that the law firm of Townsend and Townsend had an impeccable reputation.

Katie had expected to have to drive to their office in Jacksonville, but Mr. Townsend's secretary said he'd meet her here today, Monday, at ten o'clock. She'd arrived a few minutes early.

The sun beat down warmer than usual for February. Katie walked to the porch steps to get out of the bright light. The steps appeared in good shape. To test the wood, she put one foot out and cautiously stepped forward.

The front door creaked open a small slit. She gasped, and her hand went to her throat, where her heart beat hard and fast. She waited. The only sounds were blackbirds cawing and the whisper of wind.

Dare she move closer? She stumbled and reached out to prevent herself from falling. She glanced around as though she expected to see someone behind her. "Katie girl, you're letting the isolation scare you," she mumbled to herself.

Pushing open the warped door, Katie nudged herself to go in. The smell of fresh paint tickled her nose. Sunlight shone across newly polished wood floors. There was an old red brick fireplace situated against the far wall. An obviously new tan leather sofa and chairs with accompanying side tables filled the living area.

Through a large curved entrance, she moved into the dining room. Dark wood stairs curved off to the right side and led to the second floor. Crown molding edged the ceilings.

"What a beautiful old house," she whispered. "And someone has recently decided to clean you up inside." She ran her hand over an old china cabinet with sparkling glass walls and shelves. A long table with high back chairs still had the plastic covering on them.

Continuing her exploration, she went into the kitchen. Shiny new appliances filled the work area, and a small old oak table with two chairs sat in one corner. Only thing missing is a dishwasher.

The paint smell began to give her a headache, and she reached across the sink to push the window open and then went to the back door and opened it. The faint smell of roses blew in through the screen door.

"Hello, anyone here?" A male voice came from the living room.

Katie hurried back to the front of the house. A tall, thin man with thick white hair and dressed in a dark brown suit stood in the doorway, a briefcase in his hand.

"Mr. Townsend?"

"Yes, and you must be Katie Weber."

Katie smiled and stepped forward to take his outstretched hand. "I am. I got here a little early, and the house was open."

A frown crossed Mr. Townsend's face. "That's strange. My contractor assured me he'd locked up for the weekend. Oh, well, nothing appears to be disturbed."

"You're the one that has fixed up the house?" Katie asked.

Mr. Townsend nodded. "The inside anyway. How do you like it?"

"It's lovely, nice soft colors and leaving some of the old furniture, like the china cabinet, is a nice touch."

He laughed. "The china cabinet and a few items upstairs are all that's really valuable about this old place. The house itself should probably be torn down."

"Oh I hope not. Surely it can be saved."

The sound of another car had them both looking out the window. Katie got a glimpse of a black Mercedes before the driver pulled over to park.

"Good," Mr. Townsend said. "We're all here now and can get down to business."

A tall shadow cast across the door, and the man stepped into the room.

"Jake Andrews," Katie gasped.

Mr. Townsend smiled. "You know each other? That will make this easier. Please join me at the dining room table."

Jake and Katie stared questioningly at each other and followed Mr. Townsend.

"Mr. Andrews, I didn't introduce myself. I'm Harold Townsend. I've heard good things about your computer company. A friend of mine, who lives in Atlanta, says if I ever have problems with my set-up that you're the man to call." He motioned for the two of them to sit.

"Well, thank you, but I don't understand. I thought you and I had an appointment at ten this morning."

"I'm sure this is all very confusing, but I'll explain. After consideration, I decided I'd see you two together as the decision you make will affect both of you."

"Does this concern the possible inheritance?" Katie asked, and felt her face flush when both men looked in her direction.

"Yes, it does." Mr. Townsend sat and opened his briefcase, pulling out a thick manila folder. He smiled at Katie and Jake and leaned back in his chair. "I understand you both knew Mrs. Pace in the past. She named you in her will, but she added several stipulations regarding the inheritance."

"Stipulations?" Jake Andrews's deep voice edged with control.

The lawyer nodded. "You probably know that Sandstone is valuable property. It includes this original farm house and surrounding acres of prime

Florida land." Mr. Townsend shuffled papers in his hands. "You jointly inherit Sandstone Ranch, if you meet the terms of the will."

His gaze intent, he continued. "First, you must live here," his hands spread out to indicate the farm house, "for thirty days."

"B…both of us?" Katie stammered.

"Yes. However, if you don't accept the requirements," Mr. Townsend held up his hand to forestall Jake's reply, "we can conclude our business now, and the State of Florida receives the house and surrounding thousand acres."

"A thousand acres?" Katie squeaked out.

"The land will be valuable developed. The old farm house would be best torn down, as I mentioned to you earlier." Mr. Townsend looked at Katie. "Do you wish for me to proceed?"

"Go on." Jake ground out the words.

Katie flashed him an annoyed look before nodding for the lawyer to continue.

"The house has the reputation of being haunted. No one has lived here for more than a few weeks straight since 1863." He paused. "Your next stipulation is to discover the story of the house. Is it haunted or not and if so, by whom? Are there other secrets about the house?"

Mr. Townsend leaned back in his chair. "Mrs. Pace always wanted to know the true story, but she never lived in the house herself. She did have her suspicions." He stopped and cleared his throat. "After you discover what you can about the house, she requested you write an article for the local paper to finally tell the story, whatever you believe it might be." He concluded and sat back, a satisfied grin on his face. "My client was a bit eccentric, but the will is clearly written with no loopholes.

"I was Mrs. Pace's attorney for many years. I know that for various reasons she admired you both." Mr. Townsend stood and gathered his papers. "You will need to decide quickly. If you accept the terms of her will, you must move in by tomorrow afternoon. That's why I went ahead and had the place made livable.

"In a month, we will meet at my office and you can tell me what you discovered. Any questions?" he asked. He snapped his case closed and prepared to leave.

"I'll need to fly to Atlanta to make arrangements for my company during my absence," Jake said.

"As long as you're back tomorrow at dark, that's fine. I expect there will be things you need to do during the days, but this will be your home base. Here's my card. Call me with your decision."

They watched him stride out the front and go to his car. Katie went to the refrigerator and saw several cold cokes. She took two and handed one to Jake.

She laughed. "Do I look as stunned as you do?"

"Thanks for the coke, and yes, you do." He took a long swig from the can.

Katie studied the man in front of her. He bore little resemblance to the Jake Andrews she'd met Saturday night. Today, he was dressed in a gray pin-striped suit with a vest. His thick, collar length, golden brown hair shone in the sunlight coming from the kitchen window. She stared into his sky blue eyes. Reluctantly, she forced herself to look away.

Walking to the screen door, she pushed it open and stepped out onto the back stoop. Jake followed and stood close behind her.

"The place is isolated," he commented.

To put distance between them, Katie moved across the space and sat on the edge of the first step. She took a sip of her drink.

"Do you think the house is haunted?" Katie asked him.

"I believe in what I can see and what can be explained by logic and reason," Jake said, and joined her.

"I don't know. Sometimes things happen that don't always make sense."

"It's usually just someone's overactive imagination. Anyway, neither of us wants to turn down this opportunity. What's your main concern?"

"I've never lived with a stranger. Well, you're almost a stranger."

He cleared his throat, "I'm perfectly safe. You didn't seem worried about me Saturday night."

"I hadn't planned to live with you then," she said.

"You know Tom Cole is my friend, and I knew your brother, Frank, in high school. You can always ask him about me. Let's face it this is a large house. We don't have to be in each other's space all the time. It's too good of an opportunity to past up."

Katie nodded, and they both stood. She put out her hand. "I agree. Let's shake on it."

That was a big mistake Katie realized, as soon as her hand touched his. Sparks zapped up her arm, and he gave a quick yank pulling her against his hard frame. His arms wrapped around her, and his smoldering glance heated her body.

"Maybe we're both afraid of this." He lowered his mouth and pressed his lips over hers. The kiss took her breath away. His tongue moved gently around the soft lining of her mouth, while his hands pulled her body tighter against him.

Katie pushed away and retreated down the steps. Wrapping her arms tight around herself, she walked to the field of wildflowers before turning to face him.

He hadn't moved.

"I don't think I can have a casual relationship with you. If we do this," she nodded toward the house, "you have to promise to treat me as a friend, nothing more."

"I'll follow your example," he said, skirting around the promise.

"See you here tomorrow evening," she called to him.

Katie hurried to her car and slid into her seat. Turning, she headed back toward the dirt lane. At the last minute, she glanced in her rearview mirror. Jake stood on the front porch watching her drive off. She moved her eyes upward and was almost certain she saw the curtains at the upstairs window move.

A shiver moved over her. Which would be more dangerous, the ghost that she suspected lived at Sandstone, or the man?

* * * *

Jake flashed his ID and airline tickets on his way through the metal detector and took his case off the moving conveyor belt.

Gate twenty-eight occupied the end of the left wing. Stopping at a small concession stand, he ordered black coffee and watched his fellow passengers rushing from place to place. Most caught up in their own little bubble, unaware of the tide of people flowing around them.

He strode down the walkway and checked in at the gate. He sat in a nearby seat and placed his monogrammed briefcase beside his leg.

Jake thought about Katie Weber. She'd always held a certain fascination for him, her and her family. He'd seen her around town in the past. Little Katie, her three tall brothers and two sisters let her tag along with them. They always seemed to be joking and playing tricks on each other. He remembered watching them, envying them.

"Flight eighty-nine is ready for boarding." He grabbed his briefcase and threw the empty cup into the waste container.

"Welcome abroad, Mr. Andrews." The stewardess smiled in greeting. "Glad to see you're flying with us again."

"Thanks, I can find my seat. Good to see you."

Jake moved quickly to number three in first class and put his briefcase in the overhead compartment. No work this trip. His head was full of ideas and plans.

He leaned back against his seat and closed his eyes. If he received this inheritance, he and Tom's dream of building a housing development in Treehaven might become a reality. Finally, Jake had an opportunity to show the town's people that he was not his father.

Some of the old timers still watched and waited to see him fail. He resembled his father in looks, and they expected Jake to end up just like him.

"Mr. Andrews." He opened his eyes to see the stewardess standing beside his seat.

"Would you like a drink before your dinner is served?"

"No thanks, I'll pass."

She smiled. "Let me know if you want anything."

"I will." Jake watched her walk back to the galley before turning his head to look out the window. He loved the take off, the uplift into the sky.

The first time he'd flown he'd been four. He still remembered wondering how close to heaven you'd be if you stepped outside onto the fluffy white clouds.

His aunt had sat beside him and laughed at his comment. "It's a lot harder to get into heaven, young man. There ain't no plane to take you. It takes lots of good deeds and hard work." She scowled at him. "No messing around or being a crook like your Daddy."

When the four-year-old boy stepped off the plane he found how close to hell he really was. Jake shook his head. He never let those memories enter his mind. He stood and retrieved his briefcase. He'd study the contracts he'd brought with him. His past wasn't worth contemplating. Working toward a better future would take him where he wanted to go.

* * * *

After seeing Sara off on her date with Tom, Katie decided to drive to her parents' house for a visit. Sara and she had discussed the will and stipulations, and Katie had seen the concern in her friend's eyes. She knew her parents weren't going to be happy about her living at Sandstone either, but she might as well get it over with and tell them.

She knocked on the door and then let herself in through the kitchen. "Mom, Dad," she called out.

"I'm out here, Katie love." Her father stuck his head in the screened door from the porch. "Your mother has gone to her monthly bridge club meeting."

"I forgot."

"Get something to drink and join me on the porch."

Katie nodded and poured herself a glass of lemonade then headed in his direction.

Her dad held the door open. She took a seat across the table from him.

The lemonade was sweet and cold. She stared out at the lush landscaped lawn. In the twilight, she smelled the fragrances of roses, gardenias, and honeysuckle. Cardinals, blue jays and doves flew back and forth to a nearby bird feeder. "I'd forgotten how beautiful this back yard is Dad. You must spend hours working on it."

"Now that I'm retired it's easier, a joy really. Tell me about your meeting, Katie. How did it go?"

"The inheritance includes conditions to be met," Katie said.

"Conditions?"

Katie nodded and took another sip of her drink. "You know the letter mentioned Sandstone Ranch."

"Sure, the old place off 501. Actually, I'm surprised the house is still standing," her dad said. He looked intently at Katie. "Rumor was old lady Pace owned it."

"Yes, she did." Katie took a deep breath. "Jake Andrews and I are to inherit the house and land, if we live there for thirty days and discover the mystery regarding the place." The words rushed out. "And write an article for the paper with the results."

Her father stared at her. "Dad, say something."

"Jake Andrews was the boy that always got into fights in high school. There was talk around town about him being a trouble maker." Her Dad hesitated. "I heard the gossip, but Frank liked him and the several times I saw him after football practice he was always polite. Frank said Jake was treated unfairly."

"He's apparently done well for himself," Katie said. "He has his own business and Mr. Townsend mentioned hearing about his company. What do you think about all of this, Dad?"

"Have you decided to meet the terms of the will?" he asked her, a probing query in his eyes.

"Yes. It's too good an opportunity not to."

She watched him sip the last of his lemonade. "Then you have my support, Katie love, but be careful," he added. "A gift can sometimes be a two-edged sword." He stood, kissed the top of her head and went inside to answer the ringing phone.

Katie stared out across the lawn. She did remember Mrs. Pace, a tiny woman with snow white hair and a quick smile. She always had homemade cookies and cold tea for refreshments. Never did Katie dream Mrs. Pace owned anything other than the small, square, concrete home she'd lived in for years.

They'd met when Katie began her volunteer work required by the local high school. Mrs. Pace needed someone to read to her. She loved books and her eyesight was failing. What started as a three week project ended up lasting for two years until Katie went off to college.

Nightfall cast shadows across the lawn. Katie stood and stretched. How her life had changed in the past months. She 'd never have thought a year ago that she'd be back home in Florida and planning to stay in an old, reportedly haunted house with a handsome man from her past.

She heard the screen door and glanced around at her father when he returned to his seat. "You've been looking sad, my Katie."

His gentle loving voice almost brought tears to her eyes. She reached out and squeezed his hand. "You can't protect me from all the hurts, you know."

"Just remember I've still got a broad shoulder to cry on."

"Dad," she spoke out determined to change the subject. "Have you ever been to Sandstone Ranch?"

Rocking slowly in his chair, he lit his pipe. The familiar odor of pipe tobacco wafted across her nose and brought back pleasant memories.

"Once during my high school years, some of my buddies and I went out there one Halloween. You see we'd heard the rumors of it being haunted."

"Did you see anything?" Katie tried to keep the anxiety out of her voice.

"You have to understand we scared ourselves from the start. The idea of going to that house, on Halloween night of all times, had our hearts tripping and our hands slick with sweat. Of course, none of us admitted to being afraid. We stumbled around the perimeter of the house and made creepy noises to scare each other."

"You saw nothing out of the ordinary?"

"Oh, I didn't say that." Her dad puffed on his pipe. "Afterwards we all figured it was our spirited imagination and nothing more, but I've wondered. Not enough to want to go back and check it out." He winked at her.

"Wondered what, Dad?" Katie knew she had to be patient. Her dad loved to string out a tale.

"The full moon gave us a lot of light. We started to move off toward where we'd left the car and then we glanced back."

His words had Katie's heart beating faster.

"Bud Stevens and I both saw her pacing across the front upstairs room. Then, the most ungodly scream of pain echoed through the still night."

He stared across at Katie. "From then on, I've always believed in the possibility of ghosts." He grinned. "You'd have laughed if you'd seen us, four big teenage boys scrambling into the car on top of each other."

Goose bumps covered Katie's arms and legs. She moved along the porch, leaning out staring at the sliver of moon overhead. She turned to face her father.

"When I visited Sandstone today, I arrived first. The place had a desolate feeling about it." She hesitated.

Her father sat quietly, waiting for her to continue.

"Something pushed me forward, Dad, after I'd climbed the steps to the porch, and the door creaked open. So, I was wary before I ever entered the house. Inside an eerie stillness settled around me. Then after our meeting, when I drove away, I'm sure I saw the curtains in the upstairs window move. I can't get it out of my mind."

"Some things are unexplainable. It's an old house. I don't much care for the idea of you having to live there for a month, but I understand why you think you can't pass this up." He reached out and took her hand. "Actually, I'm glad you won't be alone, but I wish one of us could be with you."

"You think it's haunted, don't you?"

"Yes."

Katie squeezed his hand. "I do too," she said, then glanced at her watch. "I'd better leave. If I hurry, I can get to the library before they close. They might have some information on Sandstone."

Her Dad stood and gave her a hug. "Stay in touch. Call us if you need anything."

"Thanks, Dad. Tell Mom hello. I'll see you soon." She waved and hurried to her car. She sat for a moment looking out at the darkness around her and visualizing Sandstone. A shiver ran across her shoulders.

Chapter 3

Katie unlocked the door to Sara's townhouse and went to her bedroom. She was glad Sara wasn't home. She was anxious to read the library book titled, *Haunted Houses in Florida*, which she'd checked out. She turned on her bedside light. Flipping open the pages, she read the list of contents and found The Legacy of Sandstone Ranch, and a note about the information coming from old-timers living in the area. She kicked off her shoes, leaned against her pillows and started to read.

A young Treehaven couple married in 1861 and settled on the ranch planning to work the farm and raise a family.

Katie looked up and stared out her window to the darkened sky. She turned the switch on her lamp up another notch to give her more light.

By the next year the Civil War began and across the South all able-bodied men were encouraged to enlist. The young bride reportedly pleaded with her husband to stay and not leave her. And he did, at first. Later, as the war continued and reports of casualties filtered back to them, the husband joined the Confederate Army.

Katie imagined the despair and fears the young woman felt, and her husband had to choose between the love for his wife and the need to stand for the cause.

A lump formed in Katie's throat. That horrible war tore apart a country and also the couple. She started to read again.

He left one day and never returned. His bride received news of his death at Fredericksburg, in December 1862, two months after he enlisted.

Neighbors found her body. She lay across their bed. No evidence of foul play or illness. Rumor had it she died of a broken heart. Later, people came to believe the old house was haunted.

Feeling silly to be so emotional, Katie wiped her tears and slammed the book shut. She hated sad love stories, especially since she'd had her own disappointment with love. She'd read enough.

Determined to forget the mystery of the house for tonight, she put the book by her purse to return it tomorrow. She jumped when the phone beside her bed rang.

"Hello."

"Hi, this is Jake Andrews. I just got back to my apartment and thought I'd call."

"Oh, hi." Katie said, surprised to hear his deep velvety voice.

"I flew back to Atlanta this afternoon. As I told Mr. Townsend, I have things to take care of before I can move into the house. I wanted to make sure you haven't changed your mind."

Katie sat on the side of her bed.

"You still there?" Jake asked.

"Yes, and I haven't changed my mind."

"Did you tell your parents you'd be living with me for the next month?"

"I told my father the conditions. All of them."

"Really?"

"Yes." Katie heard the mockery in his voice.

"Maybe he doesn't remember me."

"I think he does," Katie said. "Dad said you and my brother knew each other in high school and that Frank thought you were an all right guy.,"

"Well-good. See you soon."

Katie listened to the buzz in the receiver. She hadn't expected to hear from him until they moved into Sandstone.

Her mind in turmoil and her emotions rattled, she refused to even glance at the library book. She thought of her dad's comment and knew he worried about her.

He didn't like her living with any man not her husband. He'd been displeased with Eric and happy when they set the wedding date. Eric was in her past. She'd avoided men since their breakup, but she'd find it hard to ignore Jake Andrews. He was compelling, mysterious and much too worldly for her.

The cacophony of frogs and crickets filled the night. She sat on her window seat staring at the star-filled sky.

Eric's betrayal hurt, but she had to admit things had changed between them before their split. She'd had her own doubts about their future. Still she'd tried to deny the problems. After she'd invested so much emotionally and financially, she didn't want to let go of the relationship. Finally, she had to admit it was broken beyond repair.

Now she didn't want or have time for anyone in her life. She wanted her own home, a safe haven, safe, being the operative word. Could she ever feel that way about Sandstone?

She had decisions to make, including what direction to take with her career. There were too many obstacles in the way of her starting a relationship with anyone and now she had a haunted house to deal with. Her life turned upside down these past months.

Her reaction to Jake on Saturday night had knocked her for a loop, but she'd come to her senses in time. This strong sensual pull between them confused and scared her. He struck her as a no commitment type guy and she someday, not now, wanted a home and family. She feared Jake might be able to really break her heart. Thirty days was going to be a long time to keep her guard up.

* * * *

"Thanks for helping me settle in, Annie." Katie smiled at her sister.

"I'm glad you called. I admit I was curious to see this place and to hear all about your inheritance. Bet Dad doesn't like the idea of your living here all alone with a man."

"I…"

"Hello." Jake Andrews stood in the kitchen doorway.

Dressed in faded jeans and a tee shirt, he looked dangerously handsome. The motorcycle man.

"Hi. Annie, this is Mr. Jake Andrews. Jake, Annie Cramer is one of my sisters."

"Nice to meet you," he said, putting out his hand. He looked from one to the other and raised an eyebrow. "You two don't look much alike."

Annie laughed. "Katie's the shortest one of the group and the only redhead."

"I am not a redhead," Katie protested. "My hair is dark blonde with some red in it."

Jake and Annie both laughed.

"Can we help you bring in your suitcases?" Katie asked to change the subject.

"This is it. I travel light." Jake pointed to his one suitcase and suit bag. "The only thing left in the car is my briefcase and laptop. Which room do you want me to use?"

She felt her face flush and glanced uneasily at her sister.

"I thought you might like the downstairs bedroom to the left of the dining room. There's a small bath next to it," she said.

"I am getting older. It'll save me walking up all those stairs." There was a trace of humor in his voice.

She and Annie watched him as he took his bags, and went whistling down the hall toward his room.

"Now that is a handsome man."

"I suppose," Katie said nonchalantly. She felt her sister's scrutiny. Katie busied herself putting away the rest of the groceries.

Everything about the man sent her pulses spinning. The faint aroma of his cologne lingered and the memory of his tee shirt covering a broad chest and jeans clinging to long, muscled legs brought on a gamut of conflicting emotions.

Her long lectures to herself didn't seem to be working. She'd decided to treat him as a business partner and keep everything on an impersonal basis. She flunked that test already. One look at him and her good resolutions went by the board.

"Can I help with anything in here?"

He'd returned, leaning against the doorframe looking like a GQ model.

"No, we've finished putting the groceries away," Katie said.

"I'll be in my room unpacking if you do need any help." He turned to go.

"Just a minute, Jake." Annie stopped him.

Katie saw the look of caution in his eyes. He stood politely, his body taut.

"We always have a big Sunday dinner after church at our parents'. They'd like you to join us this next weekend." Annie's sweet voice seemed to echo in the silent house. "Of course, you don't have to attend church with us, but the family would like to meet you."

"You want me to come for dinner?" His voice reflected his surprise and wariness.

Annie nodded.

"Sorry, I've already got an invitation for that day." He spoke coolly.

Katie studied his expressionless face.

Annie smiled. "Maybe another time."

"Maybe," he repeated, but Katie didn't believe him.

"Well, I'd better get home and start supper. I left my youngest with the next door neighbor. I'm glad I got to meet you, Jake." She hugged Katie and waved as she hurried out the door.

Jake stepped into the kitchen. "Have any cold cokes?

"Yes, help yourself. The weather is a bit warm for February."

"I'll reimburse you for any groceries I use." He walked around her and opened the fridge.

"Not necessary."

"I insist," Jake said, and popped open the coke can.

"Fine, I like to cook so I bought my favorite foods," she warned him.

His sexy smile lit his face. "I'm easy."

Oh yeah, she thought. She felt the heat rise to her face. She'd like to challenge him on that.

They stayed silent, as heat and desire swirled in the air around them. When he moved toward her, Katie jerked herself out of her trance. How embarrassing. She might as well drool all over him.

"Guess I'd better unpack too. Excuse me." Katie rushed out of the room and up the stairs.

The second floor held three bedrooms and a small bath that someone had remodeled adding a bear claw tub, hand shower and stand alone sink. Two of the bedrooms were small, the third, ran across the front of the house making it twice as large. This had to be the room where her father saw the ghost and where she spotted the curtains move.

She'd come upstairs earlier and left her suitcase inside the door of the front bedroom. Most certainly the best room.

A full size white wrought iron bed faced the three windows looking out across the front yard. Two matching rattan tables sat on either side of the bed. A large armoire stood against the far wall and on the other side an antique tallboy. The furnishings fit the room.

It didn't take her long to unpack and put her clothes away. She found a colorful afghan stored in the tallboy and threw it across the white bedspread. A hint of roses clung to it. The splash of red, blue, and purple gave the room some needed color. Katie ran her fingers along the yarn. She felt a hint of warmth, and yanked her hand away.

She glanced around the room, while her heart beat slowed back to normal. It needed something more. Remembering a vase packed in a box with some other odds and ends, Katie headed downstairs to search for it.

After she found the vase, she'd pick a bunch of the wildflowers blooming in the field behind the house to put in it.

* * * *

Jake looked out the screen door. Katie twirled around stopping here and there to pick flowers. Sunshine shone across her reddish blond hair sending flashes of light dancing around her head. The breeze blew across her curls and ruffled the light material of her blouse. Joy emanated from her. He wanted to be part of that joy, to reach out and capture the essence of her.

She looked toward the door, and he stepped into the shadows. He wanted her, against his better judgment, and thirty days was a long time.

Katie smiled when she came inside and saw him. "You're finished?"

"I'm all settled in. I'm going to town to see Tom. Do you need me to get anything for you?"

"I might. Can you wait while I run these upstairs?"

"Sure. It'll be a few minutes before I'm ready to leave."

"Good, I'll hurry."

Jake stood admiring her as she climbed the stairs. His hands itched to reach out and touch her soft, curvy skin. Hopefully she didn't plan on wearing such short shorts every day or he'd need treatment for high blood pressure.

She hurried back downstairs to join him, that sweet smile ever tempting him to taste her. Forcing his lustful thoughts aside, he picked up his briefcase from the floor where he'd sat it down.

"I'm going to use Tom's internet connection to keep in touch with my employees. I'm surprised this old house even has phone lines that work for the phone. I shouldn't be long. Did you think of something you need?"

"A couple of things. I'll write them down."

Jake held out his pen.

"Always prepared like a good boy scout?"

He heard the teasing note in her voice and laughed. "I doubt they'd have let me in the scout troop if I'd asked."

* * * *

Katie chuckled and wrote several items on her paper. "Here you are."

She walked to the door behind him and watched as he drove off. The house seemed quieter now. She wandered around the downstairs, opening all the windows to catch any breeze. Her steps took her down the short hall to Jake's room.

As he said, he'd put everything neatly away. In the small bath she saw his toothbrush and comb. Suddenly, she felt guilty, almost like she'd been spying on him. She walked quickly back toward the dining room.

Half the afternoon was gone. She'd—

A loud bang reverberated through the house. What was that? More sounds came from the second floor. She stepped closer to the stairs. Yes, she heard something. Mouth dry and hands clammy, she gulped for air.

What should she do? Go upstairs and check or wait for Jake? He'd laugh, and say she imagined it, then go with her and find nothing.

If she planned to live here, she'd better get over being scared of every little noise. Cautiously, she went up the steps. She thought the sounds came from her room, so she headed in that direction. The unnerving silence surrounded her.

"No!" The word erupted out of her mouth. Her beautiful glass vase lay broken on the wood floor. Flowers and water spilled from it. The doors of the armoire stood open and clothes tossed, as though by a willful child, lay around the room or hung off the side of her bed.

When Katie stepped inside, a rush of air swirled in circles around her, the faint sound of laughter echoed in her ears. Heart pounding, Katie yelled stop. The wind and laughter vanished.

Katie placed her hands on her hips and glared into the space in front of her. The quiet settled around her as she fought the urge to run downstairs.

She glanced around. There was nothing to see except the mess in her room. Anger began to replace the fear.

"Judith, I am not leaving. I plan to make this my home, so get used to it."

Nothing stirred. Katie stomped around the room gathering her clothes and hanging them in the armoire. Then, she retrieved the mop and dust pan from downstairs and cleaned the floor of glass and water.

Finished, she checked the room and closed the armoire with a definite snap. Legs still trembling, she returned to the kitchen and took a bottle of wine out of the cupboard. She'd planned to have it with dinner, but she needed something to calm her frazzled nerves. Hands shaking, she had trouble working the corkscrew.

* * * *

Jake drove quickly, turning onto highway 501 and headed for town. Katie had been smart to put their rooms on different floors. No use tempting fate. This was a month long assignment, nothing more. Nevertheless, the large farmhouse already felt too small.

He pulled into a parking space in front of Tom Cole's office. They'd been friends since elementary school and Tom was one of the few people Jake trusted.

Sara, who worked as Tom's secretary, greeted him with a big smile. "Is everything all right? I thought you and Katie were moving into Sandstone today."

"Yes, I've already dropped my things at the ranch. Is Tom available?"

"Sure, go on in."

Tom sat back in his chair, feet on his desk, the phone in his right hand and a squeeze ball in his left. He motioned for Jake to sit, as he finished up his call.

Jake sat and studied his friend. When Jake had moved in with his aunt, Tom had been one of the few boys who didn't tease the thin child, the new kid on the block. Four-years-old, withdrawn and frightened of an unknown world, Tom Cole accepted him and became his lifelong friend. Damn, there he went getting downright maudlin. If living in Treehaven had this effect on him, he was in trouble.

"Hi, man." Tom put the phone and his feet down and reached across to shake Jake's hand. "What's up?"

"You won't believe it. Has Sara told you about what happened?"

"Yes." He studied Jake's face. "It's hard to believe."

"I know," Jake agreed.

"The way I understand it, you have to find out whether there is a ghost at Sandstone." Tom said.

"You got it, and since I don't believe in ghosts, it won't be hard to show how people's imagination and stories told over the years have created this tall tale."

"Damn, that's prime real estate," Tom said.

"And large enough for our dream housing development."

"What about Katie? She gets half," Tom reminded Jake.

Jake nodded, "I'll talk to her about selling her part to me. It shouldn't be a problem to get a loan from the bank, once they review our business plan. We can buy her out with part of the money." Jake raked his hand through his hair. "Man, can you believe it. I can see it all."

Tom came around his desk and clapped Jake on the shoulder. "I...."

Sara came through the door just then with a handful of mail.

"What's going on with you two? You both have silly grins on your faces."

"Sara, my love, as you already know, Jake is going to inherit the Sandstone ranch with Katie. Isn't that a great place for our housing development?" Tom hugged her and swung her around.

"Whoa. What about Katie?"

"I'll buy her out," Jake said.

Sara raised her eyebrows. "Has anyone mentioned this plan to her?" Sara eyed the two men.

Jake wandered around the room. His hand ran along the sleek lines of a tiger, carved out of polished teak, sitting on a side table. "I haven't asked her...yet."

Sara didn't say anything. She watched Jake prowl.

"What?" Jake asked, defiance in his tone.

"Nothing, we'll see what Katie has to say," Sara said.

"You can't believe I'd let one small woman stand in our way?" Jake's voice edged with tension.

"Katie may have other ideas. We women can be stubborn when we set our minds to it."

"And I can be very persuasive, when I want something. Little Katie has met her match."

"Come on, friend," Tom said. "Let's take Sara out for coffee. Time will tell whether we see our dream become a reality."

"I can't." Jake glanced at his watch as he followed them out the door. "I'd better get back to Sandstone, but I almost forgot, can I use your empty room for an office? The farmhouse isn't equipped to handle internet connections, and I need to keep in touch with my staff."

"No problem. Use this place as your own. You may need it as a refuge after you tell Katie your idea," Tom said and laughed.

Chapter 4

Jake stood at the kitchen door and watched as Katie tilted her head back and finished the glass of wine she held in one gulp.

"Kind of early for drinking, isn't it? Or are you toasting the future?" Jake stepped inside the kitchen door and peered at Katie intently.

"Neither." She sighed and swallowed hard. "I thought I'd have a glass while I finished dinner. Do you want to join me?"

Jake's eyes went from her white face to her shaky hands.

"What's wrong?"

She shrugged her shoulders and shook her head, apparently unwilling to explain.

"Can I help?" He noted the potatoes on the counter. "I'm pretty good at peeling and I don't think you need to be handling a knife." He motioned toward her trembling hands. "Sure you don't want to tell me why you're upset? I'm a good listener."

"I don't think you'll believe me."

He leaned forward. "Why not?"

"It's so preposterous. I've been trying to think of an explanation myself, something reasonable, but nothing comes to mind."

"Take a deep breath, have some more wine and tell me what happened."

Katie glanced down at the glass of wine he'd handed her and then looked up at him. "I will. Give me a few minutes. Let's finish dinner and then we'll talk."

He watched her take a big swallow of wine and his eyes focused on her mouth, down along her neck's pearly white skin, to the shaded valley revealed by her open collar. Warm heat ran through his veins and it wasn't from the wine. Forcing himself to concentrate, he sat his glass aside and turned to his job.

During dinner, Katie told him about the incident regarding her clothes and vase and about her father's childhood story. Her hazel eyes changed with her emotion from light brown to more green with golden flecks.

"And you chose that room out of the three?"

"Well, yes. If I plan to live here I decided I'd choose the best." She grinned. "I convinced myself the ghost wouldn't frighten me away."

"You really believe in ghosts?"

"Wait and see when something happens to your room and your things. You'll believe too." Katie started clearing the table.

Jake pushed his chair back and began to help. "Maybe she likes men." He placed his plate and silverware in the sink.

"Where's the dishwashing liquid?"

"You don't have to help," Katie said.

When he frowned, she shrugged and reached below the sink to hand him the bottle.

"I'm used to fending for myself. I don't mind," he said.

"What makes you think she likes men?"

"I was joking."

"Very funny." Katie smiled, and her relaxed laughter warmed his heart. And then the lights went out.

Less then a second later, Katie jumped into his arms. "What happened?" He noticed the quiver in her voice. Then, apparently realizing she had her arms wrapped around his middle, she bumped his jaw in her hurry to pull away.

"I suspect it's the old wiring." Jake rubbed his chin and mourned the loss of her hug. "I saw a flash of lightning. I'll check the fuse box. Do you know where it's located?"

"No, and I don't have a flashlight either."

"I have one in my room." Jake strode toward the door and bumped into something. "Why is there a chair in the middle of the doorway?"

"I don't know. I put it against the wall. Maybe the ghost moved it."

"Ghosts are a fabrication made up to scare small children and naïve adults."

He pushed the chair aside and glanced back in her direction. "Stay here. I'll only be a moment."

He took two steps, and the lights came on.

"See," Katie said emphatically. "There's something here."

Jake strolled to where Katie stood. Fear showed in her eyes. Her soft body, the fragrance of her skin and the brush of her silky hair made everything in his body stand at attention.

Taking her shoulders in a firm grip, his voice softened. "Or the wiring in this old place is a hundred years old. There are no ghosts."

The lights blinked on and off, and a rush of air flew between them. She moved a little closer to him. "See," Kathy said. "You're making it angry."

Jake glanced to one side. "This window," he motioned to it, "is open and there's an evening storm coming, and gusts of wind are not abnormal."

He reluctantly let go of her shoulders and picked up his dish towel. "We'd better finish the dishes before the lights go off again. And you might as well get used to the electricity being temperamental."

But, the lights stayed on, even with the rain and lightning. Now she'd really believe the ghost was controlling things, Jake thought.

"I'm going to work in my room," he said, and hung the wet dish towel on the side of the counter. "Tom Cole is loaning me an office to use. I'll be going into town most days to contact my Atlanta staff. Thanks for the meal." He hesitated. "Are you sure you want me to sleep downstairs? I can move to one of the other rooms upstairs if you want."

She straightened her shoulders and smiled confidently. "Thanks for the offer, but I'll be fine."

He shrugged. "Yell if you need me," and strode off. He turned on his computer and stared at the screen, then put on his favorite music and tried to drown out his thoughts of Katie and how delectable she'd felt while in his arms. It wasn't working.

This whole day seemed surreal. It was this crazy inheritance and having to live with someone, after being a loner for so long, that caused his reactions to Katie. He ignored the thought that the feelings had been alive and strong on Saturday night.

Once he settled in, he'd be fine, back to his old self. Determined to do some work, he pushed his disturbing thoughts away. He was good at not dealing with emotions.

* * * *

Heavy rain beat against the window panes and brought Katie's attention away from her book. Darkness filled most of the house, except for her light in the living room. She'd half listened to Jake's music. She wasn't sure when it stopped.

"Jake," she whispered his name. He was a complex, solitary, vigilant, confusing mixture of a man and usually when he looked at her, her heart tripped faster. But, tonight his actions had soothed and his gaze had been friendly and restful. It seemed he controlled his manner at will. She wished she had the same ability.

She'd watched his face as she told him about the incident that happened while he was gone. Other than his eyes darkening, she couldn't read anything from his expression.

Katie had wanted to accept his offer to sleep upstairs, but his presence so close might create other problems plus make her look like a silly frightened woman. Even if she was one, she didn't want it to show.

The stairs stood in the shadows. She had to go to bed sometime, might as well be now. Clicking on the stairwell light, she put one foot in front of the other, wishing again she'd taken up Jake's offer. He was a long way off if anything happened.

Taking a deep breath, Katie reminded herself she was a grown woman and quite capable of taking care of herself. She peeked into her room and slumped in relief. Everything was in place.

Almost asleep, Katie heard the soft crying. A faint outline of a person paced in front of the windows, arms wrapped around the waist. The low cry continued and the figure bent forward at times. Katie froze, recalling her father's story.

A sudden flash of lightning lit the room and the ghost turned toward the bed. Chills ran along Katie's back and legs, and she yanked the covers to her throat.

The ghost like figure came closer, still only a faint outline, like an early morning mist. "Stay," Katie whispered. "I'm not here to hurt you."

The mist dissolved leaving the familiar fragrance of roses lingering. Katie lay stiff in her bed. Her eyes stared into the blackness. Afraid, she still didn't let herself contemplate running downstairs to Jake.

Katie blinked at the sun shining in and realized she'd slept. Relieved to find no evidence of her ghost, she decided to take a shower, dress, and act like it was a normal day in a normal house.

After dressing, she hurried to the kitchen. Jake followed her in.

"Where do we start?" she asked him as he raised his coffee cup to take the first sip.

"Where do you suggest?" he countered.

"I've already checked out a book from the library."

"Did you learn anything?"

She told him about the couple who'd lived in the house during the Civil war. "I'm sure it has something to do with his enlisting and leaving her alone. Maybe she's still waiting for him?"

He shrugged. "That seems too easy and unrealistic."

"Well, what do you suggest?" she snapped.

"Whoa, don't get mad at me."

"I'm not angry, but we have very little time to solve this puzzle, and you seem unconcerned."

He took his cup to the kitchen sink. His eyes glittered icy blue. "I'll start checking the internet today. Satisfied?"

Katie felt the heat from her blush. She hated the way her face turned red at the slightest inclination. Nodding briefly, she turned her head facing the living room and finished her coffee. Obviously, the next four weeks were not going to go smoothly.

She'd visit Annie. Annie used to love doing genealogy, and Katie felt a weird connection to this place. Maybe Annie could find more information about Judith Collier's family.

Jake left with a curt goodbye, and Katie went outside to sit on the back stoop. Two black birds chased each other across the sky, their feathers glistening in the sunlight. She sipped her coffee and breathed in the scent of roses from the bushes blooming by the back steps.

Jake didn't believe in ghosts or at least he wouldn't admit it. There must be some evidence around here to convince him he's wrong. It would be easier to solve the puzzle if they both worked from the same point of view.

Today, he'd dressed in a red Polo shirt and grey slacks. In casual clothes, he was ruggedly handsome. He had the looks of a man who worked hard physically and mentally.

She stood and hurried inside. Enough daydreaming about Jake. She had things to do.

At the sink, she rinsed out her cup. Annie had probably fed her kids and might possibly be free to help if Katie went now. She'd change from shorts to jeans and go.

Standing in the bedroom with sunlight pouring in, Katie almost believed she'd imagined seeing or hearing anything last night. But, she did. The house was haunted, and to inherit this house and land they had to understand why the ghost lingered here and how to get it to leave.

* * * *

Since she hadn't called ahead, Katie was relieved to find her sister home.

"Hi Annie," Katie called out and stuck her head inside the back screen door.

Annie looked away from the tiny mouth she was trying to wipe clean. "Come in, I've been thinking about you. How did the first night go?"

"Fine, I guess." Katie hugged Annie and sat down facing little Ty. She reached across touching the child's soft cheek. "Babies and small children have the most incredible skin."

After placing several toys on the high chair tray, Annie turned to Katie. "What's going on? You didn't stop by just to see Ty and me."

"I might have."

"Come on, tell me what's wrong," Annie insisted.

"Nothing, but I do need your help. Do you still do genealogy?"

"Some," she said.

"If I give you a name will you see what you can find out about the person?"

"Sure. Who is it, your ghost?"

Katie frowned. "Yes, and don't laugh."

Annie raised her eyebrows. "I wouldn't dare. Are you enjoying rooming with a hunk?"

"Jake Andrews is the other person sharing the inheritance, nothing more," Katie protested and groaned inwardly at the feel of warmth on her cheeks.

"Sure," Annie said with a smile.

"I'm not ready to have anyone in my life."

"Things don't always happen when we're ready." Annie reached across and took Katie's hand. "It's usually the opposite, when everything is going crazy in your life."

"Speaking from experience, I assume," Katie said.

"Of course, I'll have to share my expertise in the field of love with you sometime."

"For now, I need your knowledge in genealogy. My ghost's name is Judith Collier and she grew up in Treehaven. Is that enough information to get you started?"

Ty started crying, and Annie took him out of his high chair. She pulled her hair out of Ty's clutches. "I think so. Do you have any idea what I might find?"

"I feel a connection to Sandstone," Katie said. "Maybe her family and ours are related in some way."

"This should be fun. I'll start today, when this little guy," she hugged Ty, "goes to bed. Do you want to spend the day, have lunch and see me start on the hunt for Judith?"

"Thanks, but I need to do more exploring. Do you have any idea where I might go next on my search for town history?"

Annie shifted Ty to her other hip and pondered the question.

"Let me think," she said. "Mr. and Mrs. Barrows have lived on Mulberry Road for at least seventy years. They're in their nineties. I saw an article about them recently in the local paper. They might know something about Sandstone."

"Great," Katie pulled out her small notepad. "Where's your phone book?"

Katie found the number and called the Barrows. After receiving an invitation and directions, she headed to Mulberry Road.

The yellow house with white trim sat in an adornment of flower beds with tall zinnias and purple lantana flowering amongst gardenia bushes and hibiscus. A tall, thin man stood up from a rocker on the porch.

"You must be Miss Katie Weber." A lopsided smile crossed his leathery face.

"Please call me Katie, Mr. Barrows."

He nodded, "Come in, Katie. The missus is looking forward to your visit."

Mrs. Barrows was a small, round woman with a perpetual smile, every bit as welcoming as her husband. She wiped her hands on her apron and pulled Katie into a tight hug.

"We're so glad to meet you, dear. It's been a long time since a pretty young lady came to visit us. Right, Joe?"

"Right." Joe Barrows indicated a chair for Katie and sat down himself. "How can we help you?"

"Let me pour her a cup of tea first, Joe. Here you are, dear," Mrs. Barrows said.

"Thank you." Katie smiled, when Mrs. Barrows handed her the cup.

Katie explained why she needed information about Sandstone and the little she knew of the young couple who lived in the house many years ago. "I wondered if you all might know more."

"We've heard the same things you've read about," Mrs. Barrows said. "However, one of my great aunts actually knew Judith Collier as a young girl. I remember I was about ten when she told me the story. It stuck in my young mind, so sad.

"She described Judith as a quiet shy girl. Daniel Collier came to town from North Carolina or Virginia. No one knew for sure. He and Judith reportedly took one look at each other and fell in love."

Mrs. Barrows shook her head, "Her family wasn't too pleased to have her marry a stranger. You see in those days, everyone in Treehaven was either born here or came from a nearby town. Gossip had it he might be running away from something to have come so far."

She refilled Katie's tea cup with hot water, before continuing. "Judith surprised everyone by insisting on marrying Daniel, especially since rumor had it that she was close to announcing her engagement to a local man."

"Do you know who?" Katie asked interrupting.

"I think my aunt knew, but I don't remember her saying." Mrs. Barrows wrinkled her forehead. "I have some of her letters in the attic, they might name him. I'll get Joe to bring the boxes down in the next few days."

Mrs. Barrows leaned back in her chair and continued with her story. "After the wedding, they stayed at Sandstone most of the time, except for Daniel's once a week visits to town. Judith seldom came with him. She preferred to remain at home."

"Apparently she still prefers to be at home," Katie said cryptically.

"You've seen her?" Mrs. Barrows asked.

"Things have happened, and I saw something, more like a mist in my room last night. I suspect it might be her."

"Guess you know almost as much as we do," Mr. Barrows said.

"Not quite." Mrs. Barrows stood up. "Wait here, I have something to show you."

Katie took her cup and placed it in the sink.

"Here it is. I started looking for it after your call."

She handed Katie a faded picture of two women standing in front of a tree. Their long dresses molded against their legs and long hair blew around them. Both were laughing.

"The one on the left is Judith Collier," Mrs. Barrows said.

Katie stared hard at the picture. There was something vaguely familiar about Judith, but the quality of the print blurred her features. When she looked up, she saw Mrs. Barrows watching her.

"My aunt said Judith's hair color was the fiery red gold of the setting sun."

Katie touched her hair. They had about the same hair color, and there was something about her-she'd figure it out later.

Katie handed the picture back to Mrs. Barrows. "Thank you for the information."

"I'm sorry we weren't more help. I do have boxes of family mementos in the attic. I'll get Joe to bring them down."

Mrs. Barrows smiled. "I understand Jake Andrews is also part of the inheritance."

Katie's face flushed with heat.

"You must know how gossip travels in this town," Mrs. Barrows chuckled. "Maybe you and your young man will come for a visit, and we can look at the mementos. We'd like to meet him."

"Thank you. We most definitely will. Let me give you my cell phone number. Call when it's convenient for you," Katie said.

Driving home, Katie thought about the visit and the picture of Judith. She'd made a start on uncovering the mystery of Sandstone. A tingle of excitement ran through her.

Chapter 5

"There you are," Jake said, from behind the screen door.

Katie glanced around. "Get some tea and join me."

Jake grabbed some ice cubes from the fridge and dropped them into his glass. He breathed in the wonderful odors coming from the oven.

"You don't have to cook every night. I'm fine with frozen dinners or Pizza," Jake said, and settled on the step beside her.

Katie flashed him a smile. "A fast food guy. You'd never know." She glanced at his flat stomach.

"I exercise."

Katie stared back off in the distance. "If it's all the same to you, I'll continue cooking. You can join me or not, your choice."

"Your mother taught you well."

Her head whipped around. "What does that mean?"

"You exhibit all the domestic skills, cooking and making the place look like a home. I noticed some new items in the living room and on the dining room table."

"Interesting, most men never notice minor changes around the house. I bought a few things at the Bargain Barn."

Jake thought he'd best change the subject. He didn't want her to think he was encouraging her to decorate the place. And he wasn't ready to talk with her about selling all of the Sandstone property to him. Especially since this old house would be the first thing he tore down, and he sensed she wasn't going to like that idea.

"Find out anything today? You looked rather pensive when I first arrived."

"I did." Katie turned and folded her tan legs Indian style to face him. "Have you ever heard of the Barrows?"

"No, should I have?"

"I doubt it. They're a delightful elderly couple I met today, ninety and ninety-two years old respectively. I had an interesting conversation with them." She bent her head to the side. "In fact they had a picture of Judith Collier."

Jake watched the change of expressions flow across her face. Her hazel eyes gave away every emotion. He'd never met anyone like her. An overwhelming urge to reach out, take the glass from her and cup her face in his hands swept over him. He had difficulty stopping himself.

"They'd heard the story of Sandstone, of course," Katie continued, "and about Judith and her husband. Mrs. Barrow's great aunt and Judith were friends."

"Any new information or the same you gathered from the library book?"

She wrinkled her forehead for a second.

"What is it?" he asked.

She took a quick breath. "Just something I can't place or remember about the picture I saw," she stopped talking, and her body froze as he came closer.

Involuntarily, his hand went out and smoothed across her hair. The fiery red curls curved around his fingers. He looked down to see her eyes widen. Moving slowly, he lowered his head and brushed his mouth across her soft lips. She tasted like strawberries and smelled of sunshine. Her body leaned toward him.

The screen door flew open, banging against the outside wall. Jake and Katie sprang apart. Katie jumped up, grabbed her drink and ran inside muttering that she had to check on dinner.

Saved by a screen door, Jake wasn't sure whether he felt relieved or annoyed. He didn't expect it to be so hard to keep his hands off Katie. But when she was near him, she drew him like a magnet and he wanted to fold her into his arms and keep her.

He shook his head. Where did that thought come from? No way was he ready for any type of commitment. He'd always been in control. His one goal in his life was to succeed. He'd had little time for playing. He certainly wasn't the dashing bachelor most people equated him with being.

Jake stood and glanced in the kitchen at Katie. She moved briskly around the room. He felt his hand tightened around the tea glass. Being successful was still his number one goal. And Katie Weber was not a woman you had a casual affair with and moved on.

He'd best watch his step, he warned himself again. He had no time or interest in a serious relationship. He didn't want one.

* * * *

Katie set the table and finished cooking dinner. A slight tremor of excitement still flowed along her nerve endings. When Jake's mouth claimed hers, she forgot all about not falling for him. In fact, as soon as his hands touched her a sudden heat seared through her body.

She tried to remember if she'd had similar feelings for Eric when they first started dating. Although she wanted to convince herself she did, she knew better. This was different. Out of the corner of her eye, she saw Jake coming through the screen door.

"Need any help?"

"No, dinner is almost ready," she said, without making eye contact.

"I'll go change."

She let out a sigh of relief when he left the room. But when he returned in cut off jeans and a Georgia Tech sweat shirt, it did nothing to calm her frayed nerves.

Jake stepped in front of her when she headed to the dining room with a bowl of mashed potatoes in her hand. He took the bowl and sat it on the counter.

"Katie, did you run because the door flew open and frightened you, or are you afraid of me?"

His eyes stared into hers, and she looked away.

"I'm not afraid of you. I liked the kiss, but we need to concentrate on getting the inheritance." She faced him. "You're planning to return to Atlanta after this is over, aren't you?"

He didn't answer her at first, and then nodded. "Yes, my business is there."

"That's why I ran inside," she whispered.

Again the silence lengthened between them.

"We do need to work on completing the terms of the will."

He tipped her chin up. "And I definitely liked the kiss," he whispered and brushed his lips over hers lightly.

"Please close the windows," she said hoping to change the subject. "When the sun goes down so does the temperature." She picked up the bowl of potatoes and walked around him. She didn't know how to respond to his earlier comment.

The phone rang as they sat down. Jake went into the living room to answer it.

"Hello. Yes, she is. It's for you." Jake handed her the phone.

"Didn't take you long to find someone else to live with." The harsh male voice made Katie jerk and almost drop the receiver.

"Eric?"

"You know it's me. I called your parents and explained that I had some important information to discuss with you and they finally told me you'd moved to someplace called Sandstone Ranch. What's happening?"

"I don't believe my life is any of your concern. How's Monica?" she asked in a scathing tone.

"Fine! I'm calling about the house. I want it sold. There's been an offer. A little less than we wanted, but I'm willing to take it."

"Eric, I don't want you to call here again. The real estate agent can contact me with the information, and I'll decide and let her know."

"You're a spoiled bitch. I knew you'd never be able to act reasonable about any—"

Katie went to the living room and slammed the phone down, then took a deep breath. She saw Jake's eyebrows shoot up in surprise. She ignored him and went to her seat at the table.

"How's the chicken?" she asked.

"Delicious, everything is good."

She saw Jake's questioning glance, but she looked down at her plate and ignored him. Why did Eric call? Normally, he preferred to work through the real estate agent.

He puzzled her. His irritation regarding her living with a man didn't fit the Eric she knew. She ate automatically, for once unaware of the man at her side. Eric had some other reason to contact her, and his anger told her the conversation had not gone the way he'd wanted it to.

"Penny for your thoughts," Jake said, concern in his expression.

Katie hesitated. She didn't want Jake to know too much about her personal problems. She needed to protect herself emotionally by keeping a certain distance between them. He could easily become too important to her and at the end of the month, he'd leave, as he said, without looking back.

"I'd better clean up," she said and picked up her plate.

"It's OK, Katie." Jake reached out and touched her hand when she passed his chair. "I didn't mean to pry. I don't like people asking me questions."

"No, everything's all right. Really." She hurried into the kitchen and leaned against the counter. She'd wanted to pull Jake out of his seat and lean into him. Let his strength warm her, while his arms wrapped tight around her body. She shook her head, this place and Jake made her crazy. Now, Eric calls and throws more confusion her way.

"Katie." Jake came into the kitchen carrying his plate and ice tea glass. "I've got work to do. About earlier, I'm sorry I crossed the boundaries. You don't need to worry, it won't happen again."

Tears spilled down Katie's cheeks while she washed the dishes. The kiss that caused such havoc to her insides must have meant nothing to Jake. It hadn't ruffled his calm demeanor. Just as well, this wasn't the time to start a relationship and especially not one sure to end unfavorably for her.

A shiver ran across Katie's shoulders. She turned and saw the faint outline of a woman in the doorway. Tonight, Katie saw her clearer. There were no colors to her, just shades of gray. She stared at Katie.

"Judith?" Katie's voice trembled. The ghost wavered and disappeared. Katie ran into the dining room, calling Judith's name. She was gone.

"Did you say something to me?" Jake stood in the hall, shirtless, his forehead wrinkled.

"Jake Andrews, you can deny it all you want, but Judith Collier is here with us. I saw her. Why she won't show herself to you, I don't know, but she exists!" Katie took a breath and scowled at Jake.

Jake held out his hands. "Let's suppose you're right. What are we going to do about it?"

"We're going to find out why she can't move on. What happened to keep her here? Did you find anything online?" Katie looked at him accusingly.

"I'll put on a shirt and meet you in the living room. We have some things to discuss."

Katie grabbed two cokes from the fridge and joined Jake.

"Thanks." He took a long swallow of coke, then pulled a cushion from the sofa and sat on the floor. "Come down here and join me." He stretched his legs out and leaned against the couch. "I'm too full from dinner. I'll have to start exercising if you keep cooking such good meals."

"Mom's better. You'd see if you came Sunday." She saw the change in his expression.

"I can't go."

"Well, you'll miss a good meal."

Jake shrugged, "I'm getting spoiled enough with all the food you cook."

"Why don't you want to come, Jake?" Katie asked.

"To be honest, I've never been comfortable in big gatherings. I'm a fish out of water as the old cliché goes." Jake looked away from her.

"Didn't your family get together for Sunday dinners or picnics?"

He gave her an intense stare. She glimpsed the pain in his eyes, before his expression went blank. "My aunt cooked as little as possible and certainly wouldn't have put herself out to fix a big meal for a lot of people." he answered. His voice monotone and his nose crinkled in disgust. "We were lucky she fed us."

"I'm sorry."

"Don't be. I learned early on to depend on no one but myself." His eyes warned her not to say anything. "Now about this ghost," he said changing the subject.

"You remember I mentioned the picture of Judith I saw earlier today," Katie hesitated. "Well tonight I saw the ghost more clearly, and it's a woman. But I didn't see her well enough to be sure it's Judith. I just believe it is."

Jake leaned his head against the couch and appeared deep in thought. Katie didn't disturb him. The man was too good looking. Even with the shadow of a beard showing across his strong jaw, it only made him sexier.

His eyes darkened when he caught her staring.

"Perhaps the ghost feels some relationship to you, since she hasn't shown herself to me. I haven't figured out how I come into this picture," Jake said.

Katie shook her head, "I don't know. There are so many questions that need to be answered."

"Did you find anything on the internet?" Katie asked again.

"Not really. Tomorrow I'll try to research where Daniel Collier died."

"At Fredericksburg, I read that in the book I checked out from the library." Katie said. "How can that help us?"

"I'm grasping at straws. In fact, I can't believe I'm even discussing this ghost as if she were real." He'd barely finished speaking when they heard the crash. Jake jumped up and ran to his room.

Katie stood inside his doorway with her hand to her mouth. The bedspread lay half on the floor. His shirts hung from the edge of his tallboy and one hung on the bedrail, but the loud noise had been his computer. It lay upside down on the wood floor.

"You made her mad."

Jake glared at Katie. "She didn't have to throw my computer around." He bent and picked up the laptop.

"Is it broken?" Katie asked.

"I don't think so, no thanks to your friend."

"At least, you have to admit she exists." Katie saw Jake look around the room.

"I've never believed in the supernatural. I believe in science, things that can be explained, but," he closed his eyes for a moment and then surveyed his room again, "I can't think of any other explanation for this mess." His brow furrowed, and his lips thinned.

"It's frustrating and scary not to understand what's happening."

"Well, I'm not going to start talking to her," he said. "Let's leave any further discussion for tomorrow. I need to clean up this mess and make sure my computer is all right."

Katie backed out of the room and went to get the coke cans from the living room. After throwing them in the recycle bin, she leaned against the kitchen counter and looked around. "Judith," she said softly, "if it is you, how can we help?" There was no answer.

* * * *

Katie woke to gray skies and raindrops dripping from the eaves. The day reflected her mood. Almost a week gone and they still knew little about their ghost. The cold dampness seemed to seep through the walls, and Katie pulled on her warm pink robe.

After a quick hot shower, she headed downstairs dressed warmly in a white pullover sweater and jeans. Early March had turned from warm to cold overnight.

She found a note taped to the kitchen cabinet. *Gone to town. Won't be back until late tonight. Jake.*

A long dreary day stretched ahead. She could call one of her sisters, but she'd see them all tomorrow at the Sunday dinner.

It was a good day to search the house. There must be something here to help her understand Judith.

Katie climbed the stairs and went into the bathroom where she thought she'd noticed an entrance to the attic. After all, every old house had one, didn't they?

Yes, it was in the ceiling. She remembered seeing a ladder in one of the bedrooms. With that, she'd be able to reach the recessed door.

Her arms hurt by the time she got the ladder in place. She climbed the steps and pushed on the door, but it stuck. She gave it a harder shove and it opened. Moving a step further up, she looked in. Dust motes danced in the faint light. She saw nothing of any interest. No chest, just a small empty space.

Disappointed, Katie moved the recessed door back into place and climbed down. She folded the ladder and leaned it against the wall. She'd put it back later. Discouraged, she went to her bedroom and sat on the bed.

"Now is the time to help," she said to the quiet room. If Judith was around, she didn't appear. Since the night Jake found his room trashed, they'd seen no further evidence of a ghost or anything supernatural.

Katie lay on the bed and watched the clouds float by her windows. Weak sunlight tried to peek out around the storm clouds. Gradually her eyes closed.

Judith paced the floor of her bedroom. Daniel had not returned. For days, she'd hoped he would change his mind, but she'd received no word from him. She stopped pacing and looked out the front of the house. How had things gone so wrong? Had he ever really loved her? She had nothing left. Nothing, but this cold, gray, empty house.

Sometimes rage and pain consumed her. She hated the house and Daniel. Bile rushed up her throat and into her mouth, where she could taste the bitterness.

No, another part of her protested. She could never hate Daniel. He did love her. The twisted feelings, the stabbing pain in her chest, and she…

Katie bolted upright with the sound of the scream bouncing off the walls. An apparition stood at the windows, glaring at her with hollow eyes.

The ghost swooped toward Katie, and she felt fingers touch her throat and tighten. A shrill cackling laugh rang around her head. Grabbing at her neck, Katie gasped for breath. The ghostly apparition flew around her.

As quickly as it started, the choking stopped. Katie leapt off the bed and shook her head to clear it. Had she been sleeping the whole time? Her body trembled.

She swallowed, her pulse still hammered, and her arms and legs seemed unable to function. She mustn't let the fear overcome her.

"I'm staying Judith or whoever you are." Her voice sounded raspy. "You won't scare me away."

Katie managed to stagger to the bathroom. Her pale face reflected back at her. She lightly stoked her neck, smooth and white, not one visible mark.

Chapter 6

Katie walked back to the bedroom and stood at the door looking in. She'd move to another room to give the ghost time to accept people in the house. Katie wasn't about to acknowledge she was being frightened away.

But for now, she needed to get out of here. Jake, as usual, had gone to his temporary office. Ever since he'd kissed her, he'd been keeping his distance. Tomorrow was the big family dinner. She had so hoped he'd change his mind, but he hadn't.

After grabbing her bag, she locked the front door. Drops of rain started to fall. Not a good day for driving, but she only planned on going into town. She'd have her car checked. Her family took their cars to Lloyd's Auto Repair Shop. She'd leave her car there, while she went to lunch.

She drove carefully along the wet roads. Lloyd, himself, ambled toward her when she drove in.

"Howdy, Miss Weber. Having car trouble?"

"Not really," Katie said, getting out. "Thought I'd have the oil changed, the tires rotated and have you check the car for any possible problems."

Lloyd nodded his head. "That's a smart thing to do. Hear you been living in that haunted house, Sandstone."

Katie studied the man eyeing her. He looked to be about Jake's age, but he was balding and carried twenty pounds or more in his gut. His small black eyes pierced back at her.

"I'm living at Sandstone, for a while."

"Hear you've got yourself some company." His eyes stared dark and insolent. "Best be careful with Jake Andrews. He can ruin a nice girl's reputation." The words carried a hint of menace.

"What do you know about Jake?"

"Didn't he tell you?" A broad jeering grin crossed his face. "He grew up in my house."

"I thought he lived with his aunt?"

"He did. The state gave him to my mother, when his own mother rejected him."

"You're his cousin?" Katie didn't try to keep the incredibility out of her voice.

"Yep, he hates to claim us now he's gone and become so rich and successful. Folks around here speck he's done somethin' crooked along the way to get so much, so soon."

Katie took a step back from the man. "I believe he's achieved his success from going to school and working hard."

"Well, that might be what some people think." Lloyd hitched up his pants and smiled smugly. "But most don't know his history. His pa robbed a bank, went to prison and died there after getting into a fight." He paused a second. "Jake looks just like his old daddy."

"And because he and his father look alike, he'll act the same as his father?" She spit the words out.

Lloyd laughed. "I can see he's already charmed you. The girls always did like him."

Katie clenched her teeth and stepped toward the man.

A hand touched her arm. "Don't hit him, Katie. He might hit back. Hello, Lloyd."

Jake stood beside her, his blue eyes cold and a stony expression on his face. He placed a hand on Katie's back.

"It's always nice to see some people never change," Jake said. His lips curled in contempt. "Except, for putting on a few pounds and losing some hair."

Lloyd glared. "You got business here, Jake? Doubt you'd want me to work on that big Mercedes of yours?"

"I'd never let you touch anything of mine," Jake warned.

He stood close to Katie, and she felt the heat radiating from his hand into her body.

"So, that's the way it is. Didn't know you'd claimed this here young lady. Does her family know? Don't think they'll be too happy to have someone with your family background intermingle with them."

"Keep out of my business, Lloyd."

Lloyd shrugged. "She came to me." He nodded to Katie. "The car should be ready in about an hour."

Katie and Jake watched him stroll toward the garage. Katie glanced at Jake and caught a strange look on his face, anger and something else, sadness?

"Hungry? I saw you from across the street," Jake said. "Tom, Sara and I are going to eat at the Pork Barrel barbecue restaurant."

His expression, closed as usual now, gave nothing away. He had stepped back safely behind his wall.

"Sure, sounds good to me. I haven't had a chance to talk with Sara lately."

They crossed the street, and Jake held the door for her. Katie saw a hand in the back of the room wave. Jake guided her toward their table.

Tom stood. "Katie, I'm glad you joined us."

Katie was aware of Jake sliding into the booth beside her. His leg moved against hers, and she stopped herself from moving further along the seat to the wall. Every time he got close, she felt rattled.

The waitress brought two glasses of water and menus. "I'll give you all some time to decide what you want. Be back in a minute."

A country song about lost love played in the background, and the clink of silverware and hum of voices filled the wood building. Katie glanced at the menu and set it down. Sara smiled across at her.

"Jake tells us you had a couple of strange occurrences happen in the farmhouse."

"The ghost doesn't like us being there," Katie acknowledged.

"You believe in ghosts?" Tom asked.

"I'm sure you think I'm crazy, but there is no other explanation for all the things happening around Sandstone," Katie said.

"Well, that's one good thing about tearing the house down. That will get rid of any spooks." Tom's words brought three sets of eyes staring at him.

"Damn! Sorry, guess Jake hasn't mentioned our deal to you."

"Really, Tom, now you've gone and done it," Sara said, looking at Jake with a worried expression.

"What deal?" Katie moved to lean against the wall and turned toward Jake.

Jake ran his hand through his hair and swallowed. "I'd planned to talk with you."

"About what?"

"Tom and I have had a dream for years of building a development outside of Treehaven and—"

"You all decided what you want to eat?" The waitress stood at the end of the booth.

Katie eyed Jake. She wished she'd sat on the outside and she'd leave. Something told her she didn't want to hear what he had to say. "I'll have a pork sandwich. That's all."

Jake, Tom, and Sara ordered, while cautiously studying Katie's expression. Katie was sure her face glowed red with the anger boiling inside. As soon as the waitress left, she turned back to Jake. "You were saying?"

"Sandstone is the answer to our dream. We can develop the property and it will be very profitable for all of us. Homes built around a community shopping area with parks, both for ballgames and for families to enjoy." He stopped.

"I'm sorry you heard about our plans this way. We planned to offer you a good price for your share of the land, plus your choice of a lot and house," Jake added.

"Sounds like you've been planning this ever since we moved in," Katie said. She moved her water glass to make room for the waitress to put her plate down. No one spoke until the waitress left.

"I can understand you being upset, Katie," Jake said. "We don't want you to think we've been making plans behind your back."

"But you did."

Jake bit the edge of his lip, the lines of concentration deepened along his brow. "Give yourself time to think about what I've suggested. You'll see it's for the best."

"For your best, you mean." Katie glared at him, and then turned to eat her sandwich. The food tasted dry, and she drank a large sip of water trying to swallow. She knew tears were on the verge of rolling down her cheeks. She refused to cry. She'd eat this sandwich and pretend she was considering their offer. Then leave as quickly as possible.

* * * *

Jake wanted to take her into his arms. Her eyes reflected her hurt, and he felt sick, like he'd kicked a small puppy. He hated feeling guilty. It was business. Couldn't she see how it would benefit her too? His appetite was gone. No one talked, just took quick glances at each other and finished eating as quickly as possible.

Tom mouthed the word, sorry, to him. Jake shrugged. He'd put off talking to her because he suspected the conversation might not go well. There'd been many chances, but it always seemed to be the wrong time. He'd known she wasn't going to like the idea.

What was it about the old house that she liked so much? She hadn't even seen their models yet. She was being unreasonable.

"Please let me out." Katie spoke softly at his side. She nodded to the others and slid across the seat after Jake stood. "I'll pay on the way out."

"No problem, I asked you. I'll get the check."

Hot hazel eyes snapped with fire. She straightened and faced him. "I'll pay my own bill. I don't want anything from you."

He watched her march off. Red curls bounced. Fiery, passionate and stubborn, she pulled at something deep inside of him, and he didn't like it.

"Jake, man, I'm sorry. Me and my big mouth," Tom apologized.

"Don't worry. It's not over yet," Jake said, sitting back down. "I had opportunities to talk with her before this."

"I sensed Katie might not like the idea of the development," Sara added.

"Women never agree at first," Jake said. "I'll work on her." Even as he said the words, Jake regretted them. He didn't want to put pressure on Katie to change her mind.

He'd seen how much she liked the old place. Tearing the house down, even with Katie's agreement, might drive a wedge between them for good. Did it matter? He leaned back against his seat and watched the other people eating and talking. He'd always felt on the outside, wherever he went, until Katie. She'd given him a taste of what it might be like to be included.

Tom and Sara stood. "We've got to get back to work. See you later," Tom said, looking worried and sad.

Jake nodded. He stared off into the distance. In one day, Katie learned about his past and his plans. Not the best day for him.

* * * *

Katie paid Lloyd's bookkeeper and drove home. She stopped off at the Bargain Barn on the way and found a large flowered rug for the living room. The only problem, she'd never get it out of the car and into the house without help.

She didn't want to ask Jake for anything. She hadn't let herself think about the scene at the restaurant. Her chest hurt, and she was close to crying.

Parking her car in front of the house, she thought of Jake's plans to demolish it. Over my dead body, she vowed, looking at the grand old lady. So the porch leaned a little and there was other work that needed doing. When she sold part of the land, she'd have the money to upgrade the electricity and phone system. Maybe put in new windows and paint the outside. She didn't plan to part with this house.

She just needed to convince Judith's ghost to leave. She was sure it had to be Judith. There was no other explanation.

What about her attacking you? A voice in her head asked. She didn't. I'd fallen asleep. It was only a crazy dream. There'd been no marks on my neck, Katie reassured herself.

She reached in her purse and flipped open her cell phone. A familiar voice, her brother Frank, answered her call.

"Hi, this is Katie."

"Hello, I'm looking forward to seeing you tomorrow. I'd like to see Jake. Is he coming? I haven't seen him in years."

"Jake's not going to be there tomorrow. Frank, I need some help. Do you mind stopping by after work for a few minutes?"

"Not at all, I'm leaving here at four-thirty. See you shortly afterwards."

"Great." Katie snapped the phone shut. She'd move the furniture, clean the floors and be ready when Frank arrived.

At a quarter to five, Frank drove up and Jake followed just behind. She watched the two men greet each other.

Katie hurried back into the kitchen. Every other night this week Jake stayed in town late, wouldn't you know tonight he'd be here when she least wanted to see him. She listened to their deep voices in the living room. Forcing a smile on her face, Katie joined them.

"Jake and I were just getting reacquainted," Frank said. He kissed Katie's cheek and glanced around the room.

"What's the job you need help with?" he asked.

Katie motioned toward her car. "I bought a rug for the living room. I'm not able to get it in by myself." Her eyes met Jake's with a defiant glance.

"No problem. Come on, Jake, we'll bring the rug inside and then you and I can sit and visit."

Jake put down his briefcase, "Sounds good to me. I appreciate the help, but I'd have brought the rug in for Katie."

Frank looked at Katie with a questioning look. "Thought so myself, but I'm glad she called. Since you won't be with us tomorrow, it gives us a chance to catch up."

Standing at the screen door, Katie watched the two men pull the rug out and head back in her direction. They were about the same height, but Jake was the leaner of the two.

Since Frank and Susan married, he'd added a few pounds. Frank's friendly open face was a contrast to the cool unreadable expression Jake wore.

Frank's presence would help to dispel the awkwardness between Jake and her. Jake might try to apologize again, and she wasn't ready to hear it. This was one house a man was not going to take from her.

* * * *

Katie stretched and looked out the kitchen window. It promised to be a good day for a picnic. She wished Jake hadn't turned down the invitation to meet her family.

Last night, he and Frank talked while they drank a beer, and Katie was pleased to see how well the two men got along. Jake had been quiet after Frank left. He ate quickly and excused himself disappearing into his room.

"Mind if I have a cup of coffee?"

His smooth voice sent prickles of wariness cascading down her spine. Wrinkled jeans, white tee shirt, shoeless, rumpled hair and the man still looked like he stepped out of a GQ magazine. It ought to be against the law. She frowned looking down at her baggy sweats.

"I can take a hint. I'll get a cup in town," Jake said and turned to leave.

"No, sorry, I was thinking of something else. Have a cup. I'm not cooking breakfast. I'm having cereal and toast. You can fend for yourself.

Mom will stuff me with food at dinner." Katie pushed the screen door open and stepped outside.

"About today."

Katie whirled around. "Don't apologize for not going, in fact don't say anything."

"Will you get off my case? I know you're upset about the way you found out my plans for Sandstone. I should have told you from the first and asked you about selling your half to me."

"You didn't because you knew I'd say no. I like this house and I want to keep it. You can do whatever you want with your part. I'll put up a high wall between my land and your development." She snapped the words out and then regretted it, when she saw the bleak look on his face.

"I need to run an errand," Jake said, and walked away.

Darn, I didn't handle that well, and we're arguing about something that's not even ours, yet.

She decided to go upstairs and get ready. She'd go over early and help with the set-up and food.

The ladder was open and set under the door to the attic. She'd left it folded and leaning against the wall. She glanced around the bathroom. Well she didn't have time for this today. She placed the ladder back where she'd had it and went to her room.

Still, it worried her. Did the ghost want her to go up in the attic again?

Dressed in jeans, gold silk shirt, running shoes and with her make-up on, she took a last glance around her room. She'd forgotten to tell Jake about moving from the front bedroom. She wasn't sure she wanted to tell anyone about what happened yesterday.

Katie was relieved to get away before Jake returned. She was disappointed he hadn't changed his mind. She didn't really believe he had other plans for today. He had a secretive side to him, and he wasn't going to let his protective wall down for anyone.

She'd enjoy being with her family and forget Sandstone and Jake for the day. As if I'm really *not* going to think about him, she chided herself.

Chapter 7

Jake swung by and visited with Tom, but he was restless. Katie's sad eyes haunted him. He'd left his motorcycle at Tom's house and today seemed the perfect time to take a long ride.

He rode along back streets and dirt roads familiar from his childhood. He ended at the spot by the river where he and Katie went that first night. He'd known from the start she wasn't just anyone to him. That was why he didn't call her on that Sunday. He'd planned to leave town without seeing her again and then he'd arrived at the meeting on Monday and his whole world went upside down.

He still knew he wasn't for her. She needed someone warm, loving, outgoing, a man who'd been raised in a family like hers. He didn't know much about love or family and commitment just plain scared the shit out of him.

Jake rolled his head around trying to loosen the tension in his neck and shoulders. He got back on his bike and headed toward the main road. Maybe he'd catch Katie at home before she left for her parent's house.

Her car was gone, so much for that idea. He unlocked the door and started to his room when the phone rang.

"Hello, no, she's not here. You need an answer today? I'll try and get a message to her. Sure. You're welcome." Jake hung up the phone.

Katie's real estate agent wanted to talk with her. Jake looked in the phone book and found her parent's number. He could call or ride by and give her the message. He'd enjoy the motorcycle ride.

Of course he'd known somehow he'd end up here before the end of the day. He stopped his bike back from the main driveway and studied the scene in front of him.

Men and boys played a rowdy game of touch football on the side lawn. They yelled and gleefully chased the ball. The women stood on the sidelines conversing, and several younger girls crowded together whispering and giggling.

The smell of barbecue floated in the air and the sunshine beamed down on the happy picture. A Norman Rockwell type of scene, and I'm still the boy with his nose stuck on the glass pane looking in.

Stupid, he growled at himself.

I won't wallow in self pity. I've built a business and made a name for myself in Atlanta. It's this place, Treehaven that gets to me. I'll be glad when this month is over.

He started his engine and hesitated about going forward. A man came out to a car and looked in Jake's direction, then waved. Recognizing Frank, Jake knew he couldn't leave now. He rode his bike forward.

Frank put out his hand. "Hi, man, glad to see you made it after all. You're just in time for dinner."

"No, I don't want to be any bother. I have a message for Katie."

"You'll cause trouble if you don't stay." Frank nodded to the windows in the house. "I'm sure others have seen you by now." Frank slapped him on the shoulder. "They're good people. Come on in and I'll introduce you."

Jake started to protest again, but he saw Katie coming out the door smiling, and he knew there was no turning back.

Katie took his arm and directed Jake to the back yard.

"I have a message for you from your real estate agent. She wants you to call her."

"If that's what got you here, I'm glad she called. I'll ring her back after I introduce you to my family," she said and then led Jake from group to group until he had met all the couples and their children.

"There are two dozen of us. I guess it's a bit much for a person all at once," she said to Jake, while walking him toward her dad.

"Not so difficult. I knew several of them from school."

"Hi, Dad, the food smells good."

Jim Weber kissed Katie's cheek. Straightening, he studied Jake. "Jake Andrews," he said and put out his hand. "I believe we met a few times when you and Frank were in school together."

"Yes sir, a long time ago. You have a great family."

Mr. Weber nodded. "We've been blessed. Not a sour apple in the bunch."

Jake smiled and watched her father cooking.

Katie leaned toward Jake and whispered in his ear. "You're lost in thought."

"What?" Jake asked.

"What are you thinking?" she asked.

"Admiring your dad's skill with a grill."

"Right."

"You don't believe me?"

She moved closer. "I see your walls. They don't."

"Think I'll get a beer and talk with Frank. See you at the dinner table."

Jake had caught the warning from her dad. Did he think Jake might be the sour apple? His reputation in town varied according to whom you talked with, and his parental genes followed him forever.

It didn't matter. He'd never be with all the Weber family together in one place after today. This time made Katie happy, so he was almost glad Frank had stopped him from chickening out.

After this month, they might cross paths around town, or maybe not. The thought of never seeing Katie made his chest hurt.

He'd listened to Katie talk with her dad and watched the others spread around the huge yard. Children played and laughed. Two boys got into a shoving match, and their fathers spoke to them and had the two shake hands. The boys ran off together to play.

Jake felt the pain low in his gut. The scene reminded him of his favorite childhood dream. Before today, he didn't really believe it existed. But it was early yet. Something was bound to happen to spoil the day. All this happy family camaraderie couldn't last long. But it did, all the rest of the afternoon.

Jake told everyone goodbye and rode his bike to Tom's to pick up his car and one other thing, a surprise for Katie. He was glad when he got back to Sandstone that she had beat him home.

* * * *

"Katie, can you come downstairs?"

"Coming," Katie called. She ran and stopped suddenly on the third step from the bottom. "What is that?"

"It's a dog. What do you think it is?"

Katie bent her head to the side and studied the small puppy running around Jake's feet. The leash attached to the puppy's collar wrapped around his legs.

"You bought a dog to keep with you here at Sandstone?"

"The puppy is for you."

"Me?" Katie's voice squeaked. "I don't want a dog."

"Why not?"

"They're a lot of work, and he probably isn't house trained. He'll pee on my new rug."

"It's good training for when you have kids. They make messes too."

"Who said I wanted kids? Have you gone crazy?"

Jake leaned down and picked up the puppy. The pup had a shiny black coat and friendly black eyes. "I thought you'd be pleased." A pensive look crossed his face. "It's my way of saying I'm sorry. Guess I botched this too. I'll take him back."

"Where did you get him on a Sunday? You didn't have him earlier." Katie asked, as she came on down the steps and reached out to pat the puppy's head. A wet little tongue came out and licked her hand.

"Tom's Labrador had a litter of pups. This was the last one born, the runt of the litter."

Katie took the pup into her arms. "Hmm, the last born and the runt of the litter." She rubbed her chin against the soft fur. "Guess this little guy and I are destined for each other."

"My thoughts exactly." His lips curled in a half smile. "Oh, one other thing, he's a she."

"Good. I don't particularly like men much right now," Katie said, and then added. "And if you think this is going to change my mind about the house, you're wrong."

"I just wanted to see you lose your sad look and smile."

"I did not look sad," Katie said. She took the leash and set the puppy back down on the floor. "I looked mad."

Jake shook his head, "No, you're wrong. You were sad."

"Now you're trying to tell me how I feel," Katie went to step back and realized the puppy, while running in circles, had tied the leash around their feet.

Jake smiled at the dog. "Smart puppy." He looked back at Katie. "It'd be a shame to miss this opportunity." His mouth closed over hers.

Katie went still. Strong arms wrapped around her body and his mouth brushed hers. His tongue moved along the seam of her closed lips. Without thinking Katie lifted her arms around his neck and opened her mouth to welcome him.

The kiss deepened, and she melted into his body. Warm strong hands moved along her back, pulling her hips hard against his arousal. She moved her hips against him and heard him groan.

Katie's hands moved through his thick wavy hair, and a warm rush of desire raced through her. She wanted to wrap her legs around his waist and.... The puppy's bark and frantic pulling on the leash broke the spell.

"Whoa, girl." Jake untangled the leash from around their legs. The puppy ran to the stairs barking.

Dizzy from their encounter, Katie responded slowly. Without warning, Jake pushed her and the puppy hard to the side. A large, framed picture, from the upstairs hall, flew down the stairs hitting the bottom and breaking.

"What the hell?" Jake looked around from where he'd placed himself to protect Katie.

"I suppose your explanation for that is a little wind," Katie quipped.

"If it is a ghost, she's getting more aggressive." Jake reached to help Katie stand. The puppy licked Katie's face, and she laughed, pushing the pup back as she took hold of Jake's hand.

"I believe it's Judith and she wants us to leave," Katie said.

Katie feared if she told Jake about yesterday he'd be upset and tell her brother or her parents. They'd want her to move out. Whatever. She wasn't giving up on the house or the inheritance. "I'm sure if we continue to show her we aren't going anywhere, she'll stop."

"I don't want you here alone. If I can't be here you need to go to your parents' house or somewhere."

"You are not my keeper. Anyway, I have my puppy to protect me."

"This little dog?"

"Yes."

"She's going to have to grow some more before she can be a guard dog."

"She warned us just now. That's all I need."

Jake groaned. He leaned down and patted the puppy on the head. "Sorry, girl. She's expecting big things of you. Better grow fast."

"Let's give her a name." He said.

"I get to name her. You gave her to me."

"She's feisty like you and brave. Maybe we should call her little Katie."

"What makes you think I'm brave?"

"A lot of reasons."

The man was very annoying at times, but his warm blue eyes smiled at her and his kisses shook her to the core. She took a deep breath, it was best the ghost didn't like them kissing and always interrupted. It was too easy to get lost in his arms.

"Let's go get the puppy's things from my car." Jake led the way outside.

When he opened the door, Katie saw he'd placed papers and a blanket to protect the seat covers.

"I never thought you'd take a chance on a puppy messing up your automobile. You'll probably make a fine father." Katie decided to give him back some of his own medicine.

"I don't plan to ever be a dad." His unexpected cold words gave way to silence.

She caught a flash of despair cross his face. She reached out and touched his arm.

"You met a number of good examples today. My dad, brothers and brother-in-laws do a great job with their children."

"I won't change my mind." The words—clipped, sharp and final— hung in the air.

Katie stared at him. He'd warned her. She'd best remember.

She went inside and cuddled the puppy to her. Jake followed.

"What will you name her?" he asked, his voice breaking into the silent wall around them.

After studying the puppy, Katie nodded her head. "She has one little spot on the tip of her nose that looks like a smudge. I think Smudges might be a fitting name."

Jake patted the puppy. "Smudges, that's a fine name. I'll try to wake up and put her out later tonight to start training her." He placed a water bowl and a small rug for the puppy beside the back door.

"Thanks." Katie took off the leash and Smudges ran to the water bowl.

Katie walked to the stairs and started up.

"If you want to sleep down here, I'll trade rooms with you," Jake offered.

He leaned his tense body casually against the door frame to the kitchen, waiting for her answer. Out of the corner of her eye she saw Smudges, apparently tired, had settled on the small rug beside her bowls.

"I'll be fine. I don't want to stop using the upstairs, but I already decided and moved to another room." Katie said. "If I slept downstairs our ghost might think she's winning."

"Why did you move?" He asked and frowned.

"I had a silly, scary dream and decided sleeping in the front bedroom tended to make me have nightmares." She walked to the stairs.

"Maybe, I should move up there with you."

* * * *

His words stopped her. She glanced back at him, the golden lights in her eyes glinted. For a second, they just stared at each other.

His mouth went dry. Having her so close, he'd never sleep. Imagining her lying on her bed naked and her hair tousled sent an incredible rush of heat from his head to his lower body.

Her eyes flared and she looked almost as though she read his mind. He knew she felt the tension between them. He straightened and sauntered over to her, standing close enough to breathe in her sweet scent. "Or, I could sleep in your room."

She wet her lips, her eyes never leaving his. Tingles of yearning teased him. All she had to do was reach out and pull him to her. He held his breath, half afraid she would and half afraid she wouldn't. But, she turned her head away and continued up the stairs.

"Don't forget to let Smudges out," she said. "See you in the morning."

He watched her climb the steps and continued standing there until he heard the click of her bedroom door shut. Turning, he raked his fingers through his hair. The feelings Katie aroused in him continued to scare him. He'd protected his heart—forever it seemed.

Tomorrow, he decided he'd go to Atlanta and face his past. Unless he came to terms with what happened to him as a child, he had no hope of having anything to offer Katie or any other woman.

* * * *

"You're early," Katie said.

Jake turned from the stove. "I'm flying to Atlanta for the day. Want some breakfast?"

"You said you didn't cook."

"Anyone can cook a simple breakfast." He held the spatula in the air. "Well?"

"Eggs sound good." Katie smiled at Smudges sniffing around the room. "Come here, girl." She beckoned with her hand and Smudges scampered to her.

"I think you like your puppy," Jake said.

Katie sat back and stared at him. "You're all dressed up," she commented, pointing to his suit. "Do you have an important business meeting?"

Ignoring her question, he reached across the counter and pulled toast from the toaster, buttered it, and placed scrambled eggs and bacon on their plates.

"Hmm, this smells wonderful. What a treat."

"Let's eat here in the kitchen," Jake said, putting the plates on the small wooden table.

Katie took a bite of eggs and smiled. Her fresh warm openness took his breath. Smudges bark broke the spell. Jake's hand reached down to the puppy.

"Don't even think about feeding him from the table."

"Yes, Mother." Jake grinned at Smudges. "The lady's the boss. Sorry pal."

"I thought we were going to decide what to do next to get our inheritance?" Katie looked questioningly at him.

Jake looked out the window. "There's something I have to do. After today, I'll be fully involved."

"You didn't mention this trip before," Katie persisted.

"I did some thinking last night. It's only one more day. You should go to your parents' while I'm not here."

Katie took her empty plate and went to the sink. Smudges followed, tripping across her feet. "I'm going to stay here," she said, her back to him.

"We agreed you shouldn't be here alone."

"No, you said I shouldn't be here alone. If I get scared, I'll leave." She turned to him. "I promise."

"I'll cancel my flight." He headed to his room.

"Wait. That's blackmail."

He didn't answer. The peacefulness of the morning belied any thoughts of ghosts or danger, and he knew Katie fought with the idea of giving in.

Her expressions gave away the frustration and difficulty she had with the thought of accepting his demand.

"This time I'll do as you ask." The irritation in her voice also showed in those hazel eyes. "But, I'm not always going to agree with you."

He smiled. "I didn't think you would."

Chapter 8

Jake stood in front of the ornate glass doors. He was as ready as he'd ever be. His mouth dry and his hands sweaty, the cool confident business man was gone. Damn, he had to get hold of himself. The last thing he wanted was to appear nervous and needy.

The door bell echoed. Rubbing his hands on the side of his trousers, he swallowed and tried to deny the fear gripping his gut. He was that four-year-old boy waiting to see his mother.

The picture of her pale face and icy blue eyes were stamped forever on his memory. The look she'd thrown his way frightened him, and he'd shrunk closer to his aunt's side. His aunt pushed him away and ordered him to stand straight.

Jake shook his head to clear his thoughts. Today had to be different. He was a grown man, successful in his business, nothing like that boy. He'd made his success in Atlanta, where she lived. Why did he need to come here? He turned to go, and the door opened.

"May I help you?" The butler stood at attention in front of Jake.

"Yes, is Mrs. Winston in?"

"Whom may I say is calling?"

"A relative, from Treehaven."

"I'll check and see if the mistress is available. Wait here." He closed the door in Jake's face.

Jake walked to the edge of the veranda. The white southern mansion, reminiscence of *Gone with the Wind*, had broad park-like lawns and curving walkways between flowering azaleas and tall magnolia trees. Oaks hung with moss and a weeping willow bent over the edge of a small oval lake.

He chuckled at the irony. He came from the lowest and the highest in society. His father must have been some schmoozer to charm the elegant Claudia Hoffman, whose father was the patriarch of one of the richest families in Atlanta.

"Sir." The butler frowned at him.

"The landscaping is magnificent," Jake said.

The butler glanced briefly at the lawns. "Yes, well we have a very good gardener. Please come in. Mrs. Winston will see you in the parlor. She is busy. She has only a few minutes to give you." The man raised his thin nose and pointed chin at Jake.

"That's all I need," Jake said and stepped inside the marbled foyer. The ceiling soared two stories up. The staircase to the left flowed around in a circle to the second and third floor.

"Follow me, please." The butler walked briskly through the foyer to a room on the left.

It was a woman's room. Green and yellow flowered chairs, a matching sofa, dainty side tables, and a white baby grand piano filled the space. Lacy white curtains billowed in the open windows. Outside a garden bloomed full of roses and azaleas. A large fountain stood in the center and the soft whisper of the water floated inside.

Stunned by the opulence of the house, Jake almost missed the woman sitting in a chair to his right. Their only resemblance was her sky blue eyes. She studied him in shocked disbelief. The butler bowed and left shutting the double doors.

"You!" She measured him with a cool appraising glance. "You were never to come to this house. Didn't your aunt tell you to stay away?" Her cultured tones edged with ice.

Jake sauntered over and sat across from her. "She didn't tell me much. Except how you didn't want me."

Face stricken, her eyes took on a haunted look. "You look just like him." The words came out a whisper.

Jake nodded, "So I've been told. I'm not like him. I have my own business and—"

"Mother, you must speak with Father." A blond haired man strode into the room. He ignored Jake. "He says I have to be at the bank every day next week, and you know I've planned to join my friends at the Hampton's."

"Alec, you only returned from a trip two days ago. I agree with your father. Now please excuse me. I have business to discuss with my visitor."

Alec threw a quick glance at Jake and shrugged. "Whatever, Mother. I won't change my plans."

They sat in silence after Alec left. Jake nodded his head toward the door. "He's my half brother?"

"You are never," she said emphatically, "to let my family know of your existence. Is that the reason you've come, for money to buy your silence?"

Jake stood and took two steps back. "No. I came to see the person who gave me the other half of my genes. I wonder if they mixed me up in the nursery," he said. "Maybe I'm really some other family's child." He felt a perverse satisfaction seeing the flush of red on her cheeks.

"I see very little of myself in you or my father. If he," Jake motioned to the door where Alec left, "is what you produced for a son, I'm lucky you didn't raise me."

Jake felt hollow inside. What had he hoped to accomplish in seeing this woman? Recognition? Had he hoped to hear her say she loved him and missed being a part of his life, but she couldn't cope with a small child and his father's problems? It wasn't going to happen. He watched her. Her eyes darkened like billowing cumulus clouds warning of a storm.

She started to stand, but he motioned to her, "Don't get up. I know the way out. I won't bother you again."

The butler shut the front door behind him with a snap of finality. Jake opened his car door. He saw a slight figure standing by the front windows. He gave one brief nod and got into the sleek black Mercedes. He drove down the long, curved driveway and turned left onto the state highway.

Sharp pain stabbed at him. Pulling to the side of the road, he bent his head against the steering wheel. His mother didn't love him. How could he expect anyone else to give a tinker's damn?

Jake moved on automatic through the day. His employees seemed glad to see him, and he immersed himself in several problems. It helped to work and to not think. Wounds that had taken years to heal now lay open, raw and aching.

Why after seeing the Weber clan yesterday, did he ever believe things might be different for him? He was still the unwanted one, the problem shoved aside in a dark closet or insulted and watched for his father's traits to reappear in him.

He glanced around his office and listened to the bustle of movement and the voices of his staff outside the door. Here was where he belonged. Katie and her family had their life and he his. He'd best not forget.

But deep down he still felt like the little boy staring in the window of a house, seeing the home and family he wanted and not allowed to go inside.

Hopefully the next few weeks would go fast. He wanted to get the inheritance and move on. He'd have Tom start the project in Treehaven and he'd be traveling again. Life would go on the same. He'd make it.

* * * *

The woman in the mansion had watched his car go out of sight. She went to her Queen Anne desk and taking off her bracelet, with its many charms, she chose the key shaped bangle and unlocked a hidden drawer. The newspaper clippings, some yellow with age, and others from more recent years told the life of her son. The life she missed, his victories in high school athletics and his success in Atlanta. There was an article about his business and the handsome bachelor who owned it.

Her throat tightened with unshed tears. She'd kept her hands clenched to keep from reaching out and touching him. She wanted to pull him into her arms, but she didn't.

There was a phrase, too much water under the bridge, and she'd made her choice a long time ago. She'd learned well over the years to act the part given her.

She struggled to rein herself in and push him and the memories deep into her mind. Her friends would be arriving in less than thirty minutes. Determined to be ready, she went upstairs to her bedroom.

She smoothed her light golden hair. Her mirror reflected a woman with almond shaped eyes, high cheek bones, tall, thin and clothed elegantly in a tailored steel blue suit.

No one knew the girl locked within. The girl never allowed to surface, but today she clawed at the woman demanding attention. Claudia Winston glared at herself. She went to a nearby table and poured a glass of water.

The clock ticked, minutes flying by, warning her she had little time left before she must don her usual persona. Reaching for a pen and paper, she started to write a short letter to her son, Jake.

"There you are, my dear." Her husband stood in the doorway. "Aren't the girls coming today?"

Claudia crumpled the paper in her hand and threw it in the waste basket. "I started to make a list of things I need from the store, but seeing the time I realize they'll be here any moment."

"Is something wrong?" He came further into the room. "You're pale. Perhaps you should call off your meeting."

He was a good man and not bad looking at fifty-five. His blond hair had thinned across the front, but he'd maintained his slim upright figure. Not as tall or as broad across the shoulders as Jake and his father, nor as dashingly handsome, but he had taken good care of her and their spoiled son. He didn't know about Jake, and she was afraid to take the chance of his learning about her past after all this time.

She walked to him and touched his cheek. "I'm all right and anyway the ladies are on their way." She heard her polished tone and knew Mrs. Claudia Winston was back in control. Taking her husband's arm, she left the room. For a second, she glanced back at the waste basket. Her eyes closed briefly, and she swallowed around the lump in her throat. When she faced forward, the refined, elegant, society woman encased her.

* * * *

Katie pulled into the drive at three o'clock. She wasn't sure what time Jake planned on returning, but she had finished her business at the college. She'd driven to Gainesville and on the seat beside her lay pamphlets with information on the teaching courses, required for her to get certified.

She'd stopped at the market and picked out two steaks and a small hibachi. She'd have Jake grill the steaks and she'd fix a salad, then they'd make a plan. She had it all organized and under control.

There was one thing she wanted to do before he got back. She put the groceries in the fridge and went upstairs to change out of her dress into old jeans and a worn t-shirt. The ladder stood open, again, under the attic door.

After climbing the steps, Katie pushed on the recessed panel and moved it out of the way. With some difficulty, she managed to wiggle into the small space and crawl cautiously along the floor. Why had the ghost set up the ladder unless there was a reason she wanted Katie to look in the attic?

She tried to ignore the uneasy feeling creeping along her arms and in her stomach. She sneezed from the dust disturbed by her movements. Going to the window, she rubbed the dirt off the window pane with the palm of her hand and looked at the backyard. She sat for a moment and rested her chin on the window sill. When she went to move, she felt it give.

Looking closer she noticed a loose piece of wood. She tugged at the corner and pulled it away. Inside a small compartment, she found a thin book and several letters. Suddenly a strong wind whirled around the quiet attic, and a shrill noise made the hairs on her arm stand up. The air crackled with electricity.

Frightened, she clasped the book and letters to her breast and crawled along the floor. A smothering layer of dust enveloped her. She had trouble seeing because of her eyes tearing. When she tried to breathe, she tasted grit and grime.

A maniacal scream blasted her ear drums, the noise going on and on until she curled into a ball holding her hands over her ears.

Jake please come. I need you. She'd been foolish to do this on her own.

Moving carefully, she tried to locate the opening. In her fear, she'd lost her sense of direction.

Katie flung out her hand. "Go away," she yelled, but the whirlwind around her increased. Desperate to get out of the attic, Katie lunged forward, hoping to find her way out. She felt herself falling into space, head first and grabbed desperately for the ladder.

"What the hell?"

Katie regained consciousness to find Jake kneeling beside her. "What happened?"

"That's what I want to know," he said.

She raised her head and looked around. Spotting the book and letters, she reached over and picked them up from the floor where they'd fallen.

"I found these in the attic," she said.

"I thought you'd agreed to go somewhere today," he said, ignoring her find.

"I did. I got back around three and decided to check out the attic again."

"Why didn't you wait for me?"

Katie sat up straighter and ignored his question. Jake kept his arms around her. His piercing blue eyes stared at her.

"The last thing I remember was falling and grabbing the ladder, but I don't feel sore or hurt like I'd expect if I'd fallen all the way down. I was so afraid, but I must have managed to use the ladder to keep from falling the whole way." She moved her hands along her body and legs.

Jake helped her stand. He looked at the ladder knocked sideways against the wall and at the opening. "What caused you to fall?"

Did Judith cause what happened in the attic? Was that her scream? Nothing made sense. Why would she be angry when I found her papers? She wanted me to search the attic again. Katie's head began to ache.

Then she remembered the noise and the terror. The hideous laugher, the malevolent presence she'd felt close to her. No, that wasn't Judith.

What would Jake say when she told him about the other episode, the choking? He'd probably explode. She wasn't ready to tell him, not yet. But, he was still waiting for an explanation.

She brushed herself off. "I think I'll take a warm bath before dinner. Can we talk after we eat? I'm too shook up now."

"You're not cooking."

Katie grinned. "You're right. You are. The steaks are in the fridge. See you in about thirty minutes." She went into her room, shut the door and leaned against it. The house had become a lot more sinister.

She sat on the side of the bed and rubbed her arms. When the cold became palpable, it frightened her, but the warmth never scared her.

She refused to let whomever or whatever it was frightened her away. They were too close to gaining the inheritance.

She didn't know much about ghosts, but she'd never heard of one deliberately hurting a person. Hopefully this ghost only wanted to get her and Jake to leave.

Chapter 9

"Did your business go well?" Katie asked, as she rinsed the dinner dishes.

"Yes."

He put the dried plate in the cupboard. Something about the way he held his shoulders stiff and the look on his face warned her to change the subject.

"I got some information on getting my teacher's certification and my masters in finance. I'm thinking about teaching either in high school or at the college level."

"Really?" Jake said. "I can see you as a teacher."

"You can? You're not going to tell me how much more money I'd make with my MBA."

"Why should I? It's your life, and money isn't everything."

He swung the dishtowel across his shoulder and went to the fridge to pour two glasses of wine. "Join me in the living room. We'll explore your recent discoveries."

"I'll bring in Smudges first," Katie said.

She opened the screen door and watched as the puppy scampered in to the living room straight for Jake. He grinned and settled Smudges by his side, rubbing the satiny black fur. Smudges gave a happy yip. Soft warmth spread inside Katie and she swallowed past a lump in her throat. Jake would be a good husband and father. He just didn't see himself as she saw him. She waited a second and then joined him.

He sat in his favorite spot on the floor. Lamplight shone off his silky hair and made his eyes glow.

"Where do you want to start?"

"Start with the small book. Read it to me," she said.

Raising an eyebrow at her, he turned to the first page. She was surprised to see him pull glasses out of his shirt pocket.

"I only use them when reading or working long hours on the computer."

October 18, 1861, the happiest day of my life. Daniel and I were married yesterday. My parents are not pleased that I did not marry the man they preferred. Nevertheless, I'm sure Daniel is the one for me. Today, we move into Sandstone.

This is our home, to live in and raise our children. I feel complete with Daniel by my side. We will create a family and live happily ever after.

Jake raised his head. "Too bad it didn't work out for them. And you think she's our ghost?"

"It makes sense, but sometimes it's like she's two people," Katie took a deep breath before continuing. "One good and the other evil."

"What do you mean?"

"Judith seems almost caring. I feel it, but the other Judith is evil and scary."

"Have you had other experiences with the evil Judith before today?" His eyes glinted with anger. "I think you'd better explain."

Katie took a sip of wine, stalling for time. "Several days ago I was lying down, half asleep. I'm almost sure it was a dream...but I thought the ghost tried to strangle me."

Jake jumped up and paced across the floor, while Smudges ran around his feet. "And you're just now telling me this?"

"Sit down, Jake. You make me nervous when you pace."

He glared at her, then sat and swallowed half his glass of wine. "Go on."

"When I looked in the mirror there was no sign of bruising on my neck, nothing to indicate it really happened."

"And this afternoon?" he asked. "When you found this book and the letters."

"Wind blew around me and dirt and dust blinded me. My eyes watered and stung and with the screaming noise, I became disoriented." Katie stared at Jake. "I lunged forward and fell into the opening, head first."

He paused a moment and added in a softer tone, "Are you sure you're not hurt?"

"I'm sure," she said. "My theory is that Judith somehow broke my fall."

"And when did you plan to tell me all of this?" His velvet edged voice sent warning signals along her nerve endings.

"I'm telling you now. One just happened before dinner, and the other time I was convinced I dreamed it. Although after today, I'm not so sure. I guess I wanted to avoid this reaction. I knew you'd be upset."

The air around them sizzled, and Jake leaned toward her. Excitement and a tinge of fear flickered through her.

Smudges ran to them, yelping. Katie looked around the room and into the dining area. On the stairway a faint mist hovered. Smudges cuddled against Jake again. When the mist moved, the puppy whimpered. Seconds later it disappeared.

Jake's brow furrowed. "I must be tired, I'm beginning to believe Judith is here and she wants to keep us apart."

He glanced through the pages of yellowed paper. "The rest appears to be short notes on daily life and Daniel. She worried he'd go to war." He turned to the last entry.

Daniel left to enlist. His brother died in the battle of Antietam, September 17th, 1862. Daniel felt obligated to fight in his brother's place. As though endangering his life made up for the loss.

I can't go to my folks. They have not forgiven me. I won't leave Sandstone, even though it feels haunted with shattered dreams.

This is my home. Maybe I'm wrong, and Daniel will return. I don't believe it, but I have to have some hope to cling to. Damn men and wars!

Jake closed the book. "Like you, she refused to give up on this house. The damn thing ought to have been torn down years ago."

"No," Katie protested. "I think we need to learn more about Judith and Daniel."

Jake sat with Smudges in his lap. His hand ran along the puppy's back and Smudges' little eyes closed. Katie wished his hand ran along her back. When she raised her eyes, she found Jake studying her.

His gaze roamed from the top of her head, stopping briefly where her breasts swelled from the heat of his glance, and down the rest of her body.

Her breast ached to be touched, and a strong yearning went through her. Katie caught herself before she reached out for him.

She swallowed. "Give me the letters." Her voice came out low and husky. She cleared her throat and looked away from him. "I'll read them."

Gently setting the puppy aside, Jake stood. "It's enough for tonight. We'll call the older couple tomorrow. Maybe they've found more information."

"Good idea." Katie glanced at the dark stairs. The living room might seem safe, but the upstairs held secrets and darkness.

"Wait for me." Jake walked in the direction of his room. When he returned he'd changed into his pajama bottoms and carried his pillow and a blanket.

"I'm going to sleep in one of the upstairs bedrooms. I'll move the rest of my stuff tomorrow."

Katie started to protest. Jake put his finger over her lips. "There won't be any discussion. It's done."

Katie said good night and went inside her room. She leaned against the door. If there'd been a lock, she'd used it. But, she wasn't sure whether she wanted to lock the ghost out or keep herself from walking across the hall.

Torn between relief that Jake was nearby and fear she might not be able to resist the desire coursing through her veins, Katie knew there'd be little sleep tonight.

* * * *

Jake lay on the small bed looking out his window. He stared at the moon. An owl hooted in the distance. He tried to keep his thoughts away from Katie, his body still tight and hard with desire. She was only a few feet away and yet so far. He warred with himself to keep from knocking on her door.

Earlier, he'd smelled her special fragrance and mixed with the hunger in her eyes, he barely managed to restrain himself. His fingertips yearned to trail along her soft skin to the valley between her breasts. He craved the taste of her. He needed to touch her, fill her. Desire spiraled along his body, hardening him even more.

Living here with Katie and trying to keep his distance wasn't working. They had a little more than two weeks left. It might as well be forever. He didn't want to love Katie Weber. Love, the word shook him to the core.

Going to his side table, he picked up the small book. Katie hadn't noticed he'd kept it. There were parts he hadn't read out loud.

Judith never told Daniel about feeling pushed down the stairs one day. She'd caught herself in time to prevent getting hurt, and she didn't see anyone. She told herself it was her own carelessness.

But Judith feared someone was lurking around the house and whoever it was might eventually hurt her. When her husband left, it didn't matter. Without Daniel, she didn't care to live.

Jake looked forward to meeting the Barrows tomorrow. He and Katie needed to solve the mystery so they could get out of here. He'd try to convince Katie to stay away during the day, as much as possible, and at night he'd be nearby. He hoped he didn't have to battle himself and the ghost to keep Katie safe.

* * * *

Mr. and Mrs. Barrows agreed to see them and suggested they come over for coffee and cinnamon rolls. Katie and Jake decided to put Smudges in her carrying case and take her with them. No sense in taking a chance with the puppy.

"You'll love the Barrows, Jake. They're so sweet."

"I hope they can help us."

"Mrs. Barrows said she had some records in her attic. If she hasn't gotten around to bringing them down, maybe she'll let us get them."

Katie waved at Joe Barrows sitting in his rocker on the porch. She watched as the two men greeted each other. Jake wore his usual wary expression.

"Do you mind if we get Smudges and leash her to a tree?" Katie asked.

Mr. Barrows reached in the window and patted Smudges' head. "Not at all. I'll get a bowl for water."

"Katie," Mrs. Barrows came outside drying her hands on her apron. "We're so pleased to see you. And this must be your young man." She, turned to Jake.

"Mrs. Barrows, Jake Andrews."

Mrs. Barrows held Jake's hand and stared at his face. "Yep, you're as handsome as your wild daddy, but," she tipped her head to the side, "you remind me more of your granddaddy."

Jake stiffened at the mere mention of his father. Katie wished for a way to change the subject.

Mr. Barrows joined them and studied Jake. "You do," he agreed. "Bart Andrews was a fine man. Too bad you didn't get to know him. That heart attack took him away much too soon. I always thought your dad might have turned out different if his father hadn't died."

Katie saw the color leave Jake's face. She reached over and touched his arm, but Mrs. Barrows noted it too.

"You listen to me, young man. You hold your head high in this town. We've heard the rubbish they say about you. They try to compare you to your dad. You just remember your granddad was a strong, honest, hard working man and your dad didn't handle losing him very well. He was only thirteen when Bart died."

Mr. Barrows nodded. "We didn't mean to upset you."

Mrs. Barrows shuffled them into the kitchen. "Now sit here at the table and I'll pour coffee and you can eat my fresh cinnamon rolls." She leaned down and pulled out a tray of rolls fresh from the oven.

* * * *

No one ever talked open and honest to him about his family, at least not to his face, and he knew almost nothing about his grandfather. Even his aunt hadn't mentioned him. If his father had been thirteen, than she must have been ten when her father died.

Jake smelled cinnamon and Katie's hand lay warm on his arm. The concerned expression on the Barrows' faces made him force a smile.

It was a shock hearing anything good about his family. He'd never considered his grandfather was much different from his father.

Mrs. Barrows sat a large mug filled with hot coffee in front of him and a plate with two rolls covered in white frosting. He looked into her kind eyes.

"Thank you. You're the first person to ever tell me about my grandfather."

A smile broke out across her face. "Well, it's about time. Of course, we're so old, we may be the only two in town who can remember back that far, but I doubt it. Some people just like to point out the negative."

"Now what questions did you two have for us?" Mr. Barrows asked.

Jake watched Katie lick frosting off her lip before answering. If they were alone he'd lick it off for her.

"Did you have a chance to find anything else in your attic regarding Judith or Sandstone?" Katie asked, bringing him back to the present.

"Actually I planned to call you today, but you beat me to it," Mrs. Barrows said. She joined them at the table. "I found a few more photos and my aunt's diary. I read some of it last night. There are a few entries that are disturbing." She turned to her husband. "Joe, please get the things off my bureau?"

Mr. Barrows nodded and went out of the room. "I wanted to add one more thing," she said, looking over at Jake. "If you want to come over someday and talk more about your family you'd be welcome. In fact, I may have some pictures of your granddad and grandmother. A man should know the good things about his family." Mrs. Barrows patted his hand. "You're a fine young man. Bart would be proud."

"Here they are." Mr. Barrows returned holding a similar book to the one Katie had found yesterday and several photos and letters.

They spread the book and papers on the table. Jake picked up the book. "Do you mind?" he asked before opening it.

"No," Mr. Barrows said.

Jake started to read. The others sat quietly sipping coffee and eating their rolls. Jake's head came up.

"Your relative had doubts regarding Judith's death?"

Mrs. Barrows nodded. "As you see in the diary she mentions Judith being a strong woman. Judith fought her family to marry Daniel. My aunt didn't believe the story about Judith lying down and dying of a broken heart, but," Mrs. Barrows hesitated, "love can affect people in different ways. And it's not unheard of for widows to die within the first year after their spouse's death.

"Take the diary and other papers and read them. They might help you understand what happened during that time." Mrs. Barrows sorted through the papers, pulling out a faded black and white photo. "This is a picture of Judith and Daniel. I think it might have been taken on their wedding day."

Jake and Katie leaned forward eager to see the couple they were learning so much about.

"She reminds me of someone," Katie said. "I keep thinking I'll figure out who it is."

Jake took the picture and stared hard. He looked up and met Mrs. Barrows' eyes. She nodded.

"Katie, I can tell you," Jake said. "Don't you see the resemblance? She looks like you and your mother. She has your mother's height, but your facial features."

"And that lovely golden red hair," Mrs. Barrows added.

* * * *

It all fell into place. No wonder Judith looked familiar to her. "I have to talk with my sister, Annie." Katie felt exhilaration course through her. She might be a descendant of Judith's. More and more Katie felt they were coming closer to solving the mystery, and she wanted to call Annie now.

"I've asked my sister to do a genealogy study on Judith. Although I'm sure she'd have called if she found a connection to our family."

"We should be on our way. We're getting a lot of information to follow-up on and we haven't read all the papers and letters yet," Jake said. He stood. "Thank you for the delicious rolls and telling me about my grandfather."

Katie added her thanks. "We'll get the diary, papers, and photos back to you."

"Don't worry," Mrs. Barrows said, as she followed them to the front door. "Those old things have been in the attic gathering dust. I think they really belong to you." She patted Katie's arm.

Katie hugged her. "In today's world we'd never find so much hand written by the people concerned." She shrugged, "I guess future generations will learn about us through our e-mails."

Jake put Smudges in the back seat and drove to Sandstone. "You can call your sister, and I'll start reading the letters and papers from last night and the ones from the Barrows."

"Yes, all of the sudden I feel we need to hurry. That we're getting close to something. Do you feel it?" Katie asked.

"I agree. And almost half of our time is gone, so it's good thing we're finally discovering more information."

Smudges stayed close to them when they went inside. Quiet stillness filled the rooms. A chill of fear and excitement ran through Katie.

* * * *

"I'll call Annie, but first I'll order a pizza for supper," Katie said.

"Good. I'll move the rest of my stuff upstairs and start reading."

After ordering the pizza, Katie dialed Annie's number. Annie answered on the first ring. "Are you busy?" Katie asked.

"Not now, Ty's asleep. This is the only time I have to get on my computer. I've been using his nap time to look for information on Judith's family," Annie said.

"I can save you some time. Look back on our family tree, around the 1860's."

"What?" Annie sounded surprised.

"It seems Judith is probably a distant relative, since I look like her."

"You're kidding."

"No, I knew when I saw the first picture that she looked familiar. Mrs. Barrows had a better picture to show us today, and Jake recognized the likeness almost at once. She's tall like Mom, but appears to have my hair color and facial features."

"This explains why you look so different than the rest of us. Let's see I've done a lot of research on Dad's family. I'll check Mom's side."

Katie got up and paced the room.

"Here it is!"

Katie clenched the phone tighter. "What did you find?"

"One of Mom's distant grandfathers had two wives. His first wife died at age 33. He and his second wife had two children, Judith, and her younger sister. We're descendents of the sister."

"Judith is related to us."

"Yes," Annie said.

Katie sank into the nearest chair. "It sort of explains why I'm the beneficiary. Mrs. Pace must have known of the relationship."

"I agree," Annie said. "Ty is waking. I'd better go."

"Thanks, Annie." Katie sank back, her mind racing with information.

An early dinner and they'd spend the rest of the evening planning their next steps. She felt like they were on a scavenger hunt and she was anxious to find the next clue. She only hoped she'd find it in the letters and not from whatever entity roamed the second floor.

The delivery man knocked on the door. His face reflected his discomfort and desire to hurry away.

"Hum, the pizza smells good," Jake said, as he followed Katie to the kitchen. His eyebrows rose when she got a bottle of bourbon from the cabinet.

"If ever we deserved a drink it's tonight. I'm having bourbon and coke, are you?" Katie stood with her hand on her hips.

"A woman after my own heart. You can get out the paper plates for the pizza, and I'll make the drinks."

"Don't make mine too strong."

"Afraid I'll have my wicked way with you?" He wiggled his eyebrows at her.

"Not at all. The ghost would scare you away," she teased back. It was nice to relax and enjoy his company. She'd seldom seen a true smile on his strong face. His infectious grin set the tone for the evening.

Her heart skipped a beat when he handed her the drink and his hand brushed hers. Her body was so in tune to this man, as though it recognized him intuitively.

"I'll get the papers," he said. "They're in the living room."

He returned with the letters and sat beside her. "I'm going to eat this pizza while it's hot. You might want to glance at Judith's letters and we'll talk after you finish."

Katie took a bite of the hot pizza. The melted cheese blended with pepperoni, green peppers, and onions. She took a swallow of her drink and started to read the first letter.

Dear Mrs. Collier, It is with deep sadness that I inform you of your husband's death on the battlefield at Fredericksburg on December 13, 1862. Your husband fought with bravery and honor and lost his life trying to rescue a fellow soldier. May your memories of his gallantry comfort you in your time of grief. Sincerely, Col. William A. Saunders.

Katie's throat tightened, and she blinked tears away. She gently folded the letter and placed it back into the yellowed envelope. "How awful for Judith. She was probably home alone when she got this message."

"He'd have been on the list that came to town. Don't you think the townspeople came out here to comfort her?" Jake questioned.

"Maybe, but at some point she'd be alone and faced with her future without him."

"Her parents apparently didn't take her home with them," Katie added.

"I wonder if they asked and she refused. I don't think Judith wanted to give up on this house anymore than I do."

"What is it with you women? It's a house, nothing more. There are lots of houses out there. I'll build you a beautiful one, much larger, and it can be part payment for your share of the property."

"I'm not selling to you, Jake. Forget it. I'm here to stay." Katie stood and leaned across the table glaring at him.

A muscle quivered in his jaw, and his lips tightened. "We'll talk about it later. I'm as stubborn as you, and I'm not giving up."

"You've been given fair warning," she said and sat down.

Jake changed the subject, but Katie knew the issue of the house continued to stand between them. They might tiptoe around it all they wanted. It wasn't going away.

"Tomorrow, I'll go in to town and check on the computer to see if Judith's husband has any living relatives in Virginia, or at least I'll try to find the information," Jake said.

"Good." Katie picked up the other letter.

"Better take your drink and Kleenex in the other room while you read that one." Jake shook his head. "Knowing you, you'll need both. I'll clean up."

Puzzled, but wanting some distance between them, Katie did as he said and settled on the sofa. When she opened the letter, a lock of dark brown hair fell out. Her fingers touched the still soft curl.

Warmth surrounded her, and she felt Judith's presence. She'd have sworn she heard a strangled sob. Katie started reading the letter out loud.

My dearest wife, if you are reading this, I have died. I'm tucking the letter in my coat in hopes someone will forward it to you. I hope you have come to understand why I had to join the battle. Perhaps not. Women are nurturers. It is men who can't seem to settle issues in compromise. Is all this death worth it? I think not. But I ramble. I wanted you to know on this night before battle that what I think about is you and the small seemingly unimportant things in life.

Katie stopped reading to wipe her eyes and blow her nose. She took a long swallow of her drink and felt the heat settle in her nervous stomach. She took another swallow and it slid around the large lump in her throat. She imagined the brush of a hand on her forehead. "I'm so sorry, Judith," she whispered.

Katie heard Jake moving around in the kitchen. She suspected he wanted to give her this time alone. She returned her attention to the letter.

I remember the scent of you. It always reminded me of the wild roses by the steps outside the kitchen. I can hear the wind in the trees and see the deer at the edge of our forest. And I can feel the softness of your skin and hair. I never told you, but I fell in love with you from the first day and will love you until my heart stops. If love can continue after death, I'll love you always. Your husband, Daniel.

Katie finished her drink and used several more Kleenex to wipe her eyes. She went into the kitchen and stepped outside the door. The wild roses still bloomed by the back steps, and the fragrance floated on the early evening breeze. She heard the wind blow through the trees as Daniel had written, and for a second, she imagined she saw a deer at the edge of the hammock of trees.

Everything and everyone connected in some fantastic way through genes passed down and stories and a little magic.

She heard the door behind her open and arms wrapped around her. Jake's body comforted and protected her. His chin rested on the top of her head.

The stars twinkled down on them. Katie sighed. Jake nuzzled her cheek and neck with soft kisses. The sweet scent of wild roses enveloped them.

Katie felt her heart catch and tears wet her eyes. She wondered if Jake felt the connection too and what it meant for the two of them.

Chapter 10

Jake followed Katie up the stairs, tension sparking between them. Desire streaked through her. The air felt heavy like it does before a summer storm.

He touched her arm, and they stood between the rooms. His body heat enveloped her and a yearning shot through Katie. She wanted this man, but in many ways he was still an enigma. Briefly, he let you see past his armor and then he retreated behind the public mask he wore.

Katie's hand reached out and touched the rough stubble on his cheek. She ran her hand lightly across his lips. He caught hold of her hand and kissed her palm, then stared at her with those crystal blue eyes.

Her breath caught and she stepped into the warmth of him. His arms encircled her, her head rested just beneath his chin. For several moments they didn't move.

She enjoyed breathing in his special scent and letting all his body heat soak into her. It felt like coming home and that scared her. She took a step back.

His fingers lightly touched the curls around her face, slid across her cheek and caressed the side of her neck. He leaned toward her and caught her lips in a hard possessive kiss.

"You're beautiful, and I want to stay with you tonight."

The words went straight to her heart. Dare she take a chance? This man might very well hurt her, much worse than Eric did. But, she wanted his warmth and closeness and to be part of him. A ripple of excitement ran through her.

"Then stay," she whispered.

* * * *

Jake swung her into his arms and pushed her door open. Moonlight lit the room. He leaned against the door to make sure it closed before walking across the room. A chuckle escaped.

"We'll be close in that little bed," he murmured. It didn't stop him from lying down with her and pulling her tight against his body. He studied her face, and his hand roamed from her forehead, brushing across the tips of her long lashes, her turned up nose and ran across her lips. Cupping her face in both his hands, he kissed her. His tongue swept inside the warmth of her mouth. Her soft breasts and all of her body cuddled against him.

Brief kisses followed and his breath caught when her soft, warm hands touched his skin as she started to unbutton his shirt. For one second his rational brain tried to warn him, danger, danger, but it was too late. He didn't remember ever wanting anything this much.

Silencing his thoughts, he followed her lead. He pushed his jeans off after taking a condom out of his pocket. At least that took care of some danger. But, for tonight, for at least one time in his life, he wasn't the little boy looking in the candy store. He was inside, and it felt better then he ever imagined.

"Now it's my turn," he said. Quickly he unbuttoned her shirt and unfastened her bra. Her soft breast with pink nipples held him mesmerized. Bending his head, he brushed his lips across one tip and then the other. His tongue circled each and then he took one breast into his mouth.

Katie's body rose against him, and he heard her moan. After giving attention to the other breast, he reached for the waistband of her jeans and unfastened them. She helped him push them off and then her lace panties.

His lips feathered kisses across her abdomen, and he breathed in the scent of her as he went lower. Brushing his fingers through her soft hair, he sought her tender inner core. Her legs opened wider to give him access, as her fingers ran across his shoulders and into his hair.

His tongue flickered across her lower lips, and her soft gasp hardened him even more. The ache to be inside her was building. Forcing himself to take his time, he kissed her, tasted her, and then scattered kisses along the inside of her thighs.

She moaned and twisted, creating a raging fire inside him. Finally, when he wasn't able to hold off any longer, he slid up her body, held her hands above her head and moved between her legs. He plunged into her with one strong lunge.

Her body shook with tremors. She arched up to bring him closer, and he groaned. Her legs tightened, pulling him further in.

He ran his tongue along her lips. "You taste like the sweetest orange blossom honey," he whispered.

A mixture of feelings--hunger, possessiveness and tenderness—built like a crescendo as he moved faster and faster.

He held himself back until she moved upward one more time bringing him in even deeper and then she yelled out. He slid over the edge with her.

Jake kissed her face and moved to her side. His mind in turmoil, he waited for his breathing to slow. Damn, what happened? He never lost control. But he'd felt a connection with Katie. A feeling he'd guarded against in his other relationships.

He kissed her on the forehead and lay on his back with her snug against his side. After a short while her breathing slowed, and glancing at her, he saw she was sleeping.

The time crept by. He didn't sleep. Thoughts raced in his head, Katie, the inheritance, his lifestyle of traveling and keeping people at a distance. In a short time this small, cuddly woman had pushed past his protective walls, and it scared him to death.

Confused and tired, he pulled on his jeans and went to the door. He glanced at her snuggled on her side and almost went back to her. Forcing himself to leave, he shut her door quietly and went across the hall into his cold lonely room.

* * * *

Jake was on the phone when Katie came downstairs. She went into the kitchen. Obviously, he'd been up early. The coffee pot was perking and he'd poured cereal into bowls. She filled her coffee cup.

Smudges ran to Katie, and she patted her head. The puppy ran around the room and to the door. "Want to go out? Good, I need a breath of fresh air." She fastened the leash and taking her cup in the other hand went outside.

Birds chirped in the air. A hawk circled in the distance. Fluffy, white clouds floated across the canvas of the sky. She took a deep breath and the smell of honeysuckle, sweet roses, and pine filled her nostrils. Smudges pulled on the lease. Katie kept it taunt slowing the puppy down.

The caffeine in her coffee helped clear her head. If only it could wash out the questions in her mind from last night. She'd been disappointed when she woke in the early morning to find Jake gone, and the bed cold beside her. She wondered how long he stayed before escaping to his own room.

Had it been just a brief encounter to him with no deep feelings involved? Sometime just before dawn, she'd finally gone back to sleep for a few hours. When she awoke to bright daylight, she'd taken her time dressing before going downstairs.

She'd never allow him to know how right last night felt to her. At least, not unless he expressed similar feelings to her first. She needed to guard her heart. From now on Mr. Jake Andrews stayed in his own room.

Tears slid down Katie's cheeks. The feelings aroused by Jake were different from the one's she'd had for Eric. This cut much deeper.

She must get control of herself. She and Jake were partners in this mystery hunt. She'd try and ignore last night. The other was too important. Wiping her eyes, she turned around and headed to the house.

Jake stood at the screen door when she and Smudges returned. "What were you doing out there so long?"

"I needed fresh air."

"Look, I'm sorry about leaving you last night. I wasn't sleepy and I thought my restlessness might wake you up. Guess I'm used to sleeping alone."

"I understand," she lied and quickly changed the subject. "You're going to research Daniel's relatives, today?"

"Yes. Why don't you come with me and we'll both search? There's an extra computer you can use."

Her brow creased with concern. "I need to let my folks know what's going on." She bit the edge of her mouth. "I'll call them. Why don't you go on ahead, and I'll be along shortly."

She noted his hesitation, before he nodded and agreed. Katie followed him to the door and watched him leave.

A flood of emotion swept over Katie, love, despair, fear and anger. The room became hazy and Katie had the sensation that Judith hovered near-by. "Is this how you stood, Judith, watching Daniel leave that last time?" Air stirred around her and then warmth and a soft touch brushed Katie's cheek.

"We'll find the answers, Judith, about you and Daniel and the evilness that stalks the upstairs. If someone hurt you, we'll find out."

As soon as the words left her mouth, items began to fly across the room, chairs tumbled over in the dining room, and Katie swore she heard Smudges growl. But, nothing touched Katie. The warm air stayed still around her, not leaving until the house became calm and quiet again.

Grabbing her purse and Smudges, Katie flew out the door. She fastened Smudges to her chain by the large oak. The puppy had water and shade and she'd be safe here in the open. Katie'd call her folks on her way to town.

* * * *

"What's wrong?" Sara asked, coming from behind her desk to wrap her arms around Katie. "You're so pale."

"Nothing." Katie said. "I came to work with Jake."

"Sit down and I'll get you a cup of coffee. Someone else might fall for that line, but not me." Sara went to a table where coffee, cups, sugar, and a few donuts set.

She brought a cup of coffee and a donut to Katie. "Did you eat this morning?"

"I started to." Katie sighed. "The house is haunted, and sometimes it gets to me more than other times. I'm fine, really." Katie didn't want to tell her about what happened this morning.

"Is Jake in the office he's been using?"

"Yes," Sara said, before adding. "I'm your best friend, Katie. You know you can trust me."

"I do and I will explain, just not now."

Following Sara's directions, Katie found Jake working intently on his computer. She enjoyed watching him. His hands flew across the keyboard. Katie studied his strong profile. He starred at the screen through the glasses she seldom saw him wear. As though sensing her, he turned and smiled.

"Come in and find out what I discovered."

Katie moved across the room to stand by his shoulder. She bent down and looked at his screen.

"From the information I've found, I believe Daniel might be from Alexandria, Virginia or around that area. There are a good number of

Colliers living there. I'm thinking he'd be from a smaller place that would have had more farms back then. If we start on the Colliers in small towns near Alexandria, then the number decreases significantly. I thought we'd divide the calls and see if any of them are related to Daniel."

"That's a great idea," Katie pulled out her cell phone. "Let's get started. I'm really getting excited. I think we're finally on the right track."

After setting her purse on the table and pulling out a chair to sit on, Katie dialed the first number.

"Hello, Mrs. Collier? My name is Katie Weber. I'm trying to find a relative of a man who died in the Civil War in Fredericksburg. His name is Daniel Collier. Oh, sorry I bothered you."

Katie glanced across at Jake. "She just moved to the area. No southern relatives. She probably thinks I'm some kind of nut."

"I'll start calling my numbers," Jake said. The call was brief and he hung up. "I had no luck either." Jake shrugged.

Katie went to her next number. This was going to take some time. Four calls later, she got a response.

"You had two ancestors killed in the Confederate war? Did one die at Antietam and the other at Fredericksburg? Yes!

"My friend and I are living at Sandstone, where Daniel and his wife lived. We're trying to find out the mystery of the house. Most of the Treehaven residents have always believed Judith haunted it.

"I'd be glad to give you our names and you can check on us through the law firm of Townsend and Townsend. I understand you can't be too careful these days. Can we call you back later? You'll call me as soon as you check things out? Good," Katie gave her the number. "Thanks. I'll be looking forward to hearing from you."

Katie snapped her phone shut and danced around the room. "We did it. We found Daniel's relatives."

"I gathered she's going to check us out."

"I can't blame her. I'm not sure how this will help us, but I can't wait to talk with her more." Katie hesitated. "Are you going to be working late?"

Jake shook his head. "No, I'll follow you back to the ranch."

Katie frantically searched her mind for something to say. She didn't want to be in the house alone for long, but she needed time to clean the place. She wasn't sure she wanted to tell Jake about what happened earlier for fear he'd overreact. After all, Judith protected her. She'd wait and discuss it with him at home.

"I'll leave first, and you can finish what you're doing."

She saw the look Jake gave her. She'd never been good at fabricating, but he let her go without any questions.

"See you." Katie called out to Sara and practically ran out the door. All she needed was for Jake to hear Sara giving her the third degree.

Smudges slept in the shade, but raised her little head when the car got closer and started barking.

"OK, I hear you." Katie went to her and unfastened the leash. The puppy ran in circles around her feet. Katie scooped the puppy up in her arms to keep from tripping over her little body. She hugged Smudges tight as she opened the door and went inside.

Stunned, she looked all around the room and into the dining area. Everything was in place, the pillows on the sofa and the book was back on the table.

All the chairs in the dining room sat neatly in their spot around the table. How? Was she imagining things? It was real. It happened.

The sound of Jake's engine told her he had left very soon after her. Just as well she hadn't said anything. She'd look like an idiot.

Katie jumped for the phone at the first ring. "Hello. Mrs. Collier? Thanks so much for calling back."

"Your call today brought back memories of stories passed along through the years by Robert's family," Mrs. Collier's said her voice warm and friendly. "I'd like to put this on speaker phone so my husband, Robert, can be included."

"Great, my friend, Jake Andrews, can hear the conversation that way too."

"Robert hasn't been all that interested in his history, but his grandmother's tales always fascinated me, and when she died last year we inherited several boxes of mementoes."

"From the time of the Civil War?" Katie asked.

Mrs. Collier sighed. "Yes, and to be honest I've been so busy this year with my daughter graduating from college and our twenty-fifth anniversary party to plan, that I put the boxes in the attic and forgot all about them until your call."

Jake leaned forward, "Could you tell us any of the stories?"

Her voice brightened, "I remember several about the Collier boys. They'd have been Robert's very distant cousins.

"Let's see where should I start? The story goes that Mr. Collier, Jess and Daniel's father, was a stern man. When word of a possible war began to circulate, he let his two sons know he expected them to enlist. Jess was ready to go and fight for the cause. Daniel argued with his dad. They never saw eye to eye on much of anything. Daniel didn't believe in the Union splitting. His dad went into a rage and sent him away. Grandma said it broke his mama's heart."

"How do you remember all of this?"

Katie assumed it was Mr. Collier asking.

Mrs. Collier laughed. "I loved Grandma's stories, and I promised her I'd write them down and pass them along. Something," she hesitated, "I haven't done yet.

"Let me see, where was I?"

"Daniel got sent away from home," Katie said.

"Yes. He left just before the war started. Jess enlisted right after. Daniel kept in touch with his mother, so she knew where he was and from the stories told, once Daniel heard of his brother's death, he joined the army. About three months later they were both dead. The grief killed his folks. Mr. Collier died nine months later, and a year after that Mrs. Collier was gone. That side of the family totally wiped out." Mrs. Collier's voice dropped to a whisper.

"What a tragic story," Katie said. "As I mentioned earlier, Jake and I are living in the farmhouse where Daniel and his wife lived. She died shortly after his death and—I hope you won't think I'm crazy—but I think she haunts the house."

Mrs. Collier answered quickly. "Not at all. There are too many stories around this area about ghosts, especially haunting specific places, usually where they died. I've come to believe it's possible."

"Do you have any mementos available that you might be willing to send us, such as letters that might contain information?" Jake asked.

"Robert retrieved one of the boxes for me. I looked through it and found the main item I wanted to give you."

They heard the rustle of paper. Katie's heart tripped faster. People certainly wrote a lot of letters in those days.

"Ah, here it is, at the bottom of the pile. This letter has remained unopened. The family received it with his other belongings. They believed it arrived after his death and felt that it would be intrusive to open it at that time." Mrs. Collier stated frankly. "After talking with Mr. Townsend, I think you and Mr. Andrews can decide what to do with it."

Katie tried to speak and had to clear her throat first. "We'll take good care of the letter and send it back after we finish our research on the house and Daniel and Judith."

Robert spoke up and Katie heard the skepticism in his soft southern voice. "I've always taken Grandma's tales with a grain of salt. I'm sorry, but I have a hard time believing in ghosts or that a letter can be significant after all this time."

"That's why the mementos were left to me," his wife reminded him. "I think his grandmother would approve of your having the letter."

"I'd appreciate your sending it in the overnight mail," Katie said. "I'd be glad to reimburse you, whatever it costs."

"There's no need." The phone went silent for a minute. Then Mrs. Collier spoke in a soft voice. "I believe true love goes on forever. I think Daniel and Judith's story is proving it."

* * * *

The package arrived the next morning and Katie carefully opened the outside wrapper. The enclosed envelope was faded and wrinkled. Fine delicate handwriting covered the front. Katie knew instinctively that Judith had sent this to Daniel and it arrived too late.

"Is that it?" Jake asked, looking over her shoulder.

"Yes." She handed him the letter. "I have an idea. Let's check and see if we can go to Fredericksburg. I'd like to see the place where Daniel died."

"Do you think Mr. Townsend will give us permission to leave Sandstone?"

"We can always ask," Katie said. "Let's call him now?"

"He left his cell number. I'll give it a try."

Katie waited anxiously as Jake dialed and then started to talk with the lawyer.

"What did Mr. Townsend say about our trip?" Katie asked, as soon as Jake ended the call.

"No problem as long as it's related to finding out the questions surrounding Sandstone. When do you want to leave?"

"Mom and Dad will keep Smudges. We can drop her off on the way. I'll call them. Let's leave as soon as we can get ready."

Chapter 11

The road ran endlessly ahead of them. Billboards flashed by as they neared a state line and crossed into South Carolina.

Katie studied Jake's hands. His fingers held the steering wheel firmly. He wore no rings. She remembered the strength and firmness of those hands when they touched her face and body. Looking up, she saw his eyebrows raised questioningly.

She didn't say anything and turned toward the window to look out. The scenery went by in a blur as all she saw were his strong hands and his mouth curved in a sexy smile.

Her traitorous body still wanted the man sitting relaxed and confident in the driver's seat. The other night apparently wasn't an earth shattering moment for him or for her either, she told herself. You're lying, the voice whispered in her ear. She shook her head to stop her thoughts.

"Want to change places and drive?"

His husky voice startled her. "You'd let me drive your car?"

"Sure. You seem restless. Driving might help."

"I'm not restless, but I will drive."

He waved his hand at a sign. "A rest area is coming up. I'll pull in, and we can stretch our legs and change places. We need to start looking for a place to stop soon."

When he got out of the car he went around the back and opened the trunk. Sliding into the passenger side, Jake popped open a coke and handed it to Katie.

"Where did that come from?" she asked.

"I packed a cooler with drinks while you were busy with other things."

Thanks." After taking a swallow, she turned to face him. "I want to get one thing straight." She saw she had his attention. "We are going to rent two rooms wherever we have to stop."

"I agree with you," he spoke dryly.

"You do?"

"Reluctantly, yes." His hand touched her hair and smoothed the curl behind her ear. "You're very tempting, but I don't want to hurt you. I…" He hesitated and seemed to struggle for the right words. "You deserve someone who knows how to love and make a family. That isn't in me." He stared away from her. "We'd better drive. It's getting late."

Realizing she'd been holding her breath, Katie let it out. "I think you're wrong about yourself, but thank you for being honest and explaining how you feel." It was difficult to respond, but she knew she had to acknowledge what must have been hard for such a private man to say.

His face stoic, he asked, "Does this mean we can still be friends?"

For a moment she saw a wistfulness cross his face. She swallowed around the lump in her throat. It was almost impossible to go back and be only a friend to him. She'd try. It was the only option he offered.

About an hour later Katie spotted a vacancy sign, and they stopped. She had her own room, but slept little. Her mind and body was too aware of the man in the room next to hers.

* * * *

After breakfast, the receptionist gave them directions to Fredericksburg. "You might arrive in time to see a reenactment," the woman said. "The morning paper had an article about one planned for this afternoon."

"Great," Katie said. "What good timing for us." She smiled at Jake. "I'm ready to leave, are you?"

"I'll put the suitcases in the car and we'll be on our way."

They followed the directions and arrived shortly after the reenactment had started. Katie tried to picture the real battle with cannons booming and men dying. What a horrible way to die with blood and carnage the last sight you saw on earth.

She and Jake stood silent as the fake battle continued. At some point Jake took her hand, and she curled her fingers around his. Finally, the noise stopped and the men got up off the ground, clapped a few buddies on the back and started to load their cars. Gradually the field emptied, and the cars drove away.

A quiet peacefulness settled over the wide expanse of grass, dirt, and a few yellow wildflowers waving in the breeze.

"Are you ready to go?" Jake asked. "We need to find a place to stay for the night."

"All right, but I want to go to the actual battlefield tonight."

"Why?" Jake looked puzzled.

"I read or heard somewhere that ghosts tend to come out at night. Don't you think after such a horrific battle there might be lost souls still wandering the battlegrounds?"

"No, I barely believe in our ghost. Ghosts, as in plural, I can't even comprehend."

Katie walked ahead of him to the car. She glanced back. "You really need to open your mind to other possibilities." She threw him a saucy grin.

* * * *

His heart jerked. The woman was doing her best to break him down and he better not let her know how well she was succeeding. Raking his hand through his hair, he wanted to hit his head against the wall. He'd made a mess of things. Home, house, and hearth that was his Katie. No, no, no, not his. He had plans, and they didn't include a small, stubborn woman with a streak of determination wider than his.

Touching her today brought all the warm feelings back, and yet he couldn't seem to stop himself from reaching out and making contact. He, who had been told he was a cold, unfeeling bastard by several women, realized he didn't want Katie to see him that way.

He had to shore up his defenses. Marriage was not for him. He'd make a mess of it. After all, he didn't have a good example to go by. He only knew the way he didn't want it to be.

His aunt or foster mother, whatever, had yelled, complained and generally been unpleasant to her husband, children, and especially him. He had been anxious to grow up and get away. He savored his own private space, the townhouse in Atlanta.

"Are you OK?" Katie's soft voice broke into his thoughts.

Jake unlocked the car doors. "Of course."

"Whatever you were thinking about, you were far away."

"Let's find a place to stay, and then after dinner I'll drive you to the battlefield." He stared across the car top at her. "If you're sure that's what you really want."

Katie nodded emphatically. "That's what I want."

A new hotel had just opened off I95 and Jake went in to get the rooms. On his way back outside, he stopped. Katie stood beside the car. Wind blew her curls around and sunshine sparkled like flecks of gold in the deep red color.

Urges he'd never felt flooded through him making him want to protect her. He imagined her leaning down to a little girl with similar red hair and hazel eyes. He deliberately turned back into the lobby.

If he didn't get hold of himself, he'd be begging her to forgive him and start again. Digging up old memories, he thought of his mother and aunt, but he had to admit Katie was nothing like them.

"Did you get the rooms?" Katie asked, from behind him.

"Yeah, let's get settled in."

"I saw a restaurant across the street, seafood, thought we might try it," Katie said, a questioning look in her eyes.

Jake nodded and went to the car.

"Jake." Katie touched his arm. "We must go to the battlefield tonight."

Jake took a deep breath and removed her hand. He saw the swift blink of her eyes, the dampness in them, before she looked down.

"Sorry," she said.

"Guess I'm on edge. It's not every day I go looking for a ghost." But his humor fell flat.

* * * *

Katie withdrew. She remembered what Jake said about not wanting to hurt her and obviously, he planned to keep distance between them. Her food had no taste, but Jake didn't seem to have any trouble eating his meal.

He threw glances her way, but she ignored them. It seemed forever before he asked for the check and they left.

"I'll get my heavy sweater and meet you back at the car," she said, on her way to the elevator. Jake stopped at the wire shelves holding several different newspapers and other pamphlets about the town. She saw his nod.

The elevator door closed and the familiar smells, a combination of people odor, stale air, and a whiff of some type of air freshener that wasn't doing its job, made her wrinkle her nose.

She grabbed her heavy cream colored sweater and the letter. On her way through the lobby she stopped at the wire shelves and grabbed a pamphlet advertising the Fredericksburg battle. She quickly glanced over the information and the park hours jumped out at her, they closed at five.

Katie strode across to the reception desk. "Is there anyway we can get to the battleground after dark?" She pointed to the pamphlet.

"Not in the public parks, but I'm from this area and I'll draw you a map of local roads that edge part of the battlefield. There's not much to see after dark though." The man looked at her with a puzzled expression.

"I know, but I still want to make the trip." Katie deliberately kept her answer vague.

The man drew a map and listed highway numbers. "There you are."

"Thanks." Katie took the paper and hurried to the car.

"I got some new directions where we can get close to the battle area. The parks are closed," Katie said, as she slid into the car seat.. "I'm anxious to hear what Judith wrote to Daniel. I wanted to wait until we got here before we opened the letter."

They were silent the rest of the drive. Katie felt the weight of the envelope in her hands. The old paper crinkled when moved. Was this the only time Judith wrote to Daniel?

Katie directed Jake along the back highways. "Wait, slow down along here."

At night with the fields empty and quiet, they seemed a sacred place, to Katie. The moon peeked around several large clouds, and a mist seemed to rise from the musty smelling ground.

"Stop here." Katie opened the door as soon as the car stopped. The hoot of an owl in the woods broke the silence. Carefully, reverently, they moved to the edge of the field.

Jake shook out a blanket he'd brought and spread it across the damp grass. He went back to the car for a flashlight and turned off the car lights. Katie and Jake sat side by side waiting.

"What do you expect to see?" Jake whispered.

"I don't know. Can you feel the pain, the fear? I can almost taste it."

Jake didn't answer. She strained her eyes to look through the enveloping fog coming toward them.

The thick damp mist enveloped them. Then the fog lightened, and she felt Jake's hand take hers and tighten.

Faint outlines of soldiers' bodies became visible. Sadness engulfed Katie, and she gasped, wiping tears off her cheeks.

"Can you see them?" she asked. "I don't think its fog. Smell it?"

Acrid smoke rolled across the field directly at them. Katie's body shook and Jake put his arm around her. Did she hear something? Yes, men's voices, screams of pain and the pounding of canons vibrating the earth.

As quickly as it occurred, the men and battle faded from sight. Katie's heart thumped hard and fast.

"You saw it too?" Katie asked.

"Yes. I can't explain what just happened, but I did see it," Jake admitted.

Had it been real or some type of spell brought on by their determination to understand and find out the mystery of the Collier couple? Katie leaned her head on Jake's shoulder, and Jake brushed his lips across her brow. She was never sure how long they sat intertwined at the edge of chaos.

The mist began to reappear along the tree line of the forest, across the field from where they sat. Out of the haze, a group of cadaverous men in torn and faded grey uniforms stared at them.

Katie held up the envelope. "I have a letter from Judith. It came right after your death, Daniel."

As a group, the men moved forward, and Katie decided to believe Daniel's spirit was close to her. Carefully, she opened the envelope and drew out the paper. She took a deep breath. Jake's arm comforted her, and she felt his breath against her cheek. Holding the letter up to the bright moonlight, Katie began to read.

"My darling Daniel, Forgive me for not writing before. I have been thinking only of myself and about how awful it hurts to not have you by my side. I am trying to understand why you had to leave.

In my selfishness, I wanted you here. It is difficult to see how risking your life can help your family. But, I know I must accept the sacrifice you are making.

My regret is that I don't have a child with eyes the color of the morning sky to remind me of his daddy. Perhaps we can have that child in the future. Please try and take care of yourself and return home to Sandstone and me. I promise to remain here until you come. However long that may be. Your loving wife, Judith."

Stillness laid across the land, as though whatever or whoever was out there listened to Katie's voice. Katie tasted the bitterness of anguish on her tongue.

"She waits for you, Daniel," Katie said. "All these many years, she has waited at Sandstone."

No light, no sound, and gradually the faint outline of the men dissolved into the mist.

Jake hugged her. "It's time to go home, Katie. Let's go back to Sandstone."

"I'm wide awake. Let's check out and drive through the night."

"Ok by me. I'll stop and get us two big coffees at the nearest stop off I95," Jake said.

* * * *

Jake thought about their quest on the long drive home. Why did he keep calling Sandstone home? His home was the townhouse in Atlanta. Sandstone was only a temporary stop on his journey to success.

The whole scene at the battlefield unnerved him. A few weeks ago he'd have laughed if anyone suggested ghosts were real. Now, he was trying to communicate with them. He'd almost think this was all a crazy dream, if not for Katie. Katie snuggled against his side, eyes closed, body soft and warm.

They'd discovered a lot about Judith and her connection to Katie and Katie's family. But what was his relationship to all of this? He was convinced it wasn't random.

He'd almost forgotten Mr. and Mrs. Barrows. He needed to talk with them. They'd known his grandfather and liked him. Maybe they knew some family stories to tell him. When Aunt Edna talked of Jake's dad all she said was how he'd ruined their fine name in town. She never mentioned anyone else. It was time to learn more about his own ancestors and maybe find out the reason Mrs. Pace named him in the will.

Cars passed in the night, headlights starting out small becoming brighter, red taillights fading in the distance. The monotony of driving mesmerized him. He glanced at Katie dozing beside him. Road signs indicated several hotels ahead. Jake put on his blinker and moved into the exit lane.

Katie woke when the car stopped. "Where are we? Do you want me to drive?"

"No, I'm going to get us a room. We both need to rest."

* * * *

Katie climbed out of the car and checked her watch, three a.m. She stretched and waited while Jake checked them in.

"Got the room." Jake came out waving a key to room to 204.

He carried their overnight bags, while Katie followed. The air conditioner blasted icy air when Jake opened the door.

"These rooms are always so cold," Katie complained. "We'll need two blankets to get warm."

Jake chuckled. "I have a better idea if you're agreeable. Body heat works every time."

Katie hesitated. "I thought you only wanted us to be friends?"

"I'm confused Katie." He raked his fingers through his hair. "I'll get another room for me."

"No, wait. Let's just see what happens and not worry so much about our future." Katie said and slid into his arms.

Gently he helped her undress and joined her in the king size bed. He held her against his hot body and wrapped his arms and legs around her. "Better?"

"Heavenly."

"Go to sleep. We'll want to be on the road early."

"I'm not sleepy now," she whispered. His eyes widened, and a smile curved his sensuous mouth. Swirls of heat and need filled her body. She relished his touch on her face and neck. Fingers trailed to her breast.

Legs tangled as his strong hands roamed her body. She felt the hard fullness of him and waited impatiently while he slipped on protection.

He didn't hesitate before filling her full and tight. He held her face with a tender caress and scattered kisses on her cheeks and lips.

"Katie, Katie," he whispered.

He moved slowly inside her and continued to nibble on her lips and along her jaw and throat. She raised her hips to meet his and tightened herself around him. This time the lovemaking was a slow dance, and they floated up and over the top together.

Jake lay beside her, snuggled close. They didn't talk. No matter how much she had meant to stay away from Jake, her body said different. He must feel the same way. She hoped. She didn't ask. This had been too precious to try and analyze with words. Katie decided to lead with her heart.

When she woke, Jake stood by the window, dressed. He turned, and a smile ruffled fleetingly across his firm full lips. He walked across to the bed and brushed a light kiss across her mouth.

"I'll wait downstairs. We'll eat before heading on our way."

Jake, the enigma, walked out and clicked the door shut.

Chapter 12

"Home." Katie unlocked the front door and placed her overnight bag inside. "It's hot and musty in here," she said as Jake stepped in after her.

A refreshing breeze blew through when Katie opened the nearest window. She took a deep breath. "It's rained somewhere nearby." In the east, she spotted tall cumulus clouds sailing west.

"Let's wait and get Smudges tomorrow," she added.

Jake stopped on his way up the stairs with their cases. "I thought we'd plan our next step. Not much time left to complete our task to inherit this place."

"Do you feel like I do? Like there's still an important part of the puzzle missing?"

"Yes," he said, as he disappeared upstairs.

Katie frowned. Had he put their things together? Where were they in this relationship, if anywhere? Her heart ached, and she knew she'd placed herself in a vulnerable position. The ringing phone startled her, and she jerked around reaching for it.

"Katie? This is Eric. I'm in Treehaven. We need to talk."

She took the phone away from her ear and stared at it. How dare he come to her town?

"What do you want, Eric?" She didn't bother keeping the sound of irritation out of her voice. She saw Jake start down the stairs.

"I'd like for us to meet, Katie. I want to take you out to dinner. I've been in town since yesterday and haven't been able to reach you. Where have you been?"

Katie felt sure smoke was curling up and out of the top of her head. He had a lot of nerve.

"It's really none of your business, and I don't want to go to dinner with you."

She pictured him trying to regain control of his temper. The thought brought a smile to her face.

"I'm here to see you, Katie. We have some business we need to discuss. For old time's sake, can't we treat each other respectfully?"

"Like you treated me?"

"I'm sorry about that," Eric said.

Katie had to admit she was curious about what important business brought Eric to Florida. It couldn't be anything about the house as she'd been in frequent touch with their realtor.

Jake went into the kitchen, giving her privacy. "Look, I'm busy. This isn't a good time."

"Please, Katie, this is important."

Katie felt herself softening. She'd never been able to be real bitchy and make it last. "All right, but it will have to be a late lunch. I'll meet you in town at one, at the barbecue place. You can't miss it. It's the only one in the city limits."

"I know the place. Remember we ate there when I came home with you that time?"

"I'd forgotten you ever came here. See you at one. Goodbye, Eric."

Eric had his life, and she had hers. Maybe what bothered her was the way their relationship had ended. And now she'd gone out on a limb with Jake.

He stood at the kitchen screen door. He didn't turn. "The old boyfriend calls again."

Katie stuck her head in the refrigerator. "Want a coke?"

"Sure," Jake said, and stepped outside.

Katie opened the cans and took one out to him. The musty Florida smell rose from the ground trying to overshadow the sweet roses.

"He wants to meet with me. He says it's important." Katie tried to read Jake's expression. "I don't know what it's about."

He faced her. "Do you think he wants to reconcile? And if so, how do you feel about that?"

"How can you ask after the last few days?"

"We've only known each other a short time. You two have a history."

She felt her stomach sink, and a lump form in her throat. She knew her face gave away all her feelings. For once she wished she was like him and able to hide behind a bland expression.

Jake pulled the screen door open. "I want you to have what you want, Katie. I'm still afraid I might just hurt you." His voice softened. "I'm trying to be honest, and I'm not certain I'm a good risk for the long haul."

"I've got to go and finish this thing with Eric. He's here in town and I want him to understand he and I are through," Katie said her throat tight.

She went upstairs and got her purse. As she drove to town, she tried to block out Jake's words.

* * * *

Katie pulled open the heavy wood door to the restaurant and stepped into the dimness. She was beginning to really dislike this place. Fans whirled high in the ceiling and TV's set around the dining room broadcasting various sporting events. What a waste. No one heard the announcers anyway. All the tables close to the front were full. She stood just inside the door and let her eyes adjust.

"Katie." Eric waved from a table on the far side of the room, positioned in a corner.

To give the utmost privacy, she presumed. What did Eric want to discuss that required a table in a darkened corner? Katie worked her way across the room. Eric pulled out the chair for her to sit beside him.

She placed her purse on that chair and sat across from him. She wanted to smile when she saw his flush of anger. I'm in control now, big boy.

The waitress arrived promptly for their order. Katie sipped her water and waited. She'd let him tell her what he wanted.

Irritation boiled inside her. After Jake's comments, he'd left. She heard his car leaving while she dressed to come here. Her feelings for men in general ranged from pissed off to don't give a damn. It was a good time to confront Eric.

"You look good," Eric commented. "You looked tired the last time we met. I'm sorry I put you through so much while I got my degree."

Katie shrugged and didn't answer.

Eric leaned across the table. "Katie, I've come to appreciate how much you sacrificed for me. I know I've been an arrogant bastard, and I'm here to make it up to you."

"What do you want, Eric? Cut out all the flowery praise and get to it. I'm not in the mood for your lies."

He tried to take hold of her hands, but she moved them into her lap. "I'm not getting married. Monica can't compare to you. The house hasn't sold. Maybe it's a sign. Fate. Can't we go back to where we were before all of this happened?"

"Why are you really here?" Katie glared across the table. "Did someone tell you about my possible inheritance?"

"Inheritance?"

"Give it up, Eric. I'm not interested. In fact I'm not hungry either." Katie stood and reached for her purse, but he was faster and held it out of her reach.

"Sit down, Katie. I'll give this back after we finish our conversation." Eric gave her his superior smile and nodded for her to sit.

"Give me my purse, now!" Katie put out her hand.

"Is this man giving you problems, Katie darlin?" Tom Cole put his arm around Katie and snatched her purse from Eric's hand. "Down south we treat our women folk with care and respect. Guess you northern boys haven't learned that yet."

Katie almost burst out laughing at Tom's exaggerated southern accent. She thanked him for the purse and glared at Eric. "Sorry to hear about your broken engagement. It couldn't have happened to a better guy."

Tom took her arm and led her to a table where Sara waited. "How did I do, honey?"

Sara laughed. "My hero, as usual."

Out of the corner of her eye, Katie saw Eric pay the waitress and leave. She breathed a sigh of relief.

"Where's Jake? Why didn't he come with you?" Tom asked.

"Jake and I are just business partners. This had nothing to do with him."

"Ah, I see." Tom motioned to the waitress to get Katie's order. "You might as well eat. You can't deal with spooks on an empty stomach."

"Lucky we ran late today, or we'd have had lunch and been gone," Sara added.

Katie relaxed during her meal with them. Tom kept Sara and her laughing. She waved goodbye and went toward her car.

She groaned. This wasn't going to be her day. Lloyd ambled along the sidewalk in her direction.

"Howdy, Katie. Enjoying life at Sandstone Ranch?" His full lips lifted in a sneer.

"Yes, thank you."

"How polite. Jake behaving himself? The old saying is they all fall for him in the end. You falling for him, Katie girl?"

"I don't think it's any of your business." Katie unlocked her car door and rolled down the window.

"Better watch him. Heard he wants that property bad. All of it. You're the only one stands in his way and Jake always gets what he wants, one way or another. It's an Andrews's trait."

Lloyd's rough laugh grated across her skin, and Katie flinched. "Goodbye." Revving the car engine, she pulled out and hit the accelerator.

* * * *

Katie's hurt eyes haunted him. But he didn't want the responsibility or the confinement of staying home with a wife. Or maybe he wanted it too much and was afraid he'd fail at the job. He loved traveling and working out deals for his company. It's what he did best.

He'd surprised himself when he'd asked her about Eric. Was it part jealousy and part fear of how close they'd become in a short time? Did she still have feelings for Eric?

To stop his thoughts, he reached for his cell phone and called the Barrows. They were happy he called, and he soon drove into their drive. Mr. and Mrs. Barrows sat in rockers on the front porch.

"Come join us," Mrs. Barrows said. "I'll get you some ice tea. There's a nice breeze out here today and the fragrance from the gardenias is delightful." She gave him a brief hug and went inside.

"Mama loves her flowers," Mr. Barrows said. "I hate the weeding, but I learned early on it was an easy way to keep her happy so the work was worth it."

"Is that your secret of a long happy life together?" Jake teased, as he settled on the nearby wood swing.

"Pretty much. Keep the one you love happy, and they'll do the same for you. It's not very complicated."

"Well, you two have been able to live your whole life in Treehaven. It's a simpler life. Everything in the city is loud and moves fast. I'm glad to get home at night and be alone in the silence."

Mr. Barrows shook his head. "Sounds like a lonely existence, without all the color and texture of a real life."

Jake stared at him.

"Let's see if I can explain better. I see the doubt on your face." Mr. Barrows rocked his chair back and forth and took a puff from his pipe.

"Look around you." He swept his hand across to indicate the large yard. "The oak tree there is older than me. I planted the orchid tree, and it's grown strong and tall. It delights us every spring with small purple orchids trailing along the limbs in long bouquets of blooms. Birds come to the birdfeeder all year. Doves, cardinals, and blue jays are just a few of the visitors we have."

He took a breath. "This porch has a history too. My daughter's husband courted her on that very swing you sit on. Mama makes me paint the porch every few years in a different color. She says it spices up the front. Course now we're so old we've had to repeat some colors. Smells wrap around this porch—the flowers, smoke from a neighbor's barbecue and Mama's cooking. All textures of life."

He smiled at Jake. "I think you miss the flavor of life living in one of those carbon copy boxes in the city. In my mind's eye it's the difference from black and white to color." He stared off in the distance. "Of course I might be wrong."

Before Jake answered, Mrs. Barrows came through the door with three tall frosty glasses of tea and a plate of homemade cookies. "Did I miss anything?"

"You're just in time to save our guest from me boring him to death," Mr. Barrows said, with a wink to Jake.

After dispensing the tea glasses and placing the plate of cookies between Jake and them, Mrs. Barrows settled herself in a rocker. "I'm so glad you decided to come see us." She studied Jake. "I think you've come to find out more about your family."

"Yes, I have, especially about my grandfather."

Mrs. Barrows pulled a picture out of her apron pocket. "I found this among some other old photos. It was taken at a church picnic. The man second to the left is Bart Andrews, and the woman beside him is your grandmother."

Jake took the picture and leaned back against the wood slats of the swing. The man stood tall and formal looking straight into the camera. His wife, a good six inches shorter, also gave her full attention to the person taking the picture.

One man stood to his grandfather's left and another couple to their right. And then he noticed, almost hidden, his grandmother and grandfather held hands. The other couple stood rigidly apart not touching but his grandparents leaned toward each other and connected.

Mrs. Barrows' knowing eyes met his. "It was said they loved each other dearly. I think when he died your grandmother never recovered, and her children suffered for it."

"Trying to find excuses for my father?" Jake asked wryly.

"No, there's no excuse for dishonesty or stealing, but we can forgive people who do bad things, and we can care about them." Mrs. Barrows look challenged him.

Jake stared into his tea glass. "I don't remember much about him. There's a vague memory of a tall man picking me up and laughing. I remember him always smiling." Jake was as surprised by his words as the Barrows appeared to be.

Mr. Barrows nodded his head. "You'd have been what about three or four when he went to jail? I can believe you have trouble remembering him, especially with him gone so suddenly. Your memory must be etched with questions."

Jake shook his head. "I never remembered anything until now." He ran his fingers across the picture. "Grandfather, my father, and I all look very much alike."

"Yes," Mrs. Barrows responded.

Jake's mind stepped carefully around a minefield of memories, stored deep inside and trying to come out. He was the four-year-old boy scared of the dark and crying for a mother and father who'd gone away and he didn't understand why or where.

Jake yanked himself straight and swallowed around the lump in his throat. Mrs. Barrows moved to sit beside him.

"Are you all right? I'm sorry if we've said anything to upset you." Her kind eyes centered on him, and her hand patted his.

Wrapped in his cloak of self-defense, Jake pulled back from the myriad of emotions threatening to overtake him. Inside he shook, but outwardly, he became the distant man familiar to most of his acquaintances.

Reassuring Mrs. Barrows, he stood and found he still held onto the picture. "May I have this?"

"Of course, but please don't leave. We can talk about other things." She urged him to sit back down. "Did you have questions for us about Sandstone?"

Torn between leaving and staying, Jake found himself sitting. He gathered his thoughts. "Yes, I can't understand why I have been included in finding out the mystery of Sandstone. I'm not a distant relative like Katie. I can't find a connection.

Mr. Barrows emptied his pipe, and Jake watched him refill it. His gnarled hands worked slowly pulling out a bag of tobacco and tapping some into the pipe bowl. A match flared, and he took several puffs to get it started.

"I keep telling him tobacco isn't good for him," Mrs. Barrows said, a teasing smile on her face. "But he figures he'll make it to a hundred at least, and that's long enough for anyone."

Jake felt his shoulders relax. "You two are stalling. I can tell." He grinned at them.

"We've heard rumors. We don't like to pass on gossip that we don't know for sure whether it's the truth or not. You'd best talk to your aunt. I think she knows." Mr. Barrows settled back with his pipe.

"I haven't talked with her since leaving town for college."

"Then it's high time you did. Sometimes a family needs to sweep out their closets. Ask her about your grandfather's great-great cousin, Henry."

"You aren't going to tell me?"

Mrs. Barrows smiled. "We think you need to hear about him from family. We'd love to have you visit again," she said. "Bring Katie next time. She's a lovely young lady." Mrs. Barrows tipped her head to the side. "You two make a handsome couple."

"Now Mama, you go matchmaking and we'll never see them again."

Jake went down the steps to his car and waved. "We'll be back," he promised.

He got in his car and headed to Sandstone. Talk with his aunt. He hated the idea. The woman had been cold and mean, and when he left, he'd sworn to never darken her doorway again. Was it worth a visit to find out about a very distant cousin?

He glanced at the date on his watch. They were running out of time. He had to find his connection to Sandstone to solve the puzzle. He felt sure of it.

Katie had parked her car at the side of the house. Jake felt a sense of relief. Silly, it shouldn't matter whether she was here or in town with Eric. Maybe Eric came here with her.

An unfamiliar pang of jealousy flashed through him. He'd like to punch Eric for hurting Katie.

But isn't that what you're doing to her? It isn't the same; I'm hurting her a little now, so I don't hurt her a lot later. Bullshit, Jake, be honest. You're running into unfamiliar territory and it scares the shit out of you. He parked his car and leaned his head back against the head rest.

In the distance, he saw the shine of Katie's red hair and the small puppy running around her legs. He thought his heart might explode with the pain, the confusion and the raw desire.

Chapter 13

Katie heard Jake's car. She'd been home long enough to change clothes and take Smudges out for a walk. Well a run. The little puppy zipped around full of energy. She enjoyed being outside. They'd walked to the woods and in the shadowed thickness of the trees spied a doe and her baby. Smudges barked, and mother and fawn gracefully leapt deeper into the forest.

She turned and admired the old house in its late blooming beauty. This was home. She'd started strolling back when she saw Jake's car.

Her muscles tensed, and she wondered what mood he'd be in. She wanted to trust him, but nothing seemed to touch him deep enough to alter his perspective. She'd be a fool to give her heart to such a person. She'd be an even bigger fool to not admit she already had.

Jake waited at the door, an easy smile on his face.

"Hello, have you been out working on our mystery?" she asked in a light tone.

"Yes, I wanted to try and find out why I was included in the will. We know Judith's relationship to your family. We haven't found any reason why I should be involved."

Katie led the way inside the house. Coming out of the bright sunlight made it difficult to see in the shadowed room, and she stopped abruptly. Jake bumped into her.

"Sorry." His hands touched her shoulders. For a split second they stood still.

She moved first. Striding determinedly into the kitchen, she reached into the fridge and took out a jug of lemonade. She poured a glass for herself and handed one to Jake. The cold liquid ran down her parched throat, and she felt the caress of Jake's eyes on her. She must not let him entice her again.

Sitting at the far side of the old wood table she asked, "Any new news?"

He turned a chair and straddled it. "I talked to Mr. and Mrs. Barrows."

"And?"

He took the picture out of his shirt pocket. "Second from the left, my grandfather and grandmother."

Katie gingerly held the snapshot, gray with age and brittle. "You look like your grandfather."

"My father, grandfather and I all look alike."

"But different," Katie insisted.

"Apparently it wouldn't be bad to be like him." Jake motioned to the picture.

"Still nothing to indicate your relationship to Sandstone?"

"No, and I feel that's a big clue."

Katie patted Smudges head when the puppy raised her little feet up on the chair. Everything so far pointed only to her relationship to the ranch. They were missing something.

"Seeing the Barrows didn't help?" she asked.

"They preferred I got my information from family. They directed me to my aunt."

"That reminds me, I ran into Lloyd on the street. He strolled up to my car."

Jake straightened, and she sensed the tension in his body. "What did he want?"

Katie ran her finger along the frosted side of the glass. Without looking at Jake, she said, "To warn me about you."

"What?" Jake stood and slammed the table with his hand. "What the hell did he say?"

"Sit down, Jake." Her direct gaze clashed with stone cold eyes. She saw his jaw clench. "I took everything he said and compared it to the source. I don't trust him."

"Tell me anyway. There has to be some reason he cornered you."

"He didn't corner me. He just happened by."

"No, that was no coincidence."

"Whatever. He warned me you wanted this place bad, and I should be wary of you."

"How does he know anything about my plans? Neither Tom nor Sara would talk to him. Whatever. I'll let him know to stay away from you and out of our business."

Jake jumped up and went to his room. He came back with a three ring notebook.

"Let's review what we know so far about Sandstone. Judith and Daniel married and came to the ranch. Judith died here after Daniel's death on the battlefield. We think Judith is our ghost. She's your distant relative. You look like her. This explains why you are named in the will."

Jake wrote and drew squares on his paper. He glanced at Katie, a sheepish look in his eyes. "I think better with a visual picture."

Katie leaned forward. "That's good. We need to review."

Jake's brow furrowed and he started to pace around the kitchen. Smudges ran beside him barking playfully. His hands clenched in his pockets, broad shoulders stiff, he looked Katie straight in the eye.

"I have to believe I am somehow connected to this house." His shoulders slumped and he stared at the floor. When he did raise his head, Katie saw his eyes filled with despair. "All my life I've run away from my past. How ironic that to achieve our inheritance I have to stop and face it. Unpleasant as it may be."

Katie smelled the hint of roses before she saw the mist swirl around Jake. Surprise pushed through the sorrow of his expression.

"What the...," his whispered words were almost inaudible.

"I think she's accepting you, Jake."

The mist moved away and disappeared. "I don't understand, but I think it's a good sign. You need to find out what involvement your family had with Sandstone. I think Judith was letting you know whatever it is you're on the right track."

Katie felt a tug on her heart. She wanted to go to him and take him into her arms. She couldn't. Emotionally this man had her on a roller coaster and until he faced his own demons, she mustn't risk putting her heart in more jeopardy.

* * * *

Jake felt completely alone. He sensed her indecision and willed her to break through it. More than anything, he wanted to have Katie in his arms.

She avoided his stare and busied herself around the kitchen, opening and shutting cupboards as if on a quest for supper ideas.

"Why don't we go out to dinner?" he suggested. "My treat."

"No, I really want to stay home."

"Well then, how about pizza again? I'll call and have it delivered," Jake suggested.

"Sounds good, put extra cheese and veggies on mine." She hesitated. "You know, we don't have much time left to solve the mystery of Sandstone. We must stay focused. We need to talk about Judith and Daniel and read her letter again. I'll go upstairs and retrieve it."

Jake listened to her soft steps. He deserved her coolness. He'd acted like an ass yesterday. His excuse of being jealous made him realize it wasn't an emotion he was familiar with. His heart jumped with fright just admitting it.

Flipping open his cell phone, he put in their pizza order and started to go change, when he heard Katie cry out. He took the stairs two at a time and bounded into her room.

"What's the matter?"

"It's gone."

"What's gone?" Jake asked.

"The letter." Her purse lay empty, its contents strewn around on the bed. "I'm sure I put it in the side pocket of my purse."

"Maybe it fell out on your travels today. We'll retrace your steps, make some phone calls."

"No, I put it in a zippered side pocket. There was no way for it to have fallen out. It's gone."

Her woeful expression melted Jake. He sat on a chair, by the bed and pulled Katie onto his lap. Holding her close, he ran a hand along the side of her arm.

"Someone must have taken it. But, who and why?" Katie asked, puzzled.

"And how did they get it?" Jake added. "You hang onto that purse like glue."

"I found my purse open, and all my things strewn about. Someone must have come in here and taken it. But how and when?"

"Think. How long were you out walking?"

"Not long and most of the time I was in sight of the house. I lost the letter Jake. Judith's letter." Katie sobbed on his shoulder and although Jake was sorry about the lost, he had to admit he liked holding her close.

He pulled a Kleenex out of a nearby box. "Wipe your eyes. The pizza should be here soon."

"How can you think of eating?"

"I'm a man."

Katie smiled through her tears, and Jake's heart beat faster.

"Typical," she said. "The stomach has to be fed."

"After dinner we'll discuss the letter and our trip," Jake said.

Katie shuddered and hiccupped, and he almost groaned seeing her breasts rise. Jake looked at her tear-streaked face, and a sense of protectiveness floored him. She got under his skin. He couldn't deny it, and he was beginning to get tired of resisting.

He stood and set Katie on her feet. "Wash up and join me in the living room. I'll pour the wine."

"I almost never drank before coming to Sandstone," Katie said.

"I won't let you have too much." Jake wiggled his eyebrows at her making her smile. "That's better." He touched her cheek before making himself draw away and leave.

* * * *

After finishing the pizza, Katie and Jake lounged on the living room rug leaning against the sofa. He'd turned off most of the lights, leaving the glow of one small lamp near the stairs. Moonlight filtered through the thin curtains.

"Let's talk about our trip" Jake said.

"The letter is gone. The one Judith sent to Daniel about how she tried to understand his need to go to war, and how she wished she had his son."

She and Jake sat quietly. It felt like time stood still and waited, as they did, for something to happen.

"I smell the hint of roses," Jake whispered.

"She's here." Katie sensed the energy close around her and Jake. Goose bumps popped up on her arms.

"We found a relative of Daniel's," Katie said. "They had the letter you sent Daniel, unopened. We took it to the battlefield area. We believe many of the men who died there have not gone on."

A muffled sob came from the direction of the dining room. Jake turned toward the sound.

"We think he knows you love him," Katie said. "And now, he knows you wait for him to return."

Katie felt the sharp edge of Judith's pain and a sense of relief. Tears flowed down Katie's cheeks. "He loves you, Judith. I really believe he does. I read the letter at the place near where he died."

A large noise brought Katie and Jake's attention to the stairs as several chairs flew through the air, crashing on the floor below. A manic laugh echoed around the house, but it wasn't Judith. Judith's entity hovered near them. Whoever or whatever was upstairs didn't like the news they'd brought home. Maybe that was the reason the letter disappeared.

The attack ceased abruptly. Jake charged up the stairs. Smudges barked and whimpered, then ran into Katie's lap. "You're a good guard dog," she said, rubbing the puppy's fur. Concerned about Jake, she went to follow him. She was afraid of what evil lingered above them.

Jake saw her. "Stay away. I'm still checking the rooms." He rubbed the back of his neck. "Don't come up here."

She waited, as he went from room to room.

"It makes no sense. I thought I heard a chuckle, but whatever it is vanishes out of sight." Jake ran his hand along the banister as he stepped slowly down to her.

"It's malevolent and getting stronger. I'm scared of it, Jake. Do you think there might be two ghosts?"

"Or a person trying to convince us there's another ghost. I'm not going to let it hurt you." He cupped Katie's face in his hands. "If we have to, we'll leave."

He leaned close, and his lips brushed across Katie's. His own special smell surrounded her, and his tongue slid along the seam of her lips. "Our lives are more important than the ranch." His words rumbled through his strong chest, and Katie both felt and heard them.

All her resistance seeped away as she threaded her fingers through his silky hair. Parting her lips, she welcomed him. Her need built while his tongue explored the warm contours of her mouth. She cuddled closer to him, desire pulsating through her body. She ached to have him inside her. There wasn't a ghost or human that would separate them tonight.

Jake lifted her, and she wrapped her legs secure around his waist. He carried her into the living room, clicking off the lights as they went. Carefully he laid her on the couch.

His hands trembling, he removed her clothes. She helped him pull off his shirt and pants.

She gasped when the tender touch of his fingers stroked her breasts and his tongue circled around her firm aching nipple. She heard a moan and realized it had escaped from her.

Now her hands roamed freely over his warm body, through the dark hairs on his chest, down his flat stomach, to the hard silk length of him. He groaned when she moved her hand up and down and let her fingernails touch, oh so lightly, around the tip.

"Don't stop," he whispered.

"I won't," she said as she slid down his body.

Her lips closed over the tip and her tongue moved in circles around and around. Her hands gently caressed the silken length of him, and her lips followed. His fingers ran through her hair.

Lifting her head, she smiled at him and then began to cover his body with kisses as she moved upward. Her lips brushed back and forth across the soft hair on his chest.

He pulled her up the rest of the way and kissed her. His tongue slid into her mouth and caressed the softness and along the edge of her teeth.

Heat flooded her body. She wrapped her arms around him and held tight. Her skin was super sensitive to his touch.

He reached out and pulled a condom from his jeans pocket. After he rolled it on, he pulled her underneath him. He nuzzled her neck and ran his fingertips over her tender nipples, and then his lips followed.

Katie reached between them, her hand around his hardness. She whispered, "I want you in me."

"Hungry," he teased. "So am I." Centering himself over her, he slowly began to enter her. The heat and hardness of him made her want more and her body pulled him in further. Her whole body rose hungrily to meet his. The ache grew at a fevered pitch and nothing existed except them tangled together in the darkness.

"Sweet as honey, I can't get enough of you." Jake plunged harder and faster. He ravished her mouth with a deep, hard kiss.

She smelled desire on their sweat-coated bodies, and her teeth bit playfully at his lip as he drew back. "I want more," she whispered and he pounded into her deeper and deeper.

She felt their breath intermingle, raising her hips, she tightened her muscles around him, and the world exploded.

Katie awoke as Jake carried her upstairs to her room. He laid her down and curled up against her. She sighed and went back to sleep.

In the morning, he was gone. A note stuck on the fridge said there was something he needed to look into alone. Next to her cereal bowl a single red rose, from the bush by the steps, lay on her napkin.

* * * *

Jake dreaded the upcoming visit to his aunt and cousin. He'd checked the house thoroughly before he left. Katie should be safe as long as he got back well before dark. He hated leaving before talking with her, but he wanted to catch Lloyd at home. Turning his car down Snapdragon Circle, a host of memories swamped him.

Little had changed. Jake winced as he glanced around the neighborhood. The yards still had more weeds than grass, and the houses were small cinder block boxes.

A few people tried to brighten their landscape with flowers. But the sight of peeling paint and worn thin curtains drooping at the windows gave the area a general pervasive feeling of weary disenchantment.

Jake remembered walking home from school and turning into this street. He dreaded returning each day to a house full of anger and ridicule. He was the punching bag figuratively for the family.

Coming back reminded him that all his hard work and sacrifice had been worth it. He didn't ever want to live in a place like this again. He'd do almost anything to prevent it.

Noting the faded green house as he drove by, he thought of Mrs. Pace, his one good memory. She watched at her front door for the skinny little boy coming home from school, and she'd call him in for a piece of cake, a glass of milk and an occasional hug.

He'd never dreamed she'd remember him in her will or that she even owned anything but the old house she lived in. Still he felt sure there was more to the inheritance than their brief acquaintance so many years ago.

He'd moved far away from this life and he clung to his sense of accomplishment. He lived in a much different world than Treehaven and Snapdragon Circle. God, what was he doing back here? Was the inheritance worth this?

There was the house. It was too late to change his mind. He'd always known he'd have to confront his past.

Jake pulled into the driveway noting the broken concrete, weeds springing between the cracks like green tributaries and the yard, a host of sand and sandspurs. Jake eyed the dingy, pale yellow house. Perhaps he'd offer to have some repairs done. No, his aunt had no use for him, and he was on his own mission. He stepped forward and knocked on the slightly ajar door. It swung forward.

"Whoever it is, we don't want none." His Aunt Edna snatched the door further open and stared out. "Well, what do you know? Mr. Big Shot himself standing on my doorstep." Her eyes hardened. Straggly gray hair hung around her face. She'd put on weight and a plain loose cotton dress hid her short stout figure.

"Hello, Aunt Edna," Jake said.

Lloyd came into the small living room and ambled toward the door, a grin pasted across his face.

"Invite my cousin in, Mama," Lloyd said. His mother moved back, allowing Jake to enter.

An old plaid couch sat under the front windows, and a matching stuffed rocker with sagging cushions held prominence in front of the blaring TV.

"Shut the damn thing off, Lloyd, so we can hear what's brought Jake home at last."

Jake grimaced at the thought of this place being his home. She saw his expression and cackled. "Hard to admit you came from this." She threw her hand out, than leaned in closer to his face. "But you did, boy, and don't forget all I've done for you."

"Want a cup of coffee?" Lloyd asked, holding out his cup.

"Yes, thank you."

"Sit down. I can't wait to hear what brought you to these parts. Must be awful important or you'd never put your foot in here," Aunt Edna said, her contempt obvious.

Lloyd returned and handed Jake a large plain white mug. Jake thanked him.

"Take a breath, Mom, and let him talk. This should be good," Lloyd said.

Jake studied them closely. He wanted to catch their expressions when he asked about his grandfather's distant relative, Henry.

"I've been researching information about our family." He caught a quick blink of his aunt's eyes.

"Mr. and Mrs. Barrows have helped." He heard his aunt snort.

"Those old characters don't know nothin' about us. They're probably senile by now," she said.

"Far from it," Jake protested. "They gave me this picture." He handed the photo of his grandparents to his aunt.

Silently, she gazed at the picture, and after a minute gave it back to him. "So, what's brought on all this interest in the family history? Didn't see you wantin' to know anything about us before."

"I'm sure you've heard Katie Weber and I may inherit the Sandstone Ranch. The house has secrets we must learn in order to receive our inheritance." He paused for effect. "I think something about my grandfather's great great cousin, Henry, may hold part of the mystery." This time he caught the quick glance his aunt and Lloyd gave each other.

"There's a rumor about him. The Barrows aren't sure whether what they know is true. They think you know."

"This town loves to talk about our family," his aunt sneered. "Especially since your father turned out so bad." She grinned. "Do all your fancy friends know your papa was a plain old crook?"

Jake realized she hoped he'd react. Lloyd clenched his coffee cup tighter, and his aunt bared her teeth in a false smile. They didn't want to answer his question. How interesting.

"Well, can you tell me about Henry?" He threw the question back at them.

His aunt turned her back to him and went to sit on the stuffed chair. Lloyd moved and stood behind her.

"Not much of a story. Henry wanted to buy Sandstone. He offered the Colliers' a fair price, but they weren't moving. When the husband went to war, he thought for sure he'd convince the wife to sell the place to him, especially after her husband's death."

"She wouldn't?"

"Naw. According to the family stories, she laughed in his face. Said she'd stay at Sandstone where she'd lived with her husband." Aunt Edna glowered at Jake. "Stupid woman. She'd of had a good piece of change."

"That's it?" Jake let his disbelief show on his face. He wanted them to know he didn't believe that was the full story.

"Yep. Henry tried to buy the ranch several times, but the Collier woman refused to sell."

Aunt Edna looked at him with a puzzled expression in her eyes. "Never did understand why he wanted the place so bad. It's wasn't worth a lot of money like it is now." She rocked back in the chair. "What do you plan to do with all the money? That is, if you get it."

Jake ignored the question. "Why have you always hated me?" His question popped out of his mouth, surprising even him.

Lloyd frowned and took a step away from the chair toward Jake.

"No." His mother grabbed his arm. "He's right. I ain't never liked you, boy. Hate though might be too strong a word. You were nothing to me but a paycheck every month. Your high and mighty mama didn't want you, and she paid me to put up with you." Her words lashed across him, stinging like barbs in his flesh. "But why? I was four years old. What did I do to make you dislike me so much?"

"Pride. I saw it in your eyes, even at that young age. You were too good for us, and this house and this neighborhood. You looked at me with those serious eyes and reminded me of my father. He wanted us to be big important people in town. And then, he dies and Mama didn't care anymore. He left us with nothing," she shouted across the room. Lloyd put a protective hand on her shoulder.

"It's all right, Mama."

"Get out." Tears poured down her face. Aunt Edna pointed at Jake. "Go away and don't come back. I hated my father and my brother, and you remind me of both of them."

Jake stood rigid, as though his shoes had stuck to the floor. His aunt crumbled into a small ball, sobbing.

"I'm sorry," he whispered, turned and stumbled across the room. He reached the door and plunged outside taking deep breaths of fresh air. What in the hell happened in there? His head spun, and he reached for his car door. Wounded and wanting to find a place to hide, he sped away from Snapdragon Circle.

He never remembered driving back to the ranch. But he knew there was some place he had to get to, and when the car stopped, he found himself in front of the farm house.

Katie must have sensed something. She hurried to the car door and pulled it open. "What's happened?"

He tried to stand and found he had to lean on her slight figure to make it inside where he sank to his knees. Katie knelt before him and took him in her arms.

"You're home. You're home," she repeated. And in a crazy way, for that moment, he was.

Chapter 14

Katie left Jake lying on his bed, staring at the ceiling. She wasn't sure how to help him, so she headed for the kitchen. She'd bought fresh vegetables from the market earlier in the day and now she took them out of the fridge with some chicken and proceeded to make soup.

Mom always fed them chicken soup whenever they were sick or upset. She said it was good for the soul, and Katie believed her. Soon a pot of bubbling soup sent an aroma of home and hearth wafting up the stairs.

She sat at the table in the kitchen with a cup of Constant Comment tea. Whatever happened, Jake's eyes looked wounded and shocked. Where did he go this morning and what brought such a proud strong man to his knees?

She tiptoed into Jake's room and found him fast asleep. With his face relaxed and his hair falling across his forehead, he looked younger. She crept quietly back downstairs.

A feeling of protectiveness arose in her, and she wished she knew who did this to him. Fierce anger flowed through her. She would love to reciprocate and hurt them. But that wasn't something she'd really do. Striking back only caused more problems.

Walking to the kitchen door, Katie smiled at Smudges tied to the oak tree where she could run around without getting lost. She lay sleeping in the shade now.

Something drew Katie's eyes to the line of trees in the distance. She saw a large deer with huge antlers staring straight at the house. A strange feeling of comfort swept over her. She blinked her eyes, and it disappeared. She looked all around, but it was gone.

For a moment, with soup bubbling on the stove and Jake sleeping upstairs, Katie pretended her dream of having her own happy family had come true. If only.

Tonight would be difficult. How would Jake feel about her when he realized she'd seen him at his lowest point? Would it help their relationship or ruin it forever? He was a proud man with strong defenses, and he'd pulled himself inside his walls and away from her before.

What did she need to do to break down his walls for good and have his love? She wiped her hand across her face, surprised to find her cheeks damp with tears.

She never dreamed that in trying to discover the mysteries of Sandstone, she'd learn more about what she wanted in her life.

* * * *

Jake felt disoriented when he first awoke. He looked out the window, and saw the sun setting. He'd slept a good portion of the afternoon. Delicious aromas of spices and vegetables came from downstairs, and he knew Katie was cooking. He chuckled. Katie cooked when she was nervous or stressed. He'd understood that about her almost from the beginning.

He rubbed his hand across his face. What must she think? He grimaced with the thought of how he'd let his emotions take hold. His protective barrier was cracking, leaving him open and vulnerable. They had to finish here soon. And he'd return to his world, a place where he was comfortably in control.

Forcing himself to review the conversation with his aunt, he decided Henry had something to do with the Sandstone mystery. But what? Aunt Edna and Lloyd didn't plan on telling him. Did they hope he'd fail to inherit Sandstone?

After he took a shower, he'd join Katie. Maybe what they'd found so far was enough to get Sandstone.

Refreshed and in clean clothes, Jake put his head around the kitchen door. "Smells good in here."

Katie turned from the oven, holding a pan of biscuits. "Hungry?"

"Starved."

"Everything's ready. Soup, salad, and biscuits. You can pour the ice tea while I serve the soup. The salad plates are in the fridge."

"This is great," Jake said.

Katie blushed. "Thanks."

He saw the concern in her eyes, but chose to ignore it. He devoured the crisp green salad, hot chicken soup, and warm buttery biscuits. She ate little herself, picking at her salad and biscuit.

He dreaded the questions and talking about it. Women always wanted to talk, and it inevitably got him into trouble. Finally unable to eat anymore or delay the moment, he pushed his chair back from the table.

"Coffee?" Katie asked, and Jake nodded yes.

She looked sexy tonight with her shorts and blouse and a hint of floral fragrance hovering around her. Her slim tanned legs curved in all the right places, and her little butt made his hands want to reach out and cup them. Down, boy. You've got yourself in deep enough already. One more slip and you'll drown.

"Here." Katie put the mug in front of him. "What are you thinking about?"

"You don't want to know."

"I do want to know what happened today. Who did you see?"

"Aunt Edna and Lloyd."

"It didn't go well?"

Jake stared into his cup. "You might say that."

Katie felt exasperation building. "It's like pulling teeth to talk with you. Do you do this deliberately?"

Jake glanced at her and then stood and went to the sink and stared out the window.

"I asked them about Henry, my grandfather's great great cousin. The Barrows mentioned him to me, but they wouldn't tell me much about him. I think he has something to do with Sandstone." Jake turned to face her.

"Seems he wanted to buy the ranch, but Judith wouldn't sell it to him. There's some rumor concerning all this. However, no one will tell me the whole story. The Barrows indicated my aunt knew."

"And she didn't?" Katie asked.

"Oh she knows. She relishes the fact she knows and won't tell me."

"But this isn't why you were so distressed when you got home." Katie said, tilting her head back and staring at his face.

Jake forced his familiar mask back in place. "No."

* * * *

His expression blank, his blue eyes flat and cold as the ice on a frozen pond caused Katie to hesitate. If she let him retreat from her now, she'd lose him. She walked to him and took his cup away, setting it in the sink.

Holding her mouth close to his, she whispered. "You can trust me, Jake." Her lips brushed his, and she ran her hands down his arms and held his hands. "Your whole body is cold. Let me warm you."

She dropped light kisses on his cheeks, eyes and forehead. Because of his height, she stood on her toes and let her body lay against his long frame.

She'd slipped off her flip-flops, and her foot and toes caressed his legs left bare by his shorts. At first, he stiffened under her and held his mouth tight.

Breathing soft breaths on his lips, she felt a quiver along his whole body. His arms clasped her hard against him.

"Damn you," he muttered, before his mouth ravished hers and his legs brought her body in. His hands grasped her head, and he proceeded to kiss her deeply and harshly. His mouth devoured hers, and his hands raked through her hair, massaging her scalp.

Every cell in her body was on fire. She pulled her head free, kissed his ear and nuzzled his neck. Now she felt him tremble. Her hands yanked his shirt open and several buttons hit the floor. Her lips teased along his chest, sampling the taste of him, following the line of his soft hair down to the band of his shorts.

He was hard and ready for her. Her eyes challenged him to stop her. He reached down and lifted her into his arms.

She flipped off the kitchen light as he carried her past the door and up the stairs. Tonight he turned to the front bedroom and went in, kicking the door shut. Desire etched his face, the strong planes of his cheeks and nose outlined in the moonlight. His eyes shot fiery sparks at her.

Excitement and a touch of fear ran through her body. She had unleashed more emotion than he'd ever shown before, but she welcomed it. Her arms reached up to him when he laid her on the double bed.

"Tonight I want room," he growled, indicating the larger bed. He threw off his clothes. Stopping her hands, he finished undressing her. He held her face, staring into her eyes.

This time it was his turn. His lips, soft as a feather, touched her eyes, nose, cheeks, and tantalized her mouth. He moved leisurely along her body, light nibbles, soft touches, leaving a fire flickering across her skin. When he got to the heart of her, he brushed across her most sensitive point, and she moaned and moved her hips to meet his mouth. His lips and tongue licked and kissed and drove her wild. Her body bucked beneath him. She tossed and turned under him.

He stopped and stared at her. She was wet with her need for him, and her arms reached out inviting him closer as he slid into her in one smooth move.

Her legs opened wider and pulled him deeper, hard, hot, and tight in her. She threw back her head and moved up and around until he groaned and joined her in the magical dance of love.

Afterwards they lay spent, arms and legs entwined, faces almost touching. "Wow," she whispered.

Jake smiled and ran his finger along her nose and across her lips. "Wow yourself." He tucked her face into his shoulder and rubbed her back.

Katie tried to keep her thoughts at bay. Tonight she'd seduced him and brought him back to her. What did it really mean to him? Tuesday was their last day in the house. Did they have a future?

Almost as though he knew her thoughts, Jake whispered in her ear. "Sleep. Quit worrying."

She listened to his soft breathing, certain she couldn't sleep.

* * * *

She woke first, and got out of bed careful to not wake him. In the shower, cold water ran in ripples along her body. It cleared her head. She went into the smaller bedroom, dug out a pair of jeans and top, and put on her walking shoes. Smudges would want food and a run. She'd fed her early yesterday evening and left her in the new dog house she'd bought.

Weak sunlight washed across a pale sky. She heard the hum of traffic. Smudges came out of her dog house and barked while also wagging her tail in rapid circles. Katie laughed, filled with hope and happiness. She followed the tug of the leash through the dew damp grass.

In the fresh air and running with her puppy, she kept the questions at bay until they stopped for a minute and she looked back at the house. How did the letter disappear?

Who wanted to scare her away? A horrible thought crossed her mind. She remembered Lloyd's words. *"Better watch him. Heard he wants that property bad. All of it. You're the only one that stands in his way and Jake always gets what he wants. It's an Andrews's trait."*

No. She refused to think Jake might try to frighten her so she'd sell him the land. But who else would care? Could there be a second ghost? Or was it someone trying to run them off? She'd intended to talk to Jake about it yesterday, and then everything happened and she forgot.

A figure came to the screen door and stepped outside. Her heart skipped a beat. Sunlight flashed off his shiny hair, and she saw him wave.

Smudges ran around her legs, jumping at butterflies. She refused to let doubts spoil their day. Determined to forget her disloyal thoughts, she and Smudges headed back.

Jake pulled her close and hugged her before leaning down and patting Smudges. He smelled of soap and shampoo. His body was warm and tasty, she thought, kissing his neck. He pulled her into his side and stared across the field.

"Can't you see what we can do with this? Build a special community of large lots with nature all around. Plenty of trees and shrubs left for the birds and deer to hide in. It can work and not ruin the uniqueness of it all."

"That's a long speech for you. It seems you can only talk when trying to sell me on your ideas." Hurt by him mentioning the subject this morning, Katie swung away from him and went inside letting the screen door slam.

She glanced back. He stood staring after her with a puzzled expression.

"Men," she snapped. "If you don't understand I'm not going to tell you." She marched upstairs to her room and shut the door.

He followed and knocked.

"Go away."

"I don't want to leave you here alone. I'm going to see the Barrows to try and convince them to tell me more about Henry. Have you got plans to go somewhere?"

Katie heard the concern in his voice. "No. I'll be fine. Nothing much seems to happen during the day."

Jake continued to pace outside her room. "I stayed here most of yesterday," she said, then relented, "I'm going to Annie's. I'll be leaving shortly after you. Go on ahead."

"Don't wait," he said, while jiggling the doorknob. "Leave right after me."

He tramped down the stairs. Typical man, Katie thought, watching the dust swirl behind his car. Her stomach clenched at her thoughts. She'd wanted him to leave. She planned to check the house, especially his room. She hated what she was thinking. But she'd never rest until she knew for sure he wasn't the one trying to scare her into selling. Now who's not trusting? The voice in her head taunted her.

Guilt filled her when she stepped across the door frame to his room. Everything appeared to be in place. Her brothers were slobs when it came to their rooms. But Jake had his clothes hanging neatly in the armoire. His bedspread and pillow were in place. Where to start and what did she hope to find?

The room had a bedside table, armoire, and a tallboy. After checking the armoire, she went to the tallboy and started to pull out his drawers. He'd hate her for invading his privacy. She stopped. She didn't want to go any further.

Out in the hall a feeling or an imaginary nudge sent her into the front bedroom. Why? There wasn't anything here. She stared out the front windows and turned, viewing the room from that angle.

She cocked her head to the side. The armoire looked different. Moving in front of it there didn't seem to be any change. She went back to the windows. Yes, one edge stuck out a bit forward.

She pulled and put her whole body against it, but the armoire didn't budge. Opening the doors wide, she stared at the empty space. She ran her hands along the sides and leaned in to touch the back. Nothing.

Katie backed out of the armoire and stepped across the room studying it from a distance. It was tall and the top had curved carving along the edge almost touching the ceiling.

That's it. She ran back and climbed inside. The armoire looked taller outside than in. She'd never noticed before. Reaching on her tiptoes, she moved the fake top aside. Further above was another panel.

She ran downstairs for her step stool. If Jake found out about her activities today, she'd be in trouble. But she had to find out the secrets of this old house.

On the step stool, she reached the top. Her fingers felt along the edge and touched a spring. The panel came loose, and she lifted it down beside her. A hidden opening in the ceiling slid to the left.

A rope ladder fell down in front of her. With the help of the ladder, Katie climbed into the attic.

Stepping through the opening, she blinked in amazement. There were no cob webs or dust. Someone kept the place very clean. She walked to the center and looked around.

A tiny window at the front let in light. Near a far wall, she saw a huge fan. Carefully, she stepped forward. At first glance the wall looked solid. She patted her hands along the wood, feeling for any slight difference. To the far right she found a tiny knob which when turned slid a panel of wood back opening to the rest of the attic. The movable wall separated the area into two separate rooms.

Katie didn't climb through. She'd already explored that smaller space. She wanted to check out this part of the attic. Turning away, she walked carefully along the edge of the floor going toward Jake's room. Doubts came back, and she went onto her hands and knees. There. Tipping one board up, she got a grip and pulled a square section out. The opening was just big enough for a man to drop through onto Jake's bed.

Katie sank back on her heels. Did she misjudge Jake? She didn't want to believe she was wrong about him. But, who else wanted this old farm house? If they didn't inherit Sandstone Ranch, it went to the state. Anxious to get out of the attic, Katie put the section of wood floor back and climbed out through the armoire.

She needed to talk to someone. Her parents would tell her to leave and come home. Annie usually stayed calm during a crisis. She'd help Katie decide whether to stay here another night.

Katie took a deep breath. She was being silly. Jake wouldn't hurt her. He wanted her to sell the place to him, that's all. Anyway, she told Jake she was going to Annie's, so now she would.

Chapter 15

"Annie," Katie called out.

"Coming," Annie, answered. "What brings you around this morning?" She opened the front door. "Not that I'm not glad to see you, but you look like hell."

"Thanks, I didn't bother to change. I had to get out of the house."

Annie motioned Katie to go with her to the kitchen. "I'll put on the tea pot."

"Where's Ty?" Katie glanced around the room.

"Richard took him to the park. He took the day off, and thought he'd give me some free time. He really is the sweetest man." Annie went to the cupboard and took out two mugs. "I'm glad you came. We can have a talk with no children or men to interrupt. Now what has you upset?"

"I don't know where to start," Katie said, and began to pace around the kitchen.

"Start anywhere," Annie said. She went to the stove as the tea pot whistled. "Earl Grey or Constant Comment?" Annie held up the two tea bags.

"Earl Grey." Katie went to the table and sat. "I guess I'll start with yesterday when Jake came home distraught from his visit to his aunt. I cooked Mama's chicken soup."

"Comfort food, the way to a man's heart," Annie interjected.

Katie tried to smile, but instead she started to cry.

Annie rushed to her side. "I'm sorry. Here I am joking, and you're hurting." She hugged Katie.

Katie wiped her hand across her eyes and sniffled. "Everything seemed to go well last night. This morning I started to think about the things happening in the house and I began to doubt Jake."

Katie watched Annie pour the steaming hot water in the cups. She sipped the hot tea and felt warmth curl inside her.

Glancing at Annie, she continued. "I don't know if I can trust Jake. He started talking again today about how he wanted to build Sandstone into a fancy development, and he knows I hate the idea."

Guilt filled her at even thinking about Jake in such a way. By talking about her mistrust, somehow it seemed more real.

But, Annie had never been judgmental and didn't rush to conclusions. She caught the worried expression on her sister's face.

"I think someone is trying to make us, or me, leave the house."

"You mean someone besides your ghost?"

Katie nodded. "Judith is beginning to accept us. I thought we might have a second ghost, more malevolent than Judith."

"But now you think it's a real person? What changed your mind?"

Katie put more sugar in her tea and swirled her spoon around staring into the teacup. "I'm not sure what started me thinking about the possibility. I wondered, if it was a person, what could be their motive."

"How scary is this other person or ghost?" Annie asked.

"Whatever or whoever is getting more frightening every day, throwing objects down the stairs and once I thought tried to choke me, but I blamed it on Judith."

"What? And you haven't gotten out of there? The inheritance isn't worth your life." Annie's voice rose, and a frown wrinkled her brow.

"I don't believe I'll be hurt. Whoever it is wants me to leave and is trying to scare me away."

"Why do you think he or she wants you out so bad?" Annie asked bluntly.

Tears started to roll down Katie's cheeks. "I'm afraid…it's Jake." She gasped the words out.

"I can't believe he'd go to such extremes. He doesn't seem the type."

Katie stood and walked to the back window. Outside the wind blew the leaves around. Storm clouds gathered on the horizon. Chimes hanging from Annie's lemon tree tinkled in the breeze. Katie bowed her head.

"I don't want to believe it either, but today I searched the house and found a hidden passage way." She faced Annie. "It runs from the front bedroom through the attic and there's an opening over Jake's bed."

"This proves nothing. Jake may not know about the passageway. You didn't until today." Annie spoke in her calm reasonable voice.

Hope flared, and Katie stepped across and kneeled before Annie. She clasped Annie's hands. "You don't think I'm a fool to trust him?"

"Listen to your instincts, Katie. You've been living with him for almost a month. What does your heart tell you?"

"My heart hasn't always been reliable."

They both turned their heads at the sound of a car door slamming and a small voice calling Mommy.

Annie smiled ruefully. "My guys are home. Sorry we didn't have more time."

"It's fine. I needed someone to bounce my thoughts off of and you helped me. I'd better run along."

Annie caught Katie's arm as she went to leave. "Don't stay in that house alone. If Jake's gone, get out of there."

Katie tried to smile reassuringly. "Nothing serious is going to happen. I don't believe ghosts can hurt you, and if it is a person, they're trying to scare me. That's all."

"Do as I say, Katie. Don't stay alone."

"You're as bad as Jake."

"Now I know I'm right about him," Annie said, and smiled.

Katie stopped at the door to greet Richard and swing Ty into her arms. "My, you're getting to be a big boy." Katie kissed him and handed Ty to Annie. "I'm out of here. See you, guys."

* * * *

As Jake expected, the Barrows were hesitant about answering his questions. "I need to know what it is everyone seems to want to keep from me," Jake persisted.

Mrs. Barrows conceded. "I'll give you some more papers I've found. I held onto them because of the content."

Jake noted her worried expression. "It's more bad news about my family, isn't it?"

"I want you to remember your family was well liked and respected for years. Your father and your grandfather's great great cousin were the two that caused gossip and I have my doubts about the things said of your father." She finished in a rush, almost breathless, when she added the last about his father.

"How can you have doubts? He robbed a bank."

"Someone did." Mr. Barrows spoke up from across the table.

"But no one ever hinted he might have been innocent."

"He knew some tough characters from his teen years. He'd been wild as boys will, especially ones without a father to guide them," Mr. Barrows said. "There were rumors that someone wanted to get back at him."

"Revenge?" Jake asked.

Mr. Barrows ran his hand along the table's edge. He stared straight at Jake. "The police found his fingerprints on the gun. They conveniently found the gun nearby. Several men testified they saw your father running from the bank and tossing the gun."

Joe Barrows glanced across at his wife, and she nodded encouraging him. "It gave the police someone to put in jail. They didn't investigate any further."

Jake tried to suppress the emotions flooding through him—surprise, anger, hope, and a fierce determination to find out the truth.

"I hope we haven't upset you." Mrs. Barrows fluttered around him. "We didn't know whether to mention our suspicions after all these years or not." She put her hand on his shoulder. "I'll get you some fresh coffee."

All those years his aunt, uncle, and cousins taunted him about his father being a bank robber, told him he had the same genes and it would show someday. They warned he'd end up just like his old man.

The words spun around in his brain. Words and thoughts he'd never allowed into his consciousness. He'd pushed them down, forgotten half of what they'd said. Jake's stomach clenched.

"Here you are. A hot cup of coffee."

Jake heard the concern in her voice and saw the worry etched on their lined faces. He forced himself to speak.

"I'm stunned, that's all. Everyone has always told me how awful my father had been and how much I looked like him. They expected me to turn out the same way.

"I'm glad you told me. I needed to know. It gives me hope." Jake whispered the last. He took one sip of coffee and picked up the papers. "And thanks for these."

Still concerned the Barrows followed him to his car. "You'll be all right driving?" Mr. Barrows said, leaning in his window.

"I'm fine. Don't worry." He smiled at the two of them. Without thinking, he got out and hugged them.

He saw them still standing, watching his car drive out of sight. Flipping open his phone, he tried to call Katie and got a recording. He wanted to get back to Sandstone, but first he planned to stop at the local newspaper, *The Treehaven Chronicle*. They must have microfilm of papers from years ago. He hoped so.

His father might have been framed. He tried to press down the eager feelings of hope. For the first time in his life, he felt sorry for his father. Framed, sent to jail and he lost his wife and son. What a horrible life and then he was killed in prison.

Jake tried to remember the first time someone told him about his dad. He was so young. It was hard to remember. Pictures flashed into his mind, one of his mother crying and someone carrying him away.

He flinched at the memory of himself, as a small boy, yelling for his mother. Jake shook his head as though to clear his thoughts and swung into a parking space near the newspaper. Still, in his mind's eye, he heard the angry voices telling him to shut up and a small dark room with two bunk beds and older boys laughing at him. It wasn't until Jake stared into the rearview mirror that he realized he had tears in his eyes.

Jake stopped in the men's room and splashed his face with cold water, combed his hair, and pushed down the memories. The business man, the controlled Jake Andrews reflected back at him. He straightened his collar and headed out the door.

The newspaper better have the back files. Nothing was going to prevent him from finding the truth, whichever way it ended.

* * * *

Katie had stopped by her parents' house and now she headed home. She thought about Jake's plan for Sandstone as she drove. Determination stiffened her backbone. He'd have his half to do with as he pleased. She expected her half to include the house.

She'd give Eric the house in New Jersey, and she'd be completely free of him. She thought she'd known Eric after living with him for five years, but she'd been wrong. She and Jake had lived together less than a month. It was too soon to trust him.

What they felt and acted on was chemistry. She had to remember that, in case Jake left and went back to Atlanta at the end of their thirty days. Her throat went tight. She must remember this was probably a short term relationship.

When she got out of the car, the smoky delicious odor of barbecue wafted around the house and across her nostrils. The dark clouds had blown over without rain. She'd run upstairs and change before greeting Jake. It gave her time to get her thoughts in order.

Changed into clean jeans and shirt, she ran a comb through her curls. Taking the stairs two at a time, she slowed when she got to the kitchen. She'd best not act too anxious.

Jake stood at the small grill dressed in cut off jeans and no shirt. The sun glinted off his shiny hair and wide shoulders. The man looked good enough to eat.

He leaned down and patted Smudges head and the puppy cuddled closer to his leg. "You're a good girl."

When he straightened, Jake spotted her. His lips curved in a smile. "Grab a beer in the fridge for both of us."

"It smells wonderful. What are you cooking?" she asked, as she got their beers.

"Ribs and corn on the cob."

Katie pushed the screen door open with her hip and joined him on the small landing. She handed him a beer. "You look different. Find anything out today?"

"Interesting news that might turn into something good," he answered.

She watched him turn the ribs and baste them with more barbecue sauce. "Well? Are you going to tell me?"

He took a swallow of beer, and she found herself mesmerized by the movement of his throat muscles. Everything about him yelled sexy man. Maybe she was becoming one of those insatiable women, a sex maniac.

"I'd sure like to know what brought that smile to your face." Humor glinted in his eyes.

"None of your business." Katie felt her cheeks flush. "I'll be just a minute." She carried Smudges to his spot under the tree, checked his water bowl and strolled back to Jake.

"Now tell me what you found out."

"OK. The Barrows gave me more papers today, but I haven't read them yet. They also related some interesting information regarding my father."

He turned the corn and took another swig of his beer. "There is a possibility my father was framed."

Katie saw it on his face, hope. "That's great news. How wonderful if you can prove your father's innocence." She moved forward and sat on the top step. Jake joined her.

He took her hand and ran his finger along the inside of her palm and each finger. His lips followed with light kisses. Zings of desire feathered up her arm and down her body.

"I don't understand why you were mad at me this morning, but I'm sorry if I said or did something to upset you."

Katie shrugged. "Tell me more about what you discovered."

Jake continued to hold her hand and stared across the field. "I went to *The Treehaven Chronicle*. They're going to get the microfilms from around the time of the robbery out of the archives for me. I don't know if I can find anything to clear his name." Jake looked at Katie. "The Barrows said they thought he was framed, and the police went the easy route by not looking for anyone else."

Jake stood and checked on the grill Sitting down again he recaptured her hand. "Why if he was framed didn't he fight back? The stories I heard indicated he didn't put up much of a defense.

"My mother's father had plenty of money to hire a lawyer for his son-in-law. I guess he was glad to see him out of the way and he'd get his little girl back."

Katie turned partially toward Jake. "What I don't understand is how your grandparents stood by and let your mother leave her child with a person like your aunt. You are their grandchild."

A harsh laugh escaped Jake's throat. "And also my father's son," Jake added. "I'm less than nothing to them. It probably grates on them to this day that I have some of their precious genes."

Katie shook her head. "It's very confusing and how does it relate to you and Sandstone?"

"It's not clear yet. I almost forgot the papers. Let me get them. Watch the grill." He hurried inside.

He was back in a second. "Here, read them and tell me what they say while I finish our meal." He shoved the notes into Katie's hand.

Like all the other papers, these were brittle with age. Katie carefully unfolded them and started to read the fine handwriting.

"It's more like thoughts put down on paper," Katie commented. "I guess the writer is Mrs. Barrows' great aunt. She writes about her feelings regarding her friend Judith's death. At the end there's a comment noting she found it hard to believe Judith just lay down and died. She thought someone went to the farmhouse and harmed her friend. She apparently told the sheriff and he laughed at her." Katie leaned against the rail by the steps and watched Jake put the ribs and corn onto a big platter.

"Come inside, let's eat." Jake said, leading the way to the kitchen table.

Katie put the papers down on the counter and breathed in a good whiff of the aroma from the ribs. "These smell so good."

"They're my specialty."

They ate in companionable silence. Smudges howled every once in a while to remind them she wanted to eat.

"Don't worry, she's been fed," Jake commented.

"After dinner I'll let her in." Katie reached for the papers and studied the signature. "Emily must be the great aunt's name. I wonder who was sheriff at that time."

"I'll be going into town early tomorrow. If you want to go with me you can check the sheriff's office while I go to the newspaper. They may keep historical data."

The knock on the door startled them. "Who can that be?" Katie whispered.

The last rays of sun were disappearing over the horizon, and in the faint light Jake barely made out the figure of a man and woman.

"Can I help you?" he asked, and then took a deep breath seeing his aunt and cousin standing on the other side of the door.

His aunt chuckled. "Didn't recognize your own family?"

"What do you want?"

"Well for starters aren't you going to invite us in?" Lloyd asked.

"No."

"Who is it, Jake?" Katie came into the room drying her hands on a dish towel.

"No one."

Lloyd leaned around Jake. "Hello, Katie girl. My Mom and I thought we'd come out here and welcome you back to Treehaven."

"I said leave," Jake repeated himself and blocked their entrance.

"We thought you wanted to know more about Henry," his Aunt Edna said.

"You didn't want to tell me the truth before. What changed your mind?"

Aunt Edna hung her head. "I felt terrible about what I said to you. I thought I'd come out here and tell you how sorry I am and try to help."

Jake didn't believe a word. They had some motive for coming all this way.

He moved sideways and opened the door. "Come in." The quick satisfied grin on Lloyd's face didn't escape Jake's notice.

"Katie, please get us all a beer?"

Katie, who'd been standing mesmerized by the scene, blinked, nodded, and disappeared into the kitchen.

"Have a seat," Jake said. He watched the two take quick peeps around the room. "If you're looking for our resident ghost, she rarely comes out for company."

"Here are the beers. You want me to stay?" Katie asked, looking at Jake.

Jake reached out and pulled her to his side. "Yes," he said. He felt a slight resistance from her before she settled on the arm of his chair and put her hand on his shoulder.

"Looks like you two are close," Lloyd commented.

"It would seem so," Jake replied. He noted Aunt Edna looking around the room. "Looking for something or someone?"

Her head swiveled around. "No, just curious about the old place. It's in pretty good shape.

"It was repaired and cleaned before we got here."

"Goody for you," his aunt said, then seeing Katie's face she changed her tone. "I mean it's nice that they cleaned it up for you two." She glanced around again. "A place like this must be full of spooky corners and closets and secret hiding places?"

"Not really," Jake answered. "The spooky part is the ghost or ghosts."

His aunt straightened. "Two, I've never heard tell of more than one ghost, the woman that died here."

"That's what we thought," Katie said. "We may be wrong, but there seems to be another entity in the house. One who isn't nice."

Lloyd leaned forward and wrinkled his brow. "That's absurd. Another ghost has never been mentioned before."

"No one's lived here this long," Jake pointed out. He had to hide his smile watching the two of them searching the corners as if they expected a ghost to jump out at anytime.

"You were going to tell me about Henry." No sooner had Jake said his name than the lights went out. "Stay still everyone. I'll get a flashlight and some candles."

Both his aunt and his cousin stood. "I'm not staying here another minute." Aunt Edna headed for the door. "We'll talk with you another time and place. Call me." They rushed out the door before Jake had moved.

He and Katie stood side by side and watched the red taillights fade around the bend in the drive. "Now what was that all about?" Jake asked.

The lights flickered on. "She seemed ready to tell you all about Henry and the lights went off."

"Spare me. Those lights had nothing to do with our conversation."

Katie shrugged. "You believe what you want to, and I'll believe what I want."

A loud crash came from the kitchen. Food and broken china lay scattered around the floor by the sink.

"You didn't put the dishes far enough back on the counter." He quirked his eyebrow at her.

Katie set her chin in a stubborn line. "Oh yes, I did."

Ignoring him, she stooped and started to toss the bigger pieces into the wastebasket. She stood straight and glared at Jake. "And when did you start believing we had two ghosts?"

"It popped into my head. I wanted to see their reaction."

"You don't really think there are two?"

Jake pulled her to him, nuzzled her neck and whispered. "No, but with your overactive imagination, I'm sure you do," he teased and kissed the tip of her nose.

"I do and I also believe someone is trying to scare me away," Katie said.

"I did some exploring earlier today," she hesitated. "I'm ashamed to admit, that for a moment, I thought you might be the one trying to get me to leave. I needed to check out things on my own."

"What?"

"You upset me talking about your plans and ignoring how I feel about this house. I never wanted to believe it was you. I've been confused. But in my checking, I found a secret passage way to the rest of the attic.

"There's an opening in the front bedroom and over your bed. Also I found a large fan in the attic and a partition to separate the area into two spaces."

"Do you still think I might be the person?"

"No." She shook her head. "Can you forgive me?"

Jake smoothed his hand over her hair, then tipped her chin up and kissed her softly.

"I can't blame you after the way I've acted, and I didn't tell you about my own plans right away. I want to check out the area though, before I go to bed. Just to see it for myself. I'm surprised I never noticed the opening in my room. Show me?"

"Sure," she smiled and led him up the stairs.

Chapter 16

Jake dropped Katie at the sheriff's office the next morning. "I'll meet you at Tom's place around noon," Jake said, before waving and driving toward *The Treehaven Chronicle*.

A secretary sat him down in a small cubicle with all the films from the time of the robbery in 1976. Why hadn't he thought to research this information before? Because with what everyone told him about his father, he'd never felt the need to see it in writing. He'd taken their word.

Treehaven Bank Robbery. June 15, 1976. A well known local man is accused of robbing the First Bank of Florida yesterday afternoon. Eyewitnesses say they saw Kenneth Andrews running from the bank around the time of the robbery. The police found a gun in the bushes, close to the bank, with Mr. Andrews' fingerprints on it.

Jake leaned back in the hard wooden straight chair. Outside the cubicle he heard soft laughter, conversation and someone typing. He shook his head and rubbed his brow. A slight headache had lodged behind his eyes. Could his father have been so…well, stupid was the only word that came to mind? He didn't think so. It was all too cut and dried. Jake moved the knob on the machine and leaned closer to read more.

Harley (Buzz) Weedon and Dick Caudill have agreed to testify that they saw Mr. Andrews run from the bank and throw an object into the nearby bushes. The Andrews family is well known and respected in this town, and it's difficult to believe Bart Andrews' son robbed a bank.

A grainy black and white picture of the bank and one of his father handcuffed and being led into the police station figured prominently on the front page. Jake studied the pictures. A crowd had gathered around the police station, and Jake thought he spotted a light haired woman holding a small boy's hand, standing in the front line of spectators. Was that his mother and him?

Jake skipped through the files and didn't fine much more about the case until almost a year later when the trial started. It took two days for them to find his father guilty. Jake felt like a fist clutched his gut.

His Uncle Buzz, Aunt Edna's husband, testified against Jake's father. Didn't anyone suspect it might be a set-up? All the damning evidence was so readily available. Anger boiled in him, and he was thankful his uncle wasn't around. Jake feared what he might do to him if he was.

His aunt and Lloyd knew all of this. They must be laughing behind his back. Jake noted, at the end of the article, a brief statement regarding the stolen money. No one found any of the stolen goods, and his father never said what he did with it. Of course, he couldn't tell them something he didn't know. He didn't rob the bank.

"Were those the films you wanted?" The secretary stood in the door.

"Yes. Thanks." Jake started to rewind the tape.

"I'll take care of it," the secretary said. She smiled at Jake, and he noted her curvy figure and attractive brown hair and eyes.

She moved closer to him. "I'm Mari Reynolds." Her lips pursed up at him and her hand touched his arm.

Jake casually moved away, smiled and thanked her for the help. "Have to run. Thanks again." He fled out of the office.

A woman he might have been interested in a few weeks ago. Now all he thought about was Katie. He was in bad shape.

He drove to Tom's place to talk over the recent discoveries. Sara's desk was empty. Jake knocked on Tom's door and peeked around into his office.

Tom raised his head, "Come on in. We haven't seen you for a week or more. What's up?"

"We went to Virginia."

"We? Katie and you?"

"Yes, but don't get any ideas. The trip was about the mystery of the house."

"You've gotten quite involved. You still have a business in Atlanta?"

Jake made a face at him and sitting stretched out his legs. "I've been in phone contact. The guys are doing fine."

"Find out anything interesting on your trip?" Tom asked.

"So much I don't know where to start."

Jake glanced around the room. Tom's football, from the last game of their senior year, sat on a shelf. Several pictures of Tom and Sara occupied the top of a long file cabinet. He looked back to find Tom waiting patiently for him to continue.

"Did you know there was a possibility my father was framed? That he probably never robbed the bank?"

"No."

Jake stared across at his best friend. "I've been to the newspaper and read the account of the robbery and trial. They found him guilty in two days, and two of his friends, or maybe I should say enemies, testified they saw him run from the bank and toss the pistol away." Jake imagined some of the sadness and despair his father must have felt when his so-called friends betrayed him. "My Uncle Buzz testified against him."

Tom's feet hit the floor from off his desk. "Man, I swear I never heard anything. You know I'd have told you."

Jake nodded. "I know."

"What are you going to do?"

"First I'm going back to see Aunt Edna and Lloyd. They came to the house last night."

"What'd they want?" Tom asked, frowning.

"Beats me." Jake shrugged. "But I'm going to find out."

"The mystery of the house seems to be leading you in strange directions."

Jake agreed. "Ways I never expected, and not just about the inheritance and my father. Living with Katie has made me almost believe we might find what you and Sara have."

They both heard a noise in the outer office. "It's probably Katie. I asked her to meet me here." Jake turned back to Tom. "Listen we'll talk more later."

Tom came around his desk and cuffed Jake across the shoulder. "Good. I want to know the end of the story."

Katie sat on the edge of a chair. "Hi, Tom." She smiled and shook his hand.

Tom pulled her in for a bear hug. "It's good to see you. This guy being good?" He nodded at Jake.

"We're doing fine," Katie assured him. "Jake, are you ready to go?"

"Yes. See you soon, Tom. Tell Sara hello."

"I will."

Jake followed Katie to the car and opened the door for her. He walked around the back to the driver's side. He barely got in the car, before Katie turned to him.

"Guess who was sheriff?"

"Who?"

"Your Uncle Henry."

They stared at each other. "How convenient if you didn't want an investigation of Judith's death," Jake said.

"That's what I thought. No wonder he laughed at any idea of Judith dying at the hands of an intruder." Katie took a deep breath, "But that's not the only piece of information I learned from the back files at the Sheriff's. It seems Henry died at Sandstone Ranch."

"How, when?"

"It was some weird accident. There used to be an old barn out back. They theorized he went in the barn to get out of the storm. Lightning hit the barn and set it on fire. It's unclear why he didn't get out. He died in the fire."

"This is all very strange." Jake leaned his head against the side car window and watched Katie's expressions as he told her about what he'd read at the newspaper.

His hand moved involuntarily toward her and he pulled it back. What made her different from all the others? He never seemed to get enough of touching her, watching her. And they had less than a week to the end of the month.

He'd planned to go back to his life in Atlanta, and she'd stay in Treehaven. His business was in Atlanta. He enjoyed the diversity of living in a major metropolitan area. In Treehaven, he'd be bored within a month. Well, he hadn't been this month.

He twisted around in his seat and stared at the street. A few cars came toward them, and he saw several people walking along the sidewalk. This wasn't his world anymore.

"He's innocent." Katie's voice broke into his thoughts. "There's no doubt he was railroaded."

"That's what I think. How do I prove it?"

"Start with your aunt. Something tells me her husband knew who really robbed the bank and told his wife."

"We're thinking alike," Jake agreed. "Want to come with me?"

"Yes."

* * * *

Jake drove to his aunt's house. He furtively glanced at Katie to catch her expression when he turned on Snapdragon Circle. Her face only reflected an interest in her surroundings.

"See that green house, Jake?"

Jake glanced out the window. "Sure, Mrs. Pace lived there. She often greeted me on the way home from school with cookies and milk."

"I used to go there and read to her every Thursday during my junior and senior year at school," Katie said.

"She was one of the few kind adults I knew as a child." He remembered her shiny white hair and inquisitive brown eyes. "As I got older, I liked to help her by repairing things around her house or changing blown out light bulbs."

"Where did you live?" Katie asked.

He drove a short distance further. "Here we are," he said, pulling into the driveway.

"Think she'll be home?"

"That's her car under the carport."

They got out, stepped around the empty beer cans, and walked to the door. Jake raised his hand as the door was yanked open, before he could knock.

"What'd you want?"

"To continue our conversation from last night."

"See you brought your little girlfriend along. You don't mind her hearing all the family secrets?"

"No."

"Come in." Aunt Edna ushered them into the dark living room. The curtains at the window kept out most of the light. "Sit on the couch." She pointed across the room. "Don't have nothin' to offer you."

"We didn't come for a social call. Tell us about Henry." Jake thought he'd start with Henry and edge his way into asking about Buzz.

"Don't know exactly what you want to know. The story goes he was interested in that property, Sandstone, more like obsessed with it and that woman. Bet you don't know," she stopped to smirk, "he hoped to marry her, until Daniel Collier arrived."

"Really?" Jake said. "And Henry never told anyone why he wanted to buy Sandstone?"

"Supposedly, he said he had the money to buy it, and he liked the lay of the land. According to the old stories, he had planned to live there with Judith after their wedding." Aunt Edna moved one shoulder up. "He was fit to be tied when Daniel Collier married her and bought the ranch out from under him, or at least that's the way Henry saw it. He swore he'd get even." Her loud laugh crackled. "Seems to me Sandstone got even with them all."

"We found out today Henry was the sheriff, and he died at Sandstone," Katie said.

Aunt Edna flashed a dark look at Katie. "What you doin' nosin' around about my family? Tain't none of your business, girlie."

"I asked her too," Jake said. "I was busy at *The Treehaven Chronicle,* reading about my father's arrest and trial." Jake caught the sudden tightening of her mouth and saw her eyes blink. "You never told me Uncle Buzz testified against him."

She pulled her worn sweater close around her. "Weren't none of your business. He did what he had to do, his civic duty. He didn't want to, but it was his responsibility to tell the truth."

"And you never thought I should know?" Jake hesitated. "I think my father was framed, and Uncle Buzz wouldn't have known the truth if it hit him in the face.

"I want you to know I intend to prove my father's innocence and hope to find out who robbed the bank." There, he'd thrown down the gauntlet.

The words hung in the air. "Best to let sleeping dogs lie, cousin." A tall broad figure stood at the front door.

"Lloyd, I'm so glad you came home." Aunt Edna rushed to him. "They're upsetting me, and I didn't know what to do." She reached her hand out and rubbed her son's arm.

"I think it's time you two left." Lloyd glowered at them.

Jake took Katie's hand and stood. "We'll leave, but it won't stop me from finding out the truth. I think you two know who robbed the bank. Why not save me the time and tell me?"

Lloyd's lip curled back. "We don't know anything, but that your papa robbed the bank and got what he deserved. Now get out."

He stood eye to eye with Jake. Tension crackled in the air around them. Katie put her soft hand on Jake's arm.

"Come on, Jake. He isn't worth it." Turning her nose up at Jake's aunt and cousin, Katie pushed Jake toward the door.

Lloyd laughed. "She's already got you under control. What a wimp."

Jake tore his arm free and pivoted, his fist slamming into Lloyd's nose before Lloyd saw it coming.

Lloyd staggered back against his mother. He grabbed his face, and blood ran through his fingers.

"I've wanted to do that for a long time," Jake snarled at him. Jake took Katie by the arm and led her out the door.

"Don't tell me what to do, or what I shouldn't do," Jake snapped, as he opened the car door for her.

Katie blinked twice and turned her face away. They were silent on the drive back to Sandstone.

Jake stopped the car and reached across to Katie's door. "I'm sorry. I'm in a foul mood, but I shouldn't take it out on you. Don't stay here alone. Go visit a friend or someone. I'm going to Tom's to do some work." Jake steeled himself against the puzzled sad look. He needed space and time to think. "Look I'm really sorry, but I need time alone."

She jerked her head in a half nod. Relieved to see she agreed to take his advice, Jake headed toward the highway.

* * * *

Katie waited until the car disappeared from sight. She had no intention of going anywhere. Her hopes had risen when she overheard Jake's remarks to Tom. She hadn't meant to eavesdrop, but apparently, they didn't hear her enter the building. She deliberately made noise before Jake said anything more. Now she was just hurt and disgruntled.

This was a good time to stay home and clean. Cleaning always helped her think and work off tension. She'd change, get her bucket and mop, put on some loud dance music and clean the downstairs.

Smudges barked from her spot under the canopy of oak branches. "Guess you don't like my music." Katie whirled around with the mop and leaned out a window, waving to the puppy. The tension in her shoulders fell away as she hummed. Her heart almost stopped when she saw a figure standing in the kitchen doorway.

"I knocked. The music's so loud you didn't hear me."

"What in the world are you doing here? I thought you'd left days ago."

Eric's smile didn't reach his eyes. "You didn't think I'd give up so easily, did you?"

Katie shied away from him, putting distance between them. He'd dressed in cream colored slacks and a light tan shirt. It complemented his fair coloring. He was handsome. Not sexy like Jake, handsome in a more proper cool manner.

"What do you want? We said everything that needed to be said the other day."

"Katie, baby—"

"Don't call me baby!"

"You can't be serious about not wanting to see me anymore. I made a mistake."

"One the size of the Grand Canyon," Katie mumbled.

Eric's face flushed red, and his eyes tightened. "It takes two to cause a relationship to falter. You must admit you weren't as loving toward me."

"You dare to blame me for your behavior. Get out of here."

Instead, he grabbed her shoulders and pulled her toward him. "I want you back. I didn't waste five years of my life to lose you just when you're going to be worth something."

Katie struggled to get free. "And you think this will convince me to reconcile with you? Who told you about my inheritance?"

Eric grinned, a twisted sneer to his lips. "Your mom is so proud. I had no problem getting the information from her."

Finally, with one hard pull, Katie wrenched free. She stepped behind a chair and glared at him. "I'd never come back to you, not if you were the last man in the world. Get out."

"I can make it hard for you. I work for the same company you did, remember? They're going to do the annual audit next week. I can juggle the books. I'll make it look like you took more than your fair share when you left two months ago."

Katie stared. How did she ever think she loved this man? Did love make you blind? This was her fault for not ending it long ago, when she knew things had changed.

"Cat got your tongue?" Eric laughed and moved toward her.

The radio blared louder. Wind whirled around them. Eric looked puzzled.

"It's Judith."

"What…the hell. No one's here but you and me. I waited until I saw your lover leave."

A book on a nearby table flew across the room and hit him on his head. "What?" Eric whirled around and stumbled backwards as though something hit him full in his chest.

"Better run, Eric, before you get hurt."

Pale and sweating, his face marked with loathing, Eric ran to the door.

"This isn't finished, Katie. I'll do what I said if you don't marry me." His laugh scornful, he let the screen door slam.

Katie ran to the door. "Do it. My lover, as you called him, is a computer genius, and he'll prove you tampered with the program. You'll go to jail." She doubted he heard her last words. His car roared down the drive.

Katie sat on the front step. Sandstone seemed to be as much trouble for her as it had been for Judith. Did she want the house so much she'd risk everything? And where did Jake figure in all of this? Wandering around the side to where Smudges lay in the shade, Katie sat beside her and rubbed her silky coat.

Smudges jumped on her and barked excitingly. "Whoa, girl." Katie laughed and lay down on the soft grass. "What am I going to do? Life can sure be a mess at times."

Chapter 17

Jake found them under the tree, Katie laughing and rolling around with Smudges. They didn't see him. He stood in the shadows watching. Her expression changed, closed, when she spied him.

"Let's take Smudges off her leash and give her a good run," Jake said, hoping to revive Katie's earlier mood.

"You take her. I need to put away my cleaning supplies and shower."

He caught her arm as she went around him. "You didn't leave?"

"No."

"You only wanted me to believe you were leaving?"

"Yes."

He realized he'd tightened his hand on her arm. He let go. "I'll remember in the future to make sure you leave ahead of me."

She didn't answer. He watched her hips swing until out of sight. Hunger for her sent spikes of desire down his body, and he went hard. He started to take a step forward. No. He'd best keep distance between them. Whatever happened in the next few days, the end might be in sight for Katie and him. He hoped not.

Katie prepared a quick dinner, and they ate without talking. Then, she brought in a bowl of strawberries and cream and sat down with a determined look on her face. Jake wasn't sure he wanted to hear what she had to say. He started to push his chair back.

"Wait." Katie put up her hand. "You didn't eat your dessert, and I have something I need to tell you."

Jake picked up his spoon and waited. A reddish golden curl fluttered in the breeze from the fan. He started to reach out and touch it. She moved out of his reach.

"Eric came here today." Her words were soft and hesitant.

"That's why you didn't go anywhere."

"No, no. I didn't know he planned to come. I thought he'd left town."

Jake stared into her hazel eyes, flecked with green today. "What did he want?"

"He wants me to marry him, so he can have half my inheritance."

"Is he crazy?"

"No, cunning. I might need your professional assistance if he does what he's threatening."

Katie stared at her strawberries. "Will you help me?"

For a second, he didn't comprehend what she'd said. "Of course. How did he threaten you?"

Katie took a deep breath. "He said he'll fix the financial records to look like I embezzled money from my former employer. He works there. I told him you'd find out what he'd done."

"You have a lot of faith in me."

"Mr. Townsend said you were good at your job."

"I can do it. Don't worry." Jake stood and took his bowl of strawberries with him. "I'll eat these in my room. See you later."

Good exit, he thought. Let her wonder about him. You should be so lucky.

* * * *

Katie wandered through the silent house. She rubbed her arms and wrapped them around her. Blunt and to the point. He'd do it. He'd help her. His expressionless face hovered in front of her eyes. He was an expert at hiding his feelings and hers were all up front for everyone to see.

She'd taken a chance and let herself care for Jake. She'd made many mistakes in her judgment of Eric. He'd turned out to be the snake of the year and Jake…well he hadn't lied. He always said he wasn't the marrying kind. But, she clung to hope after hearing his conversation with Tom.

Going out the back door, she unfastened Smudges leash to bring her inside. The puppy ran around Katie's legs in joy.

"At least someone is glad to see me," Katie whispered into Smudges' fur, hugging her little body.

She thought of the day Jake gave Smudges to her. Jake seemed to fit so well with her family. That was her dream, not his. His plans would take him away from Treehaven. Katie's kept her here. A relationship between them didn't have much hope of working.

Katie stopped at the back door. The light in Jake's room shone around the edges of his curtain and she heard the low sound of his music.

She turned away and leveled her gaze on the edge of the forest. Standing in a streak of moonlight, the deer held his head high. He seemed to study her, and she stared back. The deer took a step forward, halted, sniffed the air, and turned to the trees. Just before he went out of sight, he looked back.

Smudges yelped and Katie loosened her grip on his body. Why did the deer seem to stare at her and the house with such intent? A shiver went across her shoulders. She hadn't seen the deer before their trip to Virginia. A horn honked in the distance. Hurrying inside with Smudges, she locked the door.

* * * *

Katie woke with an idea. Dressing quickly, she headed for the kitchen. Jake sat talking on his phone, a cup of coffee in his hand.

"I leave here at noon and arrive in Atlanta by one. I have an errand to do, but I'll check in with you guys before my return flight."

Katie wondered why he wanted to go to Atlanta again. Today was Friday. Tuesday was their last day. She poured a cup of coffee and leaned down to pet Smudges. After filling Smudges' water bowl and giving her some dog food, Katie went to the table. Jake clicked his phone shut.

"Good morning." He smiled across the table, a cautious smile.

"I overheard your conversation. You're flying to Atlanta."

"I've got some business there. I'll be back tonight."

"We only have a few more days. Our meeting with Mr. Townsend is Wednesday."

"I know."

Katie took a deep breath to push down her irritation. Dressed in his charcoal suit and polished shoes it reminded her of how he looked that Monday, almost a month ago. His jaw tightened almost imperceptivity at her study of him.

She nodded and looked away. He moved around the kitchen, rinsing his glass, and finally stopped at the door. "See you tonight. Promise me you won't stay here today."

"If you say so," she mumbled, still not looking directly at him. She sensed his hesitation, but he didn't say anything else, just left.

"And good day to you to," she mumbled. She sat at the table until certain he'd gone.

Where to start? If she only knew exactly where the barn had stood. Maybe she'd find the information at the courthouse.

Grabbing her purse, she gave Smudges a last hug and hurried to her car. A quick trip to town might save her time in the long run. Henry had to have a reason to be in the barn. What did he go back to Sandstone to retrieve?

"May I be of assistance?" the lady at the property appraisal office asked. Katie explained she hoped to find where the barn stood at Sandstone before it burned down.

"Honey, I'd love to help, but the old courthouse burned in 1899 and most of the records went with it. You might check the newspaper. If the barn burned maybe they'd have an article and a picture."

"You're so helpful. I should have thought of that. Thanks." Katie waved and rushed out. *The Treehaven Chronicle* was close-by. She took off walking, determined to find her answer today. Time was running out.

The newspaper receptionist took some wheedling, but finally consented to try and find the microfilms from that year. Katie paced back and forth across the narrow foyer.

Flushed and pleased, the woman returned with several rolls of microfilm. "You're in luck. We brought a number of old films from our warehouse the other day. These happened to be included." She motioned for Katie to follow her.

Excitement ran along Katie's spine. She'd find something in those films. She sensed it. She noted the dates and pulled out the ones soon after the date of Judith's death. At first, she saw nothing interesting. She turned the film again and read, *Lightning Burns Down Barn at Sandstone, Sheriff Dies.* They'd found the sheriff's body in the barn. The paper theorized the barn door stuck or caught fire, blocking his exit.

Katie turned the film one more turn. The picture jumped out at her. It showed the remnants of the barn where it burned to the ground. The house was barely visible to the front and right. She studied the scene. How the house and the trees set in relationship to the barn. She looked for any other landmarks. She hoped she'd be able to get close to the right spot.

"Thanks, I found what I needed." Katie waved to the receptionist and hurried outside to her car.

She'd make a quick trip to the hardware store to buy a shovel, pick, and gloves. Jake wasn't the only one with ideas. She'd surprise him tonight. Whatever she found, it was bound to answer some questions.

She flipped her phone open. "Sara, its Katie. I'll be moving back Tuesday. Is that OK with you?" Katie chuckled at Sara's answer. "I know you like having me there, and I enjoy your company, but this is only temporary. I hope to move permanently to Sandstone after the meeting with Mr. Townsend. No, I think the question about the ghosts will be resolved. See you soon, bye."

Katie knew her parents and siblings didn't like her plan to live at Sandstone. And, in spite of her bravado about staying there alone, she wasn't sure about doing it herself.

She loaded her shovel and other items into the car. A mother, pushing her baby by in a carriage, caught her attention. That's what she wanted. But she wanted her baby to have shiny brown hair, sky blue eyes, and a father named Jake.

She shook herself and got in the car. Tomorrow would take care of itself, as her father always said. Today, she had work to do.

* * * *

It didn't take Katie long to don her straw hat and gloves after a quick lunch consisting of an apple and a glass of water.

She stood to the left side of the house and moved around until she got the angle that had shown in the picture. Lifting her gaze, she studied the trees. Many of the large oaks were at least a hundred years old.

Walking to the left and forward, she studied the ground intently and then laughed at herself. Any obvious traces would be long gone.

Feeling she was at about the correct distance from the trees, she stopped. She stood in a field of weeds, sandspurs, and some grass. Taking the shovel, she dug out the first piece of dirt. She'd take only the first layer of ground and try to find something to tell her this was the area where the barn had stood.

Katie stretched and opened her bottle of water. She took a swallow and it slid down her parched throat. She'd made a line of shallow digs along a perimeter and so far found nothing. She glanced at the sky. It must be around four or five o'clock. Muscles she didn't know she had ached and sweat pasted the back of her shirt to her.

There was something here. She couldn't explain how, but she knew. Taking the rake, she brushed sand from side to side. A glint of something shiny caught her eye. Dropping to her knees, she brushed the dirt aside and found a fine gold chain with a locket. The initials on the back were worn.

She held the necklace so the full sunlight fell onto the fancy letters JLC. Rejuvenated, Katie felt a surge of energy. She resumed digging.

The tattered glove almost fell apart in her hand, a man's glove. She put the necklace in her pocket and the glove in her basket. Standing, she swayed and realized the exercise and warm sun had made her dizzy.

She'd go in, shower and wait for Jake. He'd be surprised. She believed since finding the necklace and glove so close together, they linked the sheriff to Judith. With the people involved long gone there could be no positive proof, but to her it answered some questions.

Katie leaned down to pat Smudges frolicking at her side. The puppy had stayed with her most of the afternoon, only occasionally going to sit under the shade of the oak tree. "Good girl," Katie said. A movement to her left caught her attention.

She stared hard at the trees on the other side of the house near the back. Something had moved. Maybe it was the deer. Or, maybe her imagination was running away with her. A cold shower and she'd fix supper. Hopefully Jake's business was successful.

Katie kept the necklace and glove in the bathroom with her. She'd locked the doors, but still the faint movement in the trees bothered her. After the cold shower, she put on brown slacks and an emerald colored silk blouse. The necklace felt warm in her hand. Where to keep it? A warm rush of air blew around her and caressed her neck.

"I hope you don't mind, Judith, but I think I'll wear it." Talking to a ghost probably indicated a sign of craziness. She didn't care what others thought. She felt Judith around her, more now than ever before.

After rinsing the dirt from the chain and locket, she fastened it around her neck. She started to wrap the glove in a silk scarf and hide it in her drawer, but remembering the hidden passage, she kept it with her.

Something warned her to grab the stairway rail, just before she felt the push meant to send her flying to the bottom. She fell on her knees and looked back, nothing. She grasped the rail with both hands and still holding the glove cautiously made her way downstairs. Then, a loud crazy laugh reverberated through the house and sent chills up her back.

It was after six. She expected Jake home in an hour or so. She wasn't going to let anyone or anything scare her away at this point. They were too close to success.

A mist swirled around her, and Katie smelled the scent of old roses. She had Judith to protect her.

Darkness shrouded the field and woods. Crickets chirped, and Smudges howled, looking at the stairs. Should she call one of her brothers to come and stay until Jake returned? Katie admitted to herself, she'd be scared to try to get to her car.

An ominous feeling spread through her. Shivers ran across her shoulders. Something evil haunted the house tonight. It was as though finding the glove and necklace caused a delicate balance to tip and the evil to grow stronger.

Katie went to the living room and picked up the line phone. There was no dial tone. She'd lost her cell phone. She'd discovered it gone when she went in the kitchen earlier. How, when had she lost it? She'd left the house unlocked while she worked in the field. Glancing around the room, her hand went to her throat where her heart pounded.

The threat of evil danced around her and the house. She smelled it in the closed air, a scent of fear and darkness. Her skin prickled with the feel of it, as though something crept toward her. Someone or something waited.

Chapter 18

Jake had decided sometime during the night to visit his mother once more. She had to know more about the robbery, and he wanted to know if she thought they framed his father. Today, when he stood at the fancy front door and knocked, anger pulsed through him. Everyone let him grow up feeling worthless. They took away any good feelings he might have had about his father. What kind of woman allowed her son to be treated in such a manner? He no longer felt he had to treat her with kid gloves. He came here for answers and one way or another he'd get them.

The snooty butler frowned on finding Jake at the door. "Don't give me any shit," Jake snapped. "I'm here to see my mother, Mrs. Claudia Winston."

The butler's eyes widened, and he stepped back, letting Jake inside the foyer. "Wait here. I'll let Madam know you wish to see her."

Jake watched him go to the same room, knock and enter. It only took a minute before he returned.

"Mrs. Winston will see you."

Jake stepped around him. "You don't need to lead me. I know the way."

His mother stood by the windows, shadows falling across her face. "I thought you weren't coming again. And I understand you introduced yourself as my son." Her voice was softer today, not as cold.

Jake stepped closer noting her pale, expressionless face, only the flicker of her eyes gave away any emotion.

"It's time for the charade to stop, Mother." The word came unfamiliarly to his lips. He saw her head jerk back.

"What charade?"

His lip curled in distain. "You're good. You know what I mean. Tell me the truth about my father."

She walked toward him. Her hand reached out, then fell to her side.

"You're so like him in looks."

"That's old news."

"Sit down. I can't talk having to look up at you the whole time." She walked to the nearest chair and sat gracefully. Her light floral dress floated around her thin body. She almost looked like a ghost herself. She'd lost weight since his last visit.

Jake wrinkled his forehead. "Have you been sick?" The words came out without thought.

Her eyes met his. "Not physically ill. What do you want to know, Jake?" Her voice empty, she straightened her shoulders as though preparing herself for an attack.

He felt sorry for her. That was crazy. She was the woman who'd rejected him time and again. She chose this life. He glanced around the room at the richness of the furnishings. Why ever did he feel sorry for her?

"I've come to believe my father was framed. That he didn't rob the bank and I think you knew it." Jake studied her expression as he asked his question. She was good. She let very little show.

She plucked at the pleat in her skirt before confronting him. "I did."

"Why didn't you tell someone? Why didn't you get him an attorney and fight? Why?" He heard the little boy in his voice and so did she.

"I've asked myself that question many times. He said it wouldn't help. He gave up. I was young and..." She swallowed and leaned back, taking a breath.

A knock at the door brought their attention around. "May I come in and join you?" A tall blond man stood in the entranceway. He had a strong face and kindness in his eyes.

His mother sat motionless, stunned.

"I think it's time you told me the story that makes your eyes look so sad, my dear."

Jake saw the slight nod of her head.

"Come in, Robert." She motioned with her hand toward Jake. "I'd like you to meet my son, Jake Andrews."

Jake gulped around the lump in his throat. His breath caught. He swallowed again and met her husband's eyes.

Robert Winston walked across to Jake with his hand out. "It's a pleasure to meet you." He motioned for Jake to sit, and he pulled a chair close to his wife and took her hand. "Why don't you tell me the whole story?"

Jake felt as if he'd fallen into a dream or nightmare, and it had taken on a life of its own. He was no longer in control.

"I'm not very proud of my part in the story," his mother stated. "My excuse is I was young and scared, and I'd always obeyed my parents, except when I married Jake's father." She looked directly at Jake.

"I loved him. He filled my life with laughter and joy for a short time. You were born, and we loved the miracle of having you. Your father liked to lift you up, and you'd laugh. Until the day of the bank robbery, I'd ignored my father's demand to divorce him and come home. I happily turned my back on this type of life." She glanced around the room.

"What happened that day?" Jake asked. Jake saw her husband squeeze her hand. He nodded to her with encouragement.

His mother wet her lips and continued. "He'd received a threatening letter in the mail a few weeks before the robbery. The police had arrested someone your father knew in high school, and he planned to testify against him. The man had raped a girl and Ken, your father, overheard him admit it. Ken went to the police."

"So the robbery set-up was to keep my father from testifying about the rape?"

"That's what we thought. I told Ken I'd tell the police he was with me, because he was, but he said they'd never believe me. I was his wife. I'd be expected to try and save him."

"Why didn't you at least get him a good lawyer?" Jake asked.

"My dad refused to help. He said he knew his bad blood had to show sooner or later. He demanded I come home, but I couldn't bring you. I had to leave you in Treehaven and start my life fresh."

"So you took the easy way out."

Robert Winston leaned toward Jake, and his mother stopped him with her hand. "He has a right to be bitter.

"Your father and I hoped for the best and believed in the court system and justice. I stayed for the trial. Sat in the back row and wept to hear the lies said about him. His court appointed attorney thought him guilty and didn't make much of an effort. It was a nightmare I never forgot."

Robert Winston patted her hand. "Let's take a break and order coffee." He didn't wait for the others to agree, but went to the door and stepped outside to speak with the maid.

"He's a good man," his mother said, watching her husband leave. "I've wanted to tell him about you all these years. I was afraid he'd hate me, like I hate myself for abandoning you." She stood and went to her small desk.

Jake watched her take off her bracelet. She inserted a tiny key to open a hidden drawer, pulled old papers from it, and handed them to him. It was a record of his life, his football triumphs in high school, the time he won at the science fair and his success with his business.

"I can see the questions in your eyes," she said. "I kept them to have something of you. I was proud of you, and yet I had no one to tell." Her husband returned and reached out his hand to her. She smiled at him through her tears. "At least, I thought I had no one. You can't know how happy I was to see you succeed in spite of your childhood."

Jake didn't know what to say. Restless, he stood and paced around the room. Outside the fountain still tinkled with drops of water falling from one level to the next, a busy bee flew from flower to flower gathering nectar and a golden butterfly flitted from bush to bush. The world went on while his fell apart.

Feelings of anger, frustration, and sadness all battled inside of him. He felt a strong hand on his shoulder and turned.

"Come have coffee. I can't imagine how difficult this must be for you. Join us, please."

Jake stared at his stepfather. He recognized the kindness in his face and gentleness, none of the anger and rejection Jake expected. He nodded and went back to his seat.

His mother sipped her coffee and offered him a biscuit. He declined. His stomach too tense to accept food.

She started talking again. "I implored my parents to help you and me, or to at least let me bring you here. They refused. Without a job and no income, I didn't see anyway out. My father made one more offer." Her voice was now almost a whisper. "He'd pay your father's family to take care of you until you were grown. Your aunt said she'd be happy to care for her only brother's child."

His mother looked across at Jake with tears in her eyes. "I feared she wasn't a good woman, but my father said I was being silly. Family took care of family and so I left you."

"You also managed to reject me when my aunt brought me to see you a few months later."

"You remember?"

"It's been my worst nightmare."

"She said you were having a hard time adjusting to their family, and I needed to let you know you had to live with her. I thought what I did would help you accept your new home."

"Right."

She cried now in great gulps, and her husband held her close. Anger filled him. There'd been no one to hold him, to soften the hurts and all because this woman wasn't brave enough. He stood.

"Please stay. Don't leave yet." She put out her hand.

"I have to go. I don't want to say the wrong thing because of my anger. And I have a plane to catch." Jake found himself softening his voice.

Robert Winston walked him out. "You're a smart young man. Thanks for not hurting her anymore. You may not realize or care how much you could devastate her."

Jake didn't trust himself to speak. He slipped out the door and went to his car. Today, he didn't glance back.

On the plane ride to Jacksonville, an urgent need to see Katie swept over him.

It took an extra fifteen minutes to get his luggage and then the heavy traffic slowed him, taking him more time to get out of town. He'd tried several times to phone Katie, but she didn't answer.

She might be at her parents. He flipped open his cell phone and tried to reach them and got a busy signal. After what he'd been through today, he wasn't surprised that anxiety clawed at his insides. He glanced at his watch, seven thirty. He'd be home by eight. He stepped on the accelerator.

* * * *

Katie heard a noise upstairs. Darn, she'd left her purse in her room. Without her car keys, she'd gotten herself into a corner. Smudges ran between her and the stairs barking furiously. She looked out the front door. A figure stood by a car parked far in the distance. Who was it? It looked like a woman. Why didn't she come to the door? The mist Katie had come to know as Judith darted around her and the kitchen.

Katie knew she had to handle whatever was about to happen. Jake wasn't going to get here in time. The clock showed seven-thirty and she saw no sign of him. She started up the stairs. A dark empty hallway greeted her. She switched on the light, nothing but eerie silence.

Spotting her bag on the dresser, Katie darted into her room and grabbed it. She'd take a chance and run for the car. For the first time this evening, she felt hopeful.

"Well, well, well, if it ain't pretty Miss Katie."

She knew the voice before she turned. "You." She watched Lloyd come in her room and she started to try and edge around him. He tried to grab her, and she did a trick her brothers taught her years ago. Her knee connected solidly to his groin, and he went down.

Running for her life, Katie flew down the stairs and found Jake's aunt waiting, in the living room, a small pistol in her hand.

"Going somewhere?"

"Hold the bitch for me, Mama." Lloyd stumbled partway down the steps then fell the rest of the way. He looked around and saw no one. "What the hell?"

"I think you met Judith, our resident ghost," Katie told him.

He lunged for Katie and grabbed her from behind, holding her tight against his sweaty body. She struggled to free herself, and he laughed.

"You bitch, I should have strangled you the other time, but I was careful not to leave marks." His manic laughter echoed around the room. "You thought your ghost did it."

"How—"

"A silk scarf, a little pressure on the right spots, half asleep your imagination did the rest." His laugh irritated her.

"Enough," his mother said. "Get the money and let's get out of here."

"What money?" Katie gave them a puzzled look.

Edna shoved her. "We saw you digging today and putting a package in your basket. You found the money, didn't you? You think you'll cheat us out of it after all these years. You won't, I'll kill you if need be, but I want what belongs to me."

And Katie knew, "Your husband robbed the bank. How did he lose the money?" She laughed at them. "He didn't remember where he put it?"

"Damn man died of a heart attack before he told me. Said I didn't need to know," Edna said harshly. "Wish I could get my hands on him now, I'd kill him again myself."

"I didn't find any money," Katie said. She tried again to pull free of Lloyd without success.

Lloyd partially let her go to turn her around. His hand swung out to hit her. Katie jerked loose and ran to the kitchen.

She pulled open a drawer to reach for a knife, but he was on top of her. He threw her to the floor and kicked her in the ribs. Sharp pain made her gasp for breath.

He and his mother leered over her. "Tell us where it is."

Gasping she got out the words. "I found a man's glove and a necklace, that's all."

The two towered above her, then Lloyd jerked her up to face him. "You've got one more chance. Where is it?"

Katie went to bring her knee up, and he sidestepped her. "Bitch," was the last sound she heard.

* * * *

Jake held his foot down on the accelerator the whole way. Fear gnawed at his gut. He sighed with relief when he saw the sign for Sandstone. Halfway down the dirt road, he saw the smoke and a car came careening along the road almost sideswiping him. Jake flew into the yard. His heart sank at the sight. Katie's car sat parked in front of the burning house.

He got out and Smudges ran to him, barking and running back toward the kitchen. Jake followed. The front of the house was full of flames. Taking out his cell, Jake called 911. He gave the address and closed the phone. He didn't have time to answer questions. Katie was in there, somewhere.

Jake unlocked the back door. Smoke filled the kitchen, and flames licked their way from the dining room. He saw the outline of a figure lying in front of the stove. Katie. And then he noticed no smoke covered her. A misty cloud circled and held back the smoke above her.

Jake crawled on his stomach to reach her. He felt a faint pulse. He picked her up and holding his breath, ran for the door. Smudges barked and didn't stop running around them, until Jake stood in the field away from the house.

Gently lowering Katie to the ground, Jake checked her breathing and heartbeat. Both were faint. "Katie love, come back. Please, Katie. I can't bare it if anything happened to you."

He cradled her in his arms. Tears ran down his face. The medics found them and gently pulled her from him to place her on the stretcher.

One medic touched his arm. "We'll take her to Park General Hospital. It's Katie Weber, isn't it? Should we call her family?"

"I'll call," Jake assured them and waited until the ambulance went out of sight. The firemen valiantly tried to put out the inferno, but it was too late. Katie's house burned to the ground. He flipped his cell phone open and called Katie's parents.

"What started the fire?" one of the firemen asked Jake.

"I don't know. I got here after it was already burning." He remembered the car speeding by him. He had a strong suspicion about who owned that car. He'd wait and check it out himself, before he said anything to the firemen.

"Can I look around the area with you guys?" Jake asked.

The man glanced at the fire chief. "It's not usual procedure"

The fire chief interrupted. "We'll make an exception. Meet me here in the morning. The lingering hot spots should be out, and we'll investigate. I'll have a couple of men here all night."

"Thanks. See you then," Jake checked his watch. He'd head for the hospital to check on Katie, if they'd let him in. He'd try.

Chapter 19

The short stern nurse frowned at him. "It's after visiting hours."

"I know, but I got here as soon as possible. I had to talk with the firemen. Please let me at least peek in on her."

She studied him. "You missed her parents. But I'll give you five minutes, young man. No more. She's in Room 310."

Jake flashed a smile. "Thank you."

He sped to the nearest elevator.

Her door sat partially open. Quietly, he slipped inside. Katie lay on her left side, an IV dripping into her arm. Her eyes shut, hair tousled, and her right arm snuggled close to her chin made Jake want to reach out and cuddle her. Hold her close to him and keep her safe. His fingers touched her soft curls. She never stirred.

"She's going to be fine." The short nurse had followed him to the room and put her hand on his back. "Got a slight concussion from being hit in the head and some bruised ribs. She's a lucky girl. I don't know how she kept from getting a chest full of smoke."

Jake laughed to himself thinking about the nurse's reaction if he told her a ghost had protected Katie until he got there. Another few minutes and he'd have been too late.

"The smoke and flames were filling the kitchen when I found her."

"You went in to get her?"

"Yes."

"Stay as long as you want." She patted his back. "You saved her life."

Jake collapsed into the chair next to the bed. He'd sit here for a while.

When he woke, daylight shone through the slit in the curtains. Sometime during the night, Katie had moved onto her back. This morning she had more color in her face, but Jake saw the signs of bruising on her neck, head, and arms.

He stretched. He needed to find a place to shower and change. He'd go to Tom's house. He always left some clothes there. Better hurry or the investigation would start without him. He leaned across and brushed a soft kiss on Katie's forehead. "See you," he whispered. Jake was relieved to find a police officer on guard outside Katie's door.

"The chief thought we'd better keep a check on her. Don't seem like she'd give herself a concussion." The round cheeked officer stared hard at Jake. "Where were you last night?"

"I saved her, man. Only an idiot would knock her out and then save her." Jake said in disgust.

The policeman leaned his chair back against the wall. "I heard tell of you and your father." He shrugged to indicate Katie. "I heard she's all that stands between you getting a large inheritance."

A scowl crossed Jake's face. "She'll tell you who hit her." Jake took long strides to the elevator and punched the button.

A shower and change of clothes and he'd feel more presentable. The police officer guarding Katie had obviously heard rumors around town about Jake's dad and his family. Jake didn't care what he thought of him as long as someone guarded Katie. That was important.

* * * *

Parking his car in front of the burned out house, Jake strode across to where the others stood. "Good morning."

The police chief, Carl Horseman, glared at Jake. "What are you doing here?" He turned his head to spit out his chew.

Jake nodded toward Ted Reynolds. "The fire chief said it was all right."

"He saved the girl," Chief Reynolds said. "It won't do any harm to have him around."

"So he says. Let's get on with this. Stan," the police chief barked at a young officer standing to the side. "Come here and stay glued to Jake Andrews. I want to make sure he doesn't plant any false evidence."

Jake started to speak, but the fire chief took hold of his arm and shook his head. Chief Horseman smiled as though urging Jake on. Jake forced himself to relax and back off.

The police officer came to his side. "Guess we're a pair today, Stan,"

Jake said.

"Yes, sir," Stan cleared his throat and moved closer to Jake.

They watched as the other men began to carefully sort through the debris. Being cautious, Jake and his shadow tread lightly around behind the others. An unusually warm March sun beamed down. No one said much as they followed a pattern to check for evidence of the source and accelerant of the fire.

At lunch break, Jake realized in all the confusion he'd forgotten about Smudges. "My puppy, where is she?"

"One of my men talked to Katie's dad. He took the dog over to their house," the fire chief said.

Jake leaned back against the oak tree in relief. "I can't believe I forgot her. She led me to Katie."

"Where were you yesterday?" the police chief asked.

"Atlanta."

"Can anybody verify seeing you there? Atlanta's a big city."

"My mother and her husband." Jake didn't miss the surprised expressions on some of the older faces.

Carl Horseman spit and turned back. "Heard you were a foster child."

"So? I still didn't hatch out of an egg." Jake snarled back. The police chief got under his skin. Thank God, he had Katie to tell them he wasn't the one who hurt her.

"Watch you mouth. You're not cleared yet," Carl said. "What do you think, Ted? How'd this fire start?"

"Too soon to tell, but something happened in the living room. The fire started there."

Carl stared hard at Jake. "We'll find out the truth. Never fear."

The fire chief motioned to restart the search. And Jake and his shadow went back to work.

Jake saw the flash in the dirt near where the back stoop had been. He started to lend down, and Stan stopped him.

"Sorry, sir, let me, so no one can say that it wasn't already there."

Surprised by the man's understanding, Jake pulled back. "Thank you."

Stan picked the shiny object out of the burned wood and dirt. After brushing it off, he handed the antique watch to Jake.

"I've never seen one like that, sir."

"I have." Jake wiped the watch cleaner with his shirt tail. On the back were the initials he was looking for. He'd seen Lloyd with this same watch many times. Flipping open the lid, the clock still ticked away the minutes.

In moving it around in his hand, Jake saw another small catch and he pushed on it. A separate compartment opened and the brilliant afternoon sunlight flashed off of a small piece of reddish gold hair. And the mystery of Henry and Judith fell into place.

"What you got there?" Carl Horseman came forward with his hand out.

Jake snapped the interior opening closed and handed the watch to the police chief. "Stan can tell you we found it in the dirt where the person or persons probably dropped it when they ran out of the house."

"This is old. It's probably been here for years."

"Not likely. I've seen it before," Jake retorted.

Eye to eye the two men glared at each other. "And I suppose you're going to tell me where you saw it?"

"My cousin, Lloyd, always carries it in his small pocket at the waist of his jeans."

The police chief moved the watch around in his hand. He looked from the watch to Jake. "We'll see. I plan to make a visit to talk with Miss Katie Weber. And we'll see."

Jake watched him place the watch in an evidence bag. Jake planned to visit Katie too. At least he knew she'd tell the truth.

* * * *

Katie woke slowly. Every spot on her body hurt. Where was she and what had happened? She glanced around the unfamiliar room. A straight chair and a recliner sat side by side. A TV hung from the ceiling, an IV dripped into her arm, add the antiseptic smell and she realized she was in a hospital.

"Katie love." Her father came into the room carrying flowers and her mother close behind. "How do you feel?" He bent to kiss her.

"Why am I here?" Katie asked. "Did I have an accident? Where am I?"

Her mother came to her other side and took her hand. "You moved home to Treehaven. Don't you remember living at Sandstone Ranch?"

"You mean the haunted house? No way. I'd never want to live way out there?"

She saw her mother and father exchange looks. "I'm going out to see if your doctor is here," her mother said. "Maybe we can take you home with us today."

Katie touched her head. She felt a bandage and glanced at her dad. "What's wrong with me? I can't remember anything."

Her dad patted her arm reassuringly. "Don't fret. It'll all come back. What's the last thing you do remember?"

Katie frowned. "It was raining. I'd just got home from work and had messages from you and Annie and some of my friends all encouraging me to move back home." She squeezed his hand. "I guess I did."

Her father smiled. "Yes, about two months ago."

A tall man, with dark brown hair streaked with gray, came into the room. "Well, young lady, your mother said you're having some problems with memory. I'm Dr. David Chisholm."

He took a stethoscope out of his pocket and listened to her heart. What her heart had to do with her memory she didn't know, but Katie lay still and studied the doctor. Fine lines radiated out from his eyes. He wasn't young. He'd know what he was doing. He flashed a light back and forth in front of her eyes.

"Do I pass the test?" she asked.

A small smile cracked his stern demeanor. "We'll do a CAT scan. Don't worry. The lost of memory is not uncommon and doesn't usually last very long."

Katie noted the relief on her parents face. "Define very long," Katie asked.

The doctor shrugged. "A few days, weeks, I'd say at the most a few months. It should come back gradually, but sometimes something can trigger it and everything comes flooding back. We'll see. I'll know more after the scan." After shaking their hands, he breezed out of the room.

She was frustrated and a little scared to have part of her life a black hole. Katie rubbed her forehead where a slight headache lingered.

"Jake, come in." Her mother went to the door and brought the tall, dark haired man to her bedside. His intense stare showed relief when he saw her awake.

"I'm so glad you're all right." He clasped her hand. "The police chief has some crazy idea that I hit you on the head last night, and I suppose he thinks I started the fire." Jake smiled. "He'll be here soon and you can set him straight."

"Jake." Mrs. Weber touched his arm. "Katie's doing fine, except she has no memory of the past two months."

Katie saw the color leech out of his face.

"She doesn't remember last night?"

The man they called Jake raked his hand through his hair, and for a second Katie felt a flutter of some memory, then it was gone. She didn't know him. What did he have to do with her?

His eyes seemed to plead with her to recognize him. She wanted to, but her memories eluded her. His warm hand held hers with strength, and when he smiled, it made her breathless.

"Are we friends?" Katie asked.

A light blush tinged his cheeks. He looked at her parents. "Yes, Katie. My name is Jake Andrews. We've been living at Sandstone Ranch."

"Whatever for?"

"It's a long story. Rest for now."

Katie saw her mom shake her head at Jake. He kissed Katie's hand and left the room.

* * * *

Mr. Weber followed him out. "What's wrong?"

"You mean besides Katie's lack of memory?"

"Yes."

Jake took a deep breath. "The police chief thinks I'm his number one suspect." Jake pointed to the policeman watching them closely. "Ask him. He interrogated me once already."

"Why do they think you'd hurt Katie? I understood you saved her life."

"I'm Ken Andrews' son," Jake said, sarcasm in his voice.

Katie's dad took Jake by the shoulders. Jake felt like the small lost boy again, getting ready to receive a lecture.

"It's about time the people in this town got off your back. The son does not always follow in his father's footsteps. I believe in you and so does my family."

"You might be wrong."

Mr. Weber studied him. "I'm not wrong this time."

Jake's shoulders slumped in relief, and dampness clouded his eyes. "Thank you. And it might help to know that I'm close to proving my father never robbed that bank." Jake shook Mr. Weber's hand. "I'd better go find the police chief and tell him the news about Katie's memory."

Would Carl Horseman believe his story about Lloyd and be willing to put it to the test? Jake hoped so. He was willing to risk his life to prove it.

Chapter 20

"So you want me to believe Lloyd Weedon, your cousin, hit Katie Weber and torched the house? Give me a motive." The police chief sat with his arms crossed.

In another room, Jake heard the click of an old typewriter. "I don't know. I want to wear a wire and try to get him to talk."

"And you think he'll talk to you?"

"I think he hates me. If I meet him in the dark at Sandstone, he'll see it as an opportunity to get rid of me for good. If I can get him to talk, he'll think whatever he says will die with me."

"You're willing to put your life on the line?"

"Yes."

The chief rubbed his chin and didn't say anything for several minutes. Jake began to feel uneasy. The air conditioner in the corner hummed, but didn't cool the room, and Jake wiped perspiration from his brow.

"Let me think about it," Carl Horseman said. "I'll talk with my detectives and discuss your theory. Where are you staying?"

"I've taken a room at the Terrace Inn here in town. I want to be close to Katie."

"Stay away from her. I don't want you trying to program her mind. You're still a suspect until proven otherwise."

Jake stood, his hands clenched.

The chief sneered at him. "I'll be in touch. Don't leave town."

Pink streaks colored the early evening sky. Jake wanted action now. He didn't want to wait on a man more apt to disbelieve him and throw him into jail at any moment. He had a recorder in his things at the hotel. That should work as good as a wire.

Jake taped the small recorder to his lower back and ran the microphone wire under his shirt. Talking in a normal voice, he checked to see if it recorded his words. He was ready. Instead of going to Sandstone, he'd confront Lloyd and his aunt at home.

A faint light shown through the curtains in his aunt's living room. Jake parked his car two doors down and stepped quietly to the front door. He wanted this to be a big surprise.

He heard shuffling and muted voices in response to his knock. Aunt Edna pulled the door open a notch, and Jake threw his body against it, propelling himself into the room.

"What the hell?" Lloyd jumped out of his chair spilling his beer.

"Nice to see you too," Jake said.

"Get out." Aunt Edna pointed to the open door.

"Not so fast. You came to my house uninvited. I'm returning the visit."

"Are you crazy?" Aunt Edna snarled. "You don't have a house."

Lloyd came toward Jake, his hands clenched and teeth bared. "You heard Momma. Get out."

"Not until you answer my questions. Why did you go to Sandstone?"

Aunt Edna gave out a harsh laugh. "What makes you think we went there? We don't have to tell you anything."

"You upset cause your little girlfriend got knocked around?" Lloyd put his face close to Jake's. "You afraid someone had a taste of her before they left?"

Jake knew Lloyd saw the change in his face because Lloyd jumped back as Jake's hand grabbed him by the collar. "You were there. You piece of shit." Jake's hands went around the thick column of Lloyd's throat and started to squeeze. Lloyd threw up his arms and pushed, and the two men fell on the floor.

"Stop it." His aunt pounded on Jake's head, and he broke free of his cousin and rolled to his feet. Both men stood facing each other, panting.

"I'll tell you what you want to know," Aunt Edna said. "No one will believe you even if you told them." She put herself in front of him, her hands on her large hips. "We were looking for the money. We saw Katie digging around the yard, and she found something."

"Mom shut up," Lloyd hollered.

His mother shrugged. "What can he do? I heard he's the police chief's prime suspect. They got nothin' to place us at the scene."

"Nothing except the watch and Katie."

Jake's words brought a sudden silence. He saw Lloyd reach in his pocket and his face pale. "Don't matter. It's old. Few people knew I even had it."

"More than you think," Jake said.

Lloyd came toward him. "You knew, but I plan to get rid of you, and I heard Katie don't have no memory of last night."

"How will you explain my disappearance?"

"Easy. You're a coward, and you ran away because of your guilt." Lloyd laughed. "Little Katie will find someone else to let into her bed and Treehaven will soon forget about you and your father."

"You know my father didn't rob the bank. Uncle Buzz did it."

Jake enjoyed the shocked looks on their faces. "Well if I wasn't sure before, I know the truth now."

Lloyd sat in his chair and leaned to the side. Jake realized a second too late that he was reaching for a gun. A gun now pointed at Jake's heart.

"I always disliked you," Lloyd said. "You with your good looks, effortless good grades, and a football star to boot. I waited, and somehow I knew the day would come when I'd have the upper hand."

"Anyone can have the upper hand with a gun in it. Fight me with no weapons. Just our fists," Jake taunted.

"Now why would I do that?" Lloyd laughed. "I've got you where I want you." Lloyd pointed to the chair in front of him. "Sit and I'll tell you a story before you die."

"Just shoot him. We've got to get rid of his body, and the police might arrive at anytime," Aunt Edna said.

"Patience, Mom. Jake wants to know the truth. He deserves to know before he dies.

"My pop robbed the bank and got his friend to agree they'd accuse your father. Pop told Mom he'd shown your dad the gun a couple of nights before and got him to check it out for him. Told your father he bought it to protect us from break-ins." Lloyd chuckled, "Got his fingerprints all over it. Pop wore gloves and a mask during the robbery."

Jake leaned forward. At this point he wanted to keep Lloyd talking until he figured out how to get the gun away from him. "How did your dad lose the money?"

"He hid it. Said he'd wait a year or two until the trial and after the gossip died down. He said we'd be rich after that."

"Only he never told me or anyone else where he hid it. The stupid man. That fatal heart attack hit him before he retrieved the money." Aunt Edna frowned at Jake. "That's the only reason I kept you all those years. I was going to give you to foster care, but I had to raise you. I needed what your mother sent me."

"I was family," Jake said.

"So?" Her small brown eyes sparkled with anger. "We recently found some clues that made us believe the money is somewhere around Sandstone. I didn't want you two to find it. Something had to be done."

"Why hurt Katie?"

"She fought us. We weren't about to leave a witness behind." Her laugh crackled loud and familiar.

"It was you stalking us in the house," Jake said, startled.

"Smart boy. Me, and sometimes Lloyd. We had you and your girlfriend running in circles. Tried to scare her away, but she was stupid and stubborn."

Lloyd stood and came toward Jake. "So now you can die knowing all the answers to your questions. Sucker. Did you really think I'd let you leave after coming here tonight?"

"I'd hoped so," Jake said, confronting his cousin.

Lloyd raised his arm. "Sorry about this, cousin."

Jake kicked out with his foot and threw himself to the left. Lloyd's reaction came a second to late, and Jake's foot connected with his arm. Lloyd clutched his arm and a shot rang out.

Jake threw himself at Lloyd before he recovered and wrenched the gun from his hand.

"Drop it," the voice yelled from the front door. A group of armed police stormed into the small area.

Lloyd recovered first and sat up, pointing to Jake. "He attacked me and my mother. He held the gun to force us to say things that weren't true."

Jake let the gun drop and glared at his cousin, then noticed the body on the floor. Aunt Edna lay crumbled and silent.

"Lloyd, your mother." Jake pointed to her. He watched the disbelief and fear come into his cousin's face.

"Mom." Lloyd rushed to her and pulled her body into his arms. "She's breathing, get an ambulance."

Chief Horseman pushed his way through the crowd of officers. "One's been called." Using a pen, he leaned down and picked up the gun dropping it into a bag. "This should tell us who shot Mrs. Weedon."

"It won't. I'd just taken it from Lloyd when your men burst into the room."

"Likely story. The neighbors called and said they heard noises, like a fight, from this house. I don't think Lloyd shot his own mother."

"I can prove it." Jake moved his hand to his shirt.

"Keep your hands high," the chief snapped. "Officer Brown, take this man into custody. When you get to the precinct charge him with assault and maybe murder, if his aunt doesn't survive."

"What?" Jake asked stunned by what the police chief had said. Was the man an idiot or did he have a reason to want Jake out of the way? The ambulance crew came in and took care of Aunt Edna. Handcuffs slipped around Jake's wrists and snapped shut.

Numbing cold settled in Jake's chest. Was this how his father felt when they arrested him and he knew they had the wrong man?

Jake didn't plan to sit back and let them put him in a cell without a fight. He had the resources his dad lacked. Yet a part of him feared the town would believe the sheriff and Jake would end up just like his father.

Katie wasn't safe. Lloyd must know she might get her memory back at any time and identify him and his mother. Jake's first phone call had to be to Katie's father to warn him. If anything happened to Katie, he'd lose the most valuable part of his world.

The policeman pushed his head down as Jake got into the patrol car. Neighbors stood outside in their nightclothes, staring and whispering. Jake visualized *The Treehaven Chronicle* headlines in the morning. *Son Follows in Father's Footsteps.*

* * * *

Katie stared at the streaks of light shining across the wall and floor of her room reflected from the moon out her window. She couldn't sleep. Her head hurt, but she didn't want more pain medicine to dull her brain. She felt like her memories sat behind a partially open door. At times, a picture darted across the screen in her mind. A puppy barking, a harsh face leaning over her, a man holding her close against his warm body and his silky voice repeating again and again, "Katie wake up, please wake up."

She brushed a hand across her brow and closed her eyes. Even the muted light hurt. She froze. Someone had entered her room. Slitting her eyes partially open, she saw the wide shoulders of a man silently moving toward her. Opening her mouth to scream, he jumped forward and put his thick hand across her mouth and nose, stopping her breathing.

Struggling with her attacker, she kicked and threw herself from side to side. Her hands reached out trying to dislodge him. Lights flickered across her eyes. The IV pole. She flung one arm out and connected. The metal pole hit the floor, but was the clang loud enough to get attention? Where was her guard?

"Bitch." The hand tightened around her nose. She threw one last punch toward the sound before blackness took her away.

Katie woke to find a nurse and doctor standing over her. "Where is he?"

The doctor straightened after listening to her heart. "Whoever attacked you, got away."

"How? Didn't anyone see him?"

The nurse blushed. "I got a call to the end room. The emergency light came on. The patient didn't pull it. She said some man, with a dark hat pulled low, stepped inside, excused himself and said he was in the wrong room. He probably hit the red switch on the wall."

"But my guard?" Katie asked.

The doctor patted her arm. "Try not to get excited. Your pressure is a little high."

"Not get excited!" Katie glared at the man. "A person comes into my room and tries to kill me and you say don't get excited?"

The nurse put her hand on Katie's shoulder. "The guard appeared to be asleep. Someone doctored his coffee. Here. Take this pill to help calm you and get rid of your headache."

Katie shook her head. "I want to see Jake Andrews. Where is he?" Katie's hand flew to her mouth. "I remember. I remember it all."

The doctor took out his flashlight and checked her eyes. He smiled. "It happens that way sometimes. Another stress and it opens the memory banks."

"Call Jake."

"Can't," the nurse said. "He's in jail for attempted murder."

"What? Whose?"

"I heard a little while ago when his aunt came in with a gun shot wound. They say he shot her," the nurse answered.

Katie didn't believe it and yet he certainly had reason to hate his aunt. What did she say or do to provoke him to that extent? Katie didn't know what he'd found out when he left. She remembered Lloyd and his mother at the house and she recognized the man in the shadows tonight was Lloyd.

"Get the police chief. Tell him Lloyd and his mother attacked me and set the house on fire. And I can identify the man in my room a few minutes ago, the one who tried to kill me as Lloyd Weedon."

The doctor used the bedside phone. "Get security to look for Lloyd Weedon. Check his mother's room. He tried to kill one of our patients."

Hanging up, he turned to the nurse. "Call Chief Horseman and relay Miss Weber's message." He patted Katie on the arm. "Don't worry. He'll be found."

After they left, the quiet encircled her. Jake in jail, his worst nightmare. She wanted to get to him. Reassure him. She'd never believe he shot his aunt, unless his life was in danger.

Her IV disconnected, Katie slipped out of bed and went to the closet. Fresh clothes hung neatly. Bless her mother. She put on the jeans, top and her sneakers.

Someone must have removed the guard to treat him. Good. No one looked her way. Katie, slow and quiet, crept out and around the corner to the stairs. She was going to Jake.

She made no noise going down the steps. Her head spun when she tried to hurry. Take it easy, she cautioned herself. Slow and careful, hanging onto the metal rail, Katie crept along. A single light at each landing shone through the dark. Sound didn't filter through the thick concrete walls. The faint smell of stale food and body odor hung in the air. Thank goodness she'd been on the third floor and not the eighth. Rounding the corner on the last landing, she ran into him.

"Well, well, little Katie comes and throws herself into my arms." Lloyd pulled her close against his broad body. "You're in time to be my cover out of this place." He pushed the gun against her temple. "Brought this along and it's going to come in handy."

"They'll catch you. You must know you can't get away and so far you haven't killed anyone."

"How do you know, Katie? I will, if you don't follow my instructions." He shoved the gun harder against her head.

"Think of your mother. She wouldn't want to see you in prison for life or for you to die for your crimes."

"Shut up. You talk to damn much." Lloyd put his other arm around her and pulled her down the last flight of stairs. "Open the door."

Katie pushed on the heavy metal door. They both looked out at an empty hallway.

"Dumb security guards." He laughed. "Let's go." He walked beside her, holding onto her arm and keeping the gun at her temple.

Katie's heart raced, and her eyes glanced frantically around the long, narrow hallway. She needed to find a way to escape but there was no opportunity.

Hope rose when she heard the sound of running feet, and Jake rounded the corner. They came to an abrupt halt.

"Let her go, Lloyd. This is between you and me," Jake shouted.

"Not any longer. It's much bigger now thanks to your nosing around."

Jake moved closer.

"Stay back," Lloyd said. "I'll shoot her."

Jake put out his hands. "Take me instead. You'd get more of a thrill killing me, and we both know whoever helps you escape will end up dead."

"No, Jake," Katie said. "I'll go with him. He won't shoot me, there isn't any need." Katie's eyes pleaded with Jake. She saw the relief in his expression when he realized she'd regained her memory

"This is my fight, Katie. Not yours. Why do you keep trying to get into my personal business?" The words echoed cold and hard around the narrow hall.

Katie gasped with the pain his words inflicted. His body and the tone of his voice told the world he didn't care about her. It was all about him and his father.

The grasp on her arm loosened. "Come here, before I let her go. I want this to be between you and me," Lloyd said.

"No," a new voice spoke from behind. "This is between you and the state of Florida."

Lloyd jerked partially around, bringing his gun away from Katie's face. Jake lunged, pushing her to the side. She heard the report of the pistol and fell to the floor covering her face and ears.

When Katie raised her head and turned, she saw Lloyd's body lying on the floor. Several police stood by him and medical personnel came running with a stretcher. Jake knelt beside Katie and pushed her hair off of her forehead.

"Are you all right?" His warm silky voice and the soft look in his eyes confused her.

"I'm fine." He put his hand down, and she grasped it. One tug and she stood beside him. "Thanks."

"You got your memory back? He asked.

She didn't look at him, just nodded. Tired of his mercurial mood changes and feeling weak in the knees, Katie let the nurse lead her to the elevator to return to her room.

* * * *

Jake watched her walk away. He knew he'd hurt her when he said that about staying out of his personal life. He'd wanted Lloyd to think she wasn't valuable to him. Obviously he'd convinced Katie.

Nurses and techs flew down the hall with Lloyd on the gurney to the ER. Chief Horseman strode over to Jake. "Guess I owe you an apology. I've reviewed the tape you made."

"You only jumped to the same conclusion most of the Treehaven residents already have."

"I'm not so sure about that, young man. I had a number of indignant calls regarding my putting you in jail." The chief studied him. "I was wrong." He put out his hand.

Stunned, Jake stared. Hesitantly he reached out and found his hand caught in the sheriff's strong grasp.

Jake raised his eyes and looked directly at the police chief. "Thank you, sir. If you don't need me I think I'll check on Katie." The chief waved him on his way, and Jake took the elevator to the third floor.

At the door, he heard voices. Her mom and dad stood by her bed. They hadn't seen him yet. Jake backed away. Maybe it was best to wait. He had so much to tell her and several things he wanted to do before their meeting at Mr. Townsends' office on Wednesday. He glanced once more into the room, in time to see her tearful smile and Mr. Weber lean down to comfort her.

Jake swallowed around the lump in his throat. So much had happened in the last few days. Was he the man for Katie? He wanted to be.

First on his agenda, he'd talk to the chief about exonerating his father. *The Treehaven Chronicle* should be willing to put that news on the front page. At least he hoped they would.

He wasn't sure how his mother would react to the publicity that came from all of this. He'd call Robert Winston and tell him all that had occurred. It seemed a week ago instead of only two days.

And he had to make some decisions about his own life. The next few days would go by fast with all he had to do.

* * * *

Katie sat on her parents' back porch, a frosty glass of lemonade held in one hand and *The Treehaven Chronicle* in the other. Bold headlines shouted the news that Ken Andrews' brother-in-law, Harley, "Buzz" Weedon had framed him. She imagined Jake's satisfaction must be immense to see the truth glaring up at the town's residents as they sipped their morning coffee.

Katie had heard nothing from Jake. She didn't know if he was still in town. She'd received her formal letter from the firm of Townsend and Townsend for the Wednesday morning appointment at ten. She swallowed a sip of lemonade. Her chest hurt, but it wasn't anything the doctor could cure.

Her father's comment from a month ago came to mind, a gift can sometimes be a two edged sword. She would have money enough to pay for a new home and it wouldn't be difficult to get her teaching certificate, but the house was gone and so was Jake. Money gave her material things, but that didn't help the ache in her heart.

"Hi, Katie love. I see you're deep in thought. May I join you?" Katie's dad stopped at the doorway.

"Please do." Katie motioned him to sit by her. "I was remembering what you told me weeks ago about a gift being a two edged sword. Mine certainly ended that way."

She watched her father pull his pipe from his old tan sweater pocket and pour tobacco into it. The aroma of the tobacco always reminded her of him. It lingered on his clothes and she remembered smelling it, when as a little girl he'd lifted her high to reach for passing clouds. The tobacco fragrance lingered when he comforted her about a scraped knee or a lost boyfriend.

"You're staring, Katie love. Did I spill some of your Mom's great apple pie on my shirt?" He teasingly brushed off an imaginary spot.

"I love you, Daddy."

"Well." He cleared his throat and looked out across his manicured lawn.

But Katie saw the watery glaze in his eyes. "What do you suppose happens to a ghost after a fire?"

He puffed on his pipe and rocked back and forth. The wooden rockers and porch floor created a soothing cadence to the silence around them.

"I'm not sure. Hopefully she will move on. Guess you'd have to ask one of those ghost hunters."

Katie nodded. "I like your answer. The house and all the memories held her here. Now with the house gone and the mystery solved, it should be the end."

"Where does all this leave you, Katie?"

The doves cooed by the bird feeder, and in the distance Katie heard a cardinal calling to its mate. Leaves on the trees trembled as the soft breeze flowed over their surface. Katie soaked up the quiet calmness of home.

"I must find my own way. This time I know I'll stay here in Treehaven. I plan to get my teaching certificate and hope to get a job with the local school system."

"And Jake?" Her father asked.

"Jake appears to be gone too."

They sat quietly, rocking in unison, the warmth of the afternoon slowly lessening as the sun moved further to the west. Katie knew she was safe and loved. Her parents, sisters and brothers were here to steady her as she found her way. She patted her Dad's hand. He took hers and held it snug.

Chapter 21

Sunlight sparkled off the windows of the skyscrapers. The St. John's River wove past in the background. Katie drove to the entrance of the parking garage and took a ticket. She easily found a parking place. Ten o'clock on the dot.

She hadn't wanted to arrive early. She had no idea what to say to Jake when she saw him. The silent elevator whisked her to the twelfth floor. Katie's heels sank into plush jade carpet when she stepped out. Soft music played in the background, and a hint of flowers wafted across her nose.

A woman with perfect ivory skin, cool green eyes and jet black hair sat behind a highly polished reception desk. She acknowledged Katie with a distant smile.

"May I help you?"

"I'm Katie Weber. I have an appointment with Mr. Townsend."

The woman came from around her desk. "Mr. Townsend and Mr. Andrews are in his office. Follow me."

Both men stood at her entry. Mr. Townsend smiled and came over to her. "Good to see you, Miss Weber. Please join us." He waved toward the leather chair beside Jake.

Determined to remain calm, Katie did not raise her eyes above the knot in Jake's tie when he stood. He sat when she did. Katie stared straight ahead at Mr. Townsend.

Mr. Townsend put both arms on his desk and leaned forward. "I know from the headlines in *The Treehaven Chronicle* and the local papers that you found out the truth about your father, Jake. Tell me what else the two of you discovered about Sandstone."

"Katie should tell you her connection to the place," Jake suggested.

Mr. Townsend looked at her and nodded.

"I have a feeling you already know the answers," Katie stated.

"Why don't you tell me anyway?"

"Judith Collier was a distant aunt on my mother's side. My mother and I resemble her. Judith died shortly after her husband's death during the Civil War. She and Daniel parted on unhappy terms because she didn't want him to enlist. About a week after his death Judith was found dead and everyone thought she died of a broken heart, but we think she was murdered by..." Katie stopped and for the first time looked at Jake's face. He nodded for her to continue.

"We discovered Jake's great-great-great cousin was obsessed about owning Sandstone and marrying Judith. He believed Daniel Collier cheated him out of both."

Katie took a breath. "We think when Judith refused to sell Sandstone after Daniel's death and denied any feelings for him, that he went crazy and killed her. I'm not sure how, probably some kind of poison. You'd have to have her body exhumed to know for sure.

"I also believe he was the malevolent spirit that I sensed hovering in the house, and of course Jake's aunt and cousin added to the confusion by making noises and doing things to try and scare us away."

Mr. Townsend formed an upside down V with his hands. "Your benefactor came to much the same conclusions, except she wasn't aware of the second ghost. She did suspect Judith was murdered. She'd read some old letters and heard talk. She'd be very pleased with your results verifying what she'd believed happened." He nodded. "Did you find out anything on your trip to the battlefield?"

They heard a soft knock, and Mr. Townsend glanced at the door. "Come in. I asked Velma to bring in coffee and tea." He stood and motioned for his receptionist to place the beverages and cookies on the side table by Katie.

Katie handed the coffee to the men and took a cup of tea for herself. The hot tea helped calm the butterflies in her stomach.

Jake sat quietly by her side. His grey suit did little to hide the firm hard body underneath, and Katie felt the familiar ache to touch him. His cologne filled her nostrils. A hot flush ran from her face down her body. She had to forget him. After today, she'd rarely see him. He might not ever come to Treehaven after this experience.

Jake put down his coffee. "Regarding your question about our trip, we found a distant relative who told us about Daniel Weber and his family. She sent us a letter that Judith wrote to Daniel, but he died before he could receive it. This probably sounds strange, but we read the letter aloud at the battlefield. We believe he loved and missed Judith. We took that information back to Sandstone."

Katie added, "Judith's ghost's wandered through the rooms of the house. We talked about what we found in hopes she'd understand and find peace."

The attorney rubbed his hands together. "My, my. Mrs. Pace would have loved hearing the end of this story. I'm sure she'd be satisfied that you earned your inheritance."

"I'm glad." Jake handed Mr. Townsend several papers. "Here's the story that will run in tomorrow's paper."

Mr. Townsend glanced through them.

"You've done well. Congratulations," he said, reaching across the desk to shake their hands. "It takes a few weeks to get the deed. I'll give you papers today indicating you two are the owners of the Sandstone property."

"I'd like to request you make the deed out in Miss Weber's name only," Jake said, just as Mr. Townsend started to turn away.

He swung back around. "Why?"

"No," Katie said. "You earned the inheritance too. I'm surprised you'd even suggest such a thing."

"Katie, it never belonged to me or my ancestors. We caused untold grief to your family. My relative probably killed Judith, and my cousin tried to hurt you. I have no right to the property."

Katie felt her face flush. "That's ridiculous. I won't accept it. Don't you dare alter the will," she warned the attorney. She turned to Jake. "You didn't kill or hurt anyone. You're not responsible for relatives who lived years ago or for your cousin."

Jake took her hand. "Katie, I got more than I ever believed possible. I found out the truth about my father. I learned there were people in Treehaven who believed in him and me. I don't need the ranch."

Katie blinked furiously to keep the tears at bay. "It isn't fair. I don't want it all. What about your dream, yours and Tom's?"

He smiled a crooked smile at her, and she wanted to bawl and plead with him not to go.

"We'll do it someday. On another piece of land, not on the property you love, Katie."

Katie sniffed, and Jake handed her his handkerchief. "I liked it better when you fought with me about it," she said. She stared into his eyes. Her fingers trembled with the desire to touch his familiar face, to trace across those firm warm lips. Knowing she had to get away before she made a fool of herself, she looked around to tell Mr. Townsend goodbye, but he'd left the room.

"Tell him to leave it as our benefactor wanted it. I will not accept your part." Katie ran out of the room, down the hall, and into the elevator. She thought she heard Jake call her name, but she didn't stop, not now.

* * * *

Tears ran down her cheeks as she pulled out of the parking garage. She took the long way home. She had to see Sandstone once more. She hadn't been back since the fire.

Wiping her eyes, she slowed down. No need to have a wreck and maybe hurt someone. The radio played in the background, lover's music. She sobbed again and snapped it off.

Turning down the dirt road, Katie bumped along until she turned into what had been the drive to the house. A pile of rubble greeted her, instead of the courtly old homestead. Her heart ached. She got out and wandered around the perimeter of the house. The acrid smell of smoke still lingered in the air. Her hand touched the necklace around her neck. At least that hadn't been lost.

A noise brought her head around. Dust flew as Jake drove the Mercedes into the yard and parked beside her car. He stepped out and stared across the remnants, at her. He strode toward her with determination set in the features of his face.

"You didn't let me finish."

"There wasn't anymore I wanted to hear." Again, she talked to his tie.

"Look at me."

"No." She deliberately turned her back to him and stared across at the hammock of old oak trees. The field of wildflowers stretched in front of them, only the edge browned by the fire.

Jake's hands came down on her shoulders, and his lips caressed the side of her neck. "Are you sure you don't want to hear the rest of what I wanted to say?"

She held her breath.

"I can feel you tremble. I love your little tremors and noises you make when we make love." He turned her to face him, and his lips feathered light kisses across her brow, her eyes, and her cheeks.

She lifted her mouth to his and sighed when he kissed her.

Raising his head, he pulled her into the warmth and security of his body. She breathed in the smell of him, and his strength filled her. Then, he pulled her down beside him on what was left of the back stoop.

"I've been a loner most of my life. My work took me to faraway places so I told myself I wasn't lonely and didn't need anyone." He stopped and brushed a kiss across her upturned nose. "Until you came barreling into my life, turning it upside down. I'd seen you in school and with your family." His smile reflected his humor at himself. "The perfect family. When you included me, it scared me to death. I thought I'd never fit in."

Katie took a breath to protest, and Jake placed his finger across her lips.

"Let me finish, Katie, or I might never get it out."

Katie nodded and took his hand.

"I tried to tell myself I'd have to go back to Atlanta and forget all about you. Until Friday night, when I saw you in the burning house and realized I'd give my life, in a moment, for you."

Katie felt the tears starting to flow, and Jake kissed them away.

"I realized I'd be lost without you in my world. I want to know when I open my door at the end of the day, you'll be there."

Katie put her finger across his lips. "I love you, Jake. When I didn't hear from you, I was afraid you'd gone to Atlanta and weren't coming back. The inheritance meant nothing, when I thought I'd lost you." She watched his smile light his face and his eyes sparkle.

"I spent the past two days soul searching. I'm sorry you were worried. But, I didn't want to say anything until I felt certain inside myself that I'd be a good husband and father. With your help, I will be." He threw out his arms to encompass the ranch. "I want all of this to be yours, and I also want to spend my life loving you." Jake pulled out a ring. Sunlight caught the shine of gold and diamond.

"Will you marry me, Katie, my love?"

With joyful abandonment, she threw her arms around his neck. "Yes, yes, yes."

He slid the ring on her finger. They sat with arms wrapped around each other, staring at their world surrounding them.

Katie looked down at her ring.

"Katie, the woods." Jake's voice sounded urgent.

She focused on the hammock of trees directly in front of them. At about the same spot where the large deer stood those evenings, a faint mist curled between the trees. Katie leaned forward staring hard. She saw the outline of a man with a woman held close against him. They nodded slightly toward Katie and Jake before vanishing from sight.

Katie touched Jake's hand. "Did you see them?"

"Yes, I can hardly believe my eyes."

"I want to believe it," Katie said. "I want to think Judith and Daniel have found each other, and that they've left Sandstone to us." She reached up and ran her fingers across the necklace she always wore now.

Jake smiled, took her hand and kissed her fingers. "You just reminded me. I have one more surprise." He headed to his car and returned with a roll of papers in his hand.

"This is your wedding present. I'm giving it to you early."

Katie gasped when the papers rolled open in front of her. She reached out almost afraid to touch the blueprints. "It's the plans for a house like Sandstone?" she asked.

"Pretty much, but with some modern additions like good wiring and a larger bath. I'm going to build your house for you. Not here." He motioned to the burned out house. "There in the middle of your field of flowers. I thought we'd have a lake dug here and add a fountain in honor of Judith."

Now the tears did pour down her face. "I'll only," she sniffled, "accept if you take the acres you need off the back end and build your dream development."

"You're sure?"

Katie nodded, tears in her eyes. "As long as you don't disturb my woods." She indicated where they'd last seen Judith and Daniel.

Jake swung her into his arms. "It's a deal."

"Look, let me down." Katie said.

Puzzled Jake set Katie on her feet. She went to a lone rose bush. One side had tips of brown, but on the other side, a single rose bloomed and when Katie brought it to her nose, she smelled Judith's fragrance.

"This," she pointed to the rose bush, "gets planted beside the back steps of our new home." A cool breeze fluttered by her neck and Katie smiled, knowing Judith had given her approval.

Epilogue

Jake stood beside his best man, Tom, waiting for Katie. It was still difficult to believe how his life changed the past year. Their house at Sandstone was completed. He and Katie had been involved in every detail of its rebirth. They'd managed to combine the lovely old qualities and the modern updates they both wanted.

Among the wedding guests, Jake spotted Mr. and Mrs. Barrows and Tom's wife, Sara. Behind them, he was surprised to see the sheriff, who gave him a nod.

The music changed, and he caught his breath. Katie stood at the end of the aisle dressed in a white lace gown, her smile glowing, her arm tucked in her father's. Jake prayed he'd never let her down. He'd never known much about love until she came along, but he planned to spend the rest of his life trying to be the man she deserved.

* * * *

Katie watched their guests overflow onto her parents' back lawn. It seemed like most of the town had come to wish them well. Katie would never forget the moment she saw Jake when she entered the church. Her heart jumped with joy. Her Jake, now and forever.

She didn't think he'd seen them yet, her surprise guests. She saw Jake greet several old school mates and turn. She hoped she didn't do the wrong thing inviting his mother and her family to the wedding. Moving quickly to his side, she touched his arm and saw the question in his eyes.

"I thought this should be a new beginning for all of us," she whispered.

* * * *

Jake blinked his eyes when he first saw his mother. For a second, the old resentment flared, and he knew he finally had a chance to get his revenge by turning his back on her. He stood rooted in place, and then Katie, his sweet loving Katie was beside him. With a look and a few soft words, she encouraged him.

He smiled at his mother. "I'd like you to meet my wife, Katie Andrews." Jake nodded to his stepfather. "Katie, this is my mother's husband, Robert Winston and their son, Alec."

"How do you do," Katie said, and put out her hands to his mother. "I'm so glad you came. It means a lot to Jake and me to have all of our family with us on the most important day of our lives."

"Thank you for inviting us," Robert Winston said.

Mother and son stared at each other. Jake saw the tears in her eyes. All he had to do was step forward and it would end the past. The pain of the little boy clung hard in his chest, but he swallowed and forced that image away for good.

He took a step, then another, and feeling clumsy and unsure, he wrapped his arms, at last, around the woman who had haunted his childhood dreams. Her body shuddered, and tears soaked his shoulder. He gently rubbed her back and kissed her hair.

When he raised his head, he caught a glimpse of tears in the eyes of *his* family. Holding onto his mother with one hand, he reached out to his stepfather and his half-brother with the other. He didn't have to look for Katie. She'd wrapped her arms around him and his mother.

Home was not a house. These people around him and Katie's family were home. He'd finally found himself inside the circle, and it was everything he'd dreamed.

THE END

WWW.RACHELMCNEELY.COM

ABOUT THE AUTHOR

For as long as I can remember I wanted to write and have a book of mine published. Sometimes life gets in the way, or we let it.

I grew up in the South and lived with an aunt and uncle from the time I was ten until I graduated from high school. Both my aunt and uncle worked long hours, giving me a lot of time alone. With my love of reading and an active imagination, I was never bored.

I wrote my first story at the age of eleven or twelve and read it to my neighborhood friends. They, of course, thought it was wonderful. My story did not have a happy ending. My heroine died a tragic death. I was in my melodramatic phase.

My first published work was a Mothers Day poem. The local newspaper had a contest between the local high schools. I won. The prize was ten dollars and having my poem printed in the Sunday paper, on Mothers Day. I won't say what year.

My aunt was a practical woman and worked all her life. You did not write for a career. You studied and got a sensible job that kept a roof over your head and food in your stomach.

Consequently, my first career was nursing. During my mid life crisis, I went back to school and earned my masters degree in social work. These were good choices, but in the back of my mind, those characters kept knocking on the door and reminding me of my dream job, writing.

I did write during those years, everything from poems, short stories, and longer love stories. They filled my desk drawers and the bottom of my closet.

With three grown children, three grandchildren, a very supportive husband and many friends encouragement I finally got serious. I decided in 2004 that it was time to commit to my dream, make some goals and start on my new career. They do say the third times the charm.

My first goals; Join a writer's group and a critique group, attend a writer's conference, and oh yes, write a book.

My first big shock: Not everyone thought I was a great writer. Like any other career you had to study, read, take classes, and write, write, write. Who would know following your passion could be so much work? But also so much fun.

BookStrand

www.BookStrand.com

Printed in the United States
149248LV00009B/28/P